Devonshire

Look for these titles by *Lynne Connolly*

Now Available:

Triple Countess Trilogy
Last Chance, My Love (Book 1)
A Chance to Dream (Book 2)
Met by Chance (Book 3)

Secrets Trilogy
Seductive Secrets (Book 1)
Alluring Secrets (Book 2)
Tantalizing Secrets (Book 3)

Richard and Rose Series
Yorkshire (Book 1)
Devonshire (Book 2)
Venice (Book 3)
Harley Street (Book 4)
Eyton (Book 5)

Coming Soon:

Richard and Rose Series
Darkwater (Book 6)

Devonshire

Lynne Connolly

A Samhain Publishing, Ltd. publication.

Samhain Publishing, Ltd.
577 Mulberry Street, Suite 1520
Macon, GA 31201
www.samhainpublishing.com

Devonshire
Copyright © 2009 by Lynne Connolly
Print ISBN: 978-1-60504-438-5
Digital ISBN: 978-1-60504-349-4

Cover by Natalie Winters

First Samhain Publishing, Ltd. electronic publication: January 2009
First Samhain Publishing, Ltd. print publication: December 2009

Chapter One

The door to the parlour opened and my sister-in-law bustled inside. A gust of wind followed her stocky shape and some of the pasteboard invitations on the mantelpiece fluttered to the floor. I put down my book and stood, then bent to retrieve the cards. We couldn't accept most of them. We were still in mourning, our shield from our importunate neighbours, but not for much longer.

Martha held a wicker basket covered with a fine linen cloth. "Rose, dear, I have some treats for old Mrs. Hoarty in the village. Will you take them to her?"

Restless and bored, I was glad of any distraction. "I'd love to."

I tucked the invitations back behind the clock to join the others. "Never mind," Martha said, following my wistful look. "We should be able to attend social events again soon."

"The end of this month. I never thought I'd miss attending those dreary functions, but I'd welcome anything that killed some time."

Martha smiled. "Never mind," she repeated, and then went, as was her way, to the heart of my dissatisfaction, "I'm sure he'll be here soon."

She meant my betrothed and beloved, Richard Kerre, Lord Strang. After a month apart, I missed him terribly. And I could not distract myself by attending the local social functions, although invitations arrived every day, not unconnected, I suspected, with the news of my betrothal. But we were in mourning, for cousins we had only met once, and felt little for. But since my brother James had inherited the title they'd held, we had to enter the required period of three months' full mourning and three months' half.

"Is Lizzie coming?" I paused before the mirror to tidy my hair. I'd never found a maid who could cope with my thick, curly chestnut mane, and it was forever tumbling out of its pins. I sighed and tucked the loose strands away. I smiled at my reflection, then sighed again. No, I still couldn't see it.

"What is it, dear?" Sharp-eyed Martha had seen my doubt.

I turned away from the mirror. "I still can't see why he should want me. Why not choose Lizzie?" I smoothed the folds of my gown, and shook it out at the back. It was of plain grey wool, one I'd had made after my father died. That reminder of deeply felt, sincere mourning, was one reason I felt like a hypocrite now. On the first day of April, we reverted to wearing colours again and a full social life. I could hardly wait.

"Lord Strang has fallen head-over-heels for you." Martha smiled. She had a pleasant smile that made everything she said reasonable. She always denigrated her homely looks, but I don't think she had ever been properly aware of that smile. "And you with him. You brightened, just at the mention of his name then. Don't ask why, dear, just accept it."

I still felt I would wake one day and still be Miss Golightly of Devonshire, the overlooked elder sister of the beautiful Lizzie. I had resigned myself to the role of dependant old maid long before I met Richard, thinking my future would consist of caring for nieces and nephews, not children of my own. Years of constant denigration by the local belles had given me a feeling of inferiority I found hard to shake off.

I turned away to give myself time to regain my composure and then looked back at my sister-in-law. It had happened to her, too. My brother James was tall and handsome, but he'd fallen in love with homely Martha, and after ten years of marriage, was still in love with her.

When I left the parlour with Martha, the sounds of the

manor house became more noticeable. We walked through to the small hall, and I heard the shouts and clanging coming up from the kitchen below, a state of constant activity, mingling with childish cries from the nursery above. "Have you given the children a holiday from their studies?"

"Mr. Somerfield is ill." Martha referred to the tutor who came in every day. "I couldn't see to it myself, so I decided they could make do with the nursery maids today." Martha and James had three children. With my sisters Lizzie and Ruth and my brother Ian, it made for an overcrowded dwelling place, but I was used to it and hardly noticed any more.

I found my sturdy leather shoes and sat on one of the hard hall chairs to put them on. I fumbled with the heavy brass buckles. The sound coming from the children upstairs rose around me. "I'll send them outside soon," mused Martha, as though she had read my thoughts.

"Not to go to Mrs. Hoarty's," I said, not without some alarm. "She's much too fragile to cope with small children."

Martha sighed. "I'm afraid she is. But she's a patient soul, never complains."

A door at the back of the hall opened and in swept Lizzie, already wearing her outdoor shoes and cloak. Her attention went to the basket at my feet. "Has Martha asked you to go to Mrs. Hoarty's? May I come with you, Rose? If I have to stay in much longer listening to that noise, I swear I'll run mad."

Lizzie lit up the hall with her beauty and vitality. Even before our recent change of fortune, she'd been the queen of Devonshire society, and now she was even more alluring to the local beaux. A shame the mourning kept her from them. She felt it badly, and knew her chief rival, Eustacia Terry, would steal a march on her in her absence. Lizzie had a different mother than I, accounting for her golden beauty and my own dark colouring, but I wasn't jealous. Her sweet, generous nature precluded that, but sometimes, in the recesses of my secret self, I longed for some of that dazzling loveliness for myself. Especially since I'd met Richard. I would love to be beautiful for him.

Pushing my thoughts to the back of my mind, I answered her with a smile. "Mrs. Hoarty would be happy to see you. How can you make mourning look so good?"

"Well black suits me better than it does you. Your skin has a creamy tone that looks best with a touch of colour." She grinned. "We'll be out of black soon, and then we'll show them."

I laughed, and was still laughing when I ran up the stairs to my room to fetch my cloak.

I'd never thought of my bedroom as small before, but crammed with items for my trousseau it seemed to have shrunk in size. The jewel bright colours of the rich satins and silks mocked my dull grey wool gown.

Stopping at the bed, I picked up a blue satin petticoat and smoothed my fingers over its sensuous softness, caressing it before I put it back. I'd never spent so much money on clothes before, and the total cost of the treasure laid out here made me dizzy. The petticoats and gowns had all been sewn and embroidered by the best craftsmen Exeter offered. Some fabrics, lace and ribbons had been brought up from London, just for me.

If I had married a local man, I would have embroidered many of my linens myself, but the suddenness of my engagement left no time for that, so these too were brought in. Richard wouldn't wait for me to sew my trousseau. He'd only been deterred from marrying me immediately because of our state of mourning and the pleas of his family and mine.

Ranks of delicate satin shoes faced me from their station by the window. All for me. In one startling month my brother had become an earl and I'd met and fallen in love with the most astonishing man I'd ever met. That he loved me back continued to astonish me.

The maid would put most of these things away later, and return my bedroom to its quiet, comfortable self. I grinned. The cabin of a pirate ship might look like this after a raid. I would probably be expected to dress in this finery every day after I married. The thought intimidated me, made me feel foolish, a fraud. I liked to dress in something simple, preferably something I could get into with a minimum of help, not spend hours on my toilette.

On impulse, I crossed to the dressing table and picked up the scent bottle. At least I could smell good. I anointed my wrists and throat in some of the perfume before I left with my plain cloak to join my sister downstairs.

Lizzie and I left the house and went down the drive. "You don't mind walking all the way to the end of the village?"

Lizzie laughed. "I can manage."

"You couldn't when we were little and had to walk to Church." Our father had insisted that we walk on Sundays, one tradition my brother James thankfully hadn't followed. "You were always the one who complained the loudest, and ended up being carried."

Lizzie gave me an unrepentant grin. "It worked every time."

I tipped my head back and breathed in the sweet air of my native county. March brought winds and the promise of spring, growing warmer towards the end of the month, but a nip remained in the air. The sun gained in confidence as spring approached, not a trace of rain hung in the sky.

The wrought iron gates at the end of the drive had rusted into their places, so seldom were they closed. A road ran past the gates, leading to the other large house in the district, Peacock's. When we glanced along the path, we saw our neighbours and friends, Tom Skerrit and his younger sister Georgiana, walking towards us.

Tom led his favourite hack. I assumed Tom was heading for the smithy. That meant they would be going our way, so we stopped to wait for them.

"Good morning, Tom."

"Good morning, Rose, Lizzie." We stood on no ceremony with the Skerrits. I smiled in greeting to Tom and his pretty sister. Tom was as familiar to me as my own reflection in the mirror, so I rarely noticed his appearance, but this morning,

11

with a sense of what I might soon lose, I studied him closer. It would be strange not to have him as a neighbour any more.

Tom was tall and dark, and preferred to wear his own hair rather than a formal wig. While not precisely handsome, he possessed a friendly countenance out of which gleamed a pair of amused grey eyes. He would be a good catch for someone. At one time, local society assumed it would be me, but he'd never asked and I'd never pushed the possibility. We had run together almost as brother and sister, and as far as I knew, he'd never thought of me in any other way.

Georgiana looked fetching today, wearing an Indian muslin gown printed with little flowers and a red cloak. I was envious that she didn't have to wear boring black or grey. The blue of her gown matched her eyes to perfection.

"Trusty dropped a shoe?" I asked when they caught up.

Tom cast an anxious look at the horse. "Yes, so I thought I'd take him at once."

A hill stood between Golightly Manor and the village. We chatted while we climbed it. The slope wasn't particularly gentle, but we were all used to it, so didn't get out of breath. The new grass felt crisp and springy beneath our feet, and I savoured the sensation, knowing I wouldn't have it for much longer. Nothing would ever be the same again. I was leaving something I loved behind.

Lizzie and Georgiana walked ahead, chatting about the latest fashions and my upcoming wedding. I followed behind with Tom. We had to walk a little slower to let Trusty find his feet when he stumbled, and to ensure we didn't go over anything that might get into the horse's hoof. I was in no hurry.

Tom turned to me, a question in his eyes. "You never told me what Hareton Abbey was like. I know it was dirty, and abandoned, but why won't your brother use it?" James had inherited Hareton Abbey with the title, and we'd travelled up there the previous year.

"If it was cleaned and put in order," I told him, "it would still be impersonal. It's far too large and badly built."

"Badly built?" Tom sounded surprised. Hareton was reputed to be one of the great houses of the country in its day, but my friend hadn't seen the devastation that abandonment had wrought on it.

I stared up at the blue sky as we crested the hill. It was the same sky in Yorkshire, though it hadn't seemed so at the time. "Yes. James was pleased when he heard that. It gave him the excuse he needed to come home. We didn't know anyone there, and Martha would never have been happy. It's a much better idea to rebuild the Manor."

A bird soared overhead, singing. A Devonshire bird.

"What will happen to the Abbey?" asked my old friend.

I returned my attention to him. "Nothing. It can't be sold because it's part of the entail. James will leave it to rot, or perhaps rent it out. He'll move all the treasures he wants here and sell the rest. The dowager countess, Lady Patience, is living in the Dower House, and I don't think she'll willingly set foot in the Abbey again. The place is doomed, Tom." I wasn't sorry. The Abbey had become a place of misery and suffering. Its stones had seemed to weep in the damp autumn weather last year.

Tom smiled at my dramatic words, as I had meant him to. I didn't want him to ask any more. The events of that time were privy to our family alone, and safer if they remained so. And what had happened to me was only for me and one other to know.

Tom's horse stumbled, enabling me to drop the subject. We stopped to allow Trusty to recover, and I gave my friend a statement of fact, hoping he wouldn't realise I was drawing him away from the personal aspects of our visit. "The third earl had the old building torn down and rebuilt, but he didn't keep his eye on the builders. Hareton might be grandiose, but it needs completely rebuilding to make it habitable again. We don't like it, so why bother?"

Tom grinned again and gave me a deliberate up and down scan. My old grey gown wasn't the height of fashion and had definitely seen better days, but I recognised his regard as

13

friendly teasing. I didn't mind that from Tom. "I thought you'd come back the grand lady."

"You know me better than that." I looked down with a rueful smile. My clothes could best be described as serviceable; the gown, the sturdy leather shoes I loved and had repaired regularly, and my unornamented black cloak. There was nothing about me to indicate any change in my situation.

"You'll be a countess one day."

I wished he hadn't mentioned it. It wasn't something I wanted, but Richard went along with the title, and I definitely wanted him. "Maybe." I smoothed my skirt, a habitual gesture when I felt nervous or unsure, feeling the rough woollen cloth under my hand. It gave me a small measure of assurance.

"It's suitable now you're an earl's sister. It's what's expected of you by most people." I shook my head in denial but he continued, "You know you don't have to? That James can settle a jointure on you so you can live as you always wanted to— independently?"

He reminded me of something I'd always dreamed about, something I'd often shared with him.

"If it had been anyone else I wouldn't have considered it," I told him. Tom frowned, puzzlement apparent on his face.

Lizzie heard the last part of the conversation. She stopped and turned around to address him. "You'll understand, Tom."

Tom stared at me, but he didn't pursue the subject. "And how did you find Hareton Abbey compared to Eyton?" Eyton was the main house belonging to my future parents-in-law, Lord and Lady Southwood. I'd visited them after Christmas, but came away when a large house party arrived. I was still in deep mourning and it wasn't proper for me to attend a large gathering yet.

Richard had written that the visitors were disappointed not to meet me. He also said the visitors were tedious, and he would try to get away as soon as he could. We wrote to each other every day, but I still missed him; his presence, his touch, and his reassurance. As well as the thrill he gave me by touching me, kissing me and caressing me. We hadn't repeated our one afternoon of lovemaking. Although I'd wanted to, Richard told me he wanted me with no slur on my name. An early pregnancy would not help me. My heart lifted when I thought that soon, so close to our wedding day, he might consent to make love to me again. If we found another opportunity. I just wanted him. I hadn't realised it was possible to miss someone so much.

I breathed in the fresh, green air of my native land, detecting the faint tang of the sea, not far away. "I liked Eyton much better. It's smaller than Hareton, but the family rooms are much more comfortable, and it's run like a great house of that kind should be." I looked around. "I'll miss this." Devonshire was such a beautiful part of the world, but I was so used to it I rarely allowed myself to notice. The sky was bright blue, the grass intensely green, more so than anywhere else I knew.

Everyone at Eyton had been kind, but I was still bemused by my fate, by the family welcoming me. I knew Richard's family and his erstwhile lovers resented me and doubted if a country girl, who was until recently, firmly in the ranks of the gentry, would do for their son. However, if Richard's father wanted an heir, he would have to accept his son's choice of bride. Richard had made that clear to him.

"Lord and Lady Southwood are somewhat taken aback by their son's sudden decision after years of urging him to marry," I remarked.

Tom chuckled. "About as surprised as I was when you came back betrothed. All so sudden. I'd never have thought it of you, Rose."

I didn't want to talk about it yet, and I wasn't sure what to tell him, how to explain it. "The state rooms are beautiful, but not as—well, impersonal as the ones at Hareton. Actually, Eyton and Hareton aren't that far apart. Fifty miles or so, no more."

I smiled when I remembered the short journey to Eyton and the relative privacy afforded by a travelling coach.

Tom looked at me in puzzlement. "What is it, Rose?"

"Oh, nothing."

Lizzie and Georgiana stopped at the top of the hill. They were staring at something, but we couldn't see what it was until we caught up with them. We followed their stares.

A solitary figure led a heavily laden packhorse; his gaze fixed on the ground in front of him. The man was dressed in a heavy serge coat, hat pulled low over his eyes. He was walking around the hill, heading for the land that belonged to Tom's father, Sir George Skerrit, seemingly oblivious to our presence.

I realised what the man must be about, but before I could stop him, Tom called out "Hi, you!" and after thrusting the reins of his horse at his sister, he plunged down the hill.

Chapter Two

I lifted my skirts and followed my friend as fast as I could. The ground was firm and dry under my feet and I kept up with him easily in my sturdy leather shoes. I was afraid for Tom. He could be impulsive and hot-tempered, and I didn't want him to get into trouble now. The man he was about to confront was the kind we in Devonshire were used to ignoring because of the burden his horse carried.

The man stopped his packhorse and waited for Tom. He would never have outrun him. "Where do you think you're going?" Tom demanded, his voice loud and hard.

"Peacock's, sir," came the gruff response, thick with the Devonian accent. When he looked up, I recognised him as one of the villagers from Darkwater.

"Why are you going, Cooper?"

The villager looked at me sharply when I used his name. "I been told to."

Tom indicated the burdened animal with one sweeping gesture of his arm. "What's on the horse?"

Cooper stared at the animal in surprise, as though he'd forgotten its existence. It looked back at him knowingly. "There's some French wine and some tea, and some lace."

Tom cursed. "You know my father doesn't take smuggled goods."

"Who said anything about smuggling?" The man smiled. "Just a present, is all. From my master."

The bird above us was still singing, not a care in the world, but the atmosphere below grew tense. This could be dangerous.

"Lord Hareton is your master." Tom straightened and despite his well-worn country clothes, he radiated authority.

The man looked at me and bowed low, sweeping off his hat now he no longer needed it as a disguise. It revealed greasy black locks tied back in a parody of fashion. "My lady."

I put up my chin. "Lord Hareton wouldn't send me smuggled goods," said Tom. "So who are you calling your master?"

The man didn't take his eyes from my face. "I should say my employer. Mr. Cawnton."

"Cawnton." The name was like a red rag to a bull to Tom. The Cawnton brothers ran most of the smuggling enterprises on this part of the coast. It was hard to ignore their presence, especially at the dark of the moon, but we usually managed it. "My father won't receive anything from Cawnton, you know that." Tom threw up his arms in exasperation and let them drop to his side with a resounding smack.

"My orders is to deliver them," Cooper reiterated, his accent broadening, every inch the stupid peasant—except that he wasn't. His calmness threatened Tom's agitation, and as far as I could see, he was winning the encounter, provoking Tom's temper shamelessly.

"It's an insult." Tom glanced at me. "You shouldn't be here. I'll deal with this."

"Don't be foolish, Tom. It concerns me as much as you. James had a delivery yesterday."

The man turned smug, smiling broadly in his triumph, but Tom was perturbed by what I'd said. "What did he do with it?"

"Gave it back. With thanks, but a refusal."

Tom spun around to confront Cooper again. "Why are you doing this?" A cry born more of exasperation than any desire for knowledge.

The man said nothing, but met him stare for stare. The only sounds were Tom's heavy breathing, the jingle of the harness and the stamp of the horse's hooves. The bird was still singing. Its persistence irritated me.

"My father won't have anything to do with it, you know." The new steadiness in Tom's voice relieved me. The pause must have given him a chance to regain his composure.

"That's up to him. My orders is to deliver the goods." The smell of unwashed humanity reached me and I was hard put not to wrinkle my nose. Those clothes he wore had seen more seasons than my grey gown, but far less soap.

"I can give you our answer now," Tom said. "We won't let you run the goods over our land, much less use our storehouses and barns."

"Mr. Cawnton would be sorry to hear that." A menacing tone entered Cooper's voice.

Tom took a quick breath, and his voice lifted again. "Are you threatening me?" The man's insolence and Tom's quick temper threatened to turn this encounter into something dangerous. I hoped my presence might deter them but I doubted it.

The man moved as though shifting his position, but when he did so his heavy coat moved aside. We saw the two serviceable pistols stuck in his belt, and the heavy Navy cutlass slung around his waist. Tom stared at Cooper in silence. I held my breath, not daring to move. If Tom attempted any violence he would come out the loser. He was not armed and these men didn't respect authority.

Cold fear clutched at my stomach. "Come away, Tom." I tried to keep my voice steady. Another fraught pause followed. "Your father will send a message to Cawnton."

"Dear God, I hate this." To my relief Tom turned away from Cooper to me. "No, it wouldn't be right to brawl with this man with you here. But understand this," and he turned back to confront Cooper again, "you won't get any joy from my father."

With a deliberate action that underlined his decision, Tom turned his back and strode away, leaving me to scamper behind him.

The harness jingled as Cooper and his laden horse continued on their way, and we rejoined the other two. I breathed out in a long sigh of relief, which Lizzie saw. She raised an eyebrow in query. "So what was all that about?"

"One of Cawnton's men." She grimaced. "He's trying to persuade Tom's father to lend him some barns, and let him move the goods over his land."

"I don't know why he doesn't," Lizzie said. "They'll do it anyway. And whom does it hurt? They're just running a few bits and pieces ashore."

"A few bits and pieces?" Tom's face was a mask of astonishment and fury, the heavy brows beetling over his eyes. "Smuggling is the most lucrative business in Devonshire. They make more from one run than a year working in the fields. You must know how well organised they are, Lizzie, and what they do here." His voice was louder than it needed to be, and I hoped the other man hadn't heard. Sound carried a long way in the country.

Lizzie shrugged. "People don't complain."

"Naturally they don't," came the swift reply, but in a more normal tone. "They're either well paid or terrorised into silence. That's the part I don't like. They shouldn't have so much power they can rule a whole county. If the Cawntons aren't stopped, it won't be long before they have the whole of Devonshire under their control."

"You might be exaggerating there, Tom." I took his arm and pulled him into motion. We walked towards the village below, in the opposite direction to Cooper.

Tom took back the reins of his horse. "They're clever. And quiet, but their influence increases every year. My father is worried about them, Rose. You're lucky you'll soon be away from here and all this."

I wasn't sure. I would miss my home, even this less comfortable part of it. "You're right, Tom, when you say that with smuggling wealth comes power. The Cawntons rival the local gentry, but they're on the wrong side of the law."

He sniffed. "Parliament takes little notice of the Trade, and they send too few men of too little ability to combat it. Have you seen the latest excise officer in Exeter?" I shook my head. Tom made a derisive sound between his teeth, indicative of his opinion of the unfortunate man.

We reached Darkwater and strolled up the long street. The village consisted of one long track made from centuries of trodden down dirt, fringed by cottages. Some had gardens at the front, some at the back. Villagers, busy cultivating their plots looked up from their business to acknowledge us.

"James plans to renovate these, now he can afford it," I commented.

"They should be grateful," said Tom, still miffed from our recent encounter with Cooper, "but I doubt they will be. If the Cawntons are using most of them they could probably afford to renovate their houses themselves."

The small cottages might appear picturesque, but I knew what they looked and smelled like inside. The aroma of cooking reached us from some of the open doors, no doubt from the large pot many of the inhabitants kept bubbling over the fire all day, only adding another chopped onion or some cabbage when the contents ran low.

"Why should they?" I said. "James owns most of these cottages. Most of them are our workers."

"By day." There was no persuading Tom out of his present mood, so I turned my mind to other things and walked on in silence.

"Sorry," Tom muttered after a few minutes. "It makes me angry, that's all."

"You see more of it than we do," I said. "With your land bordering the sea, you get more trouble than we do."

"Aye." We stopped to let Trusty free himself from a shallow rut. Tom grinned, his cloudy mood dispersed as it had come. "They're all talking about you," he confided, as we acknowledged the greetings of people along the busy street.

"Just me, or the rest of the family?"

"Oh, all of you. But especially you. Copies of old newspapers have been circulating like wildfire. Your Lord Strang has quite a reputation."

I smiled. "I know. You're not the first person to tell me that, you know. He told me himself, and his brother told me, and then Lizzie. It might have been a conspiracy to put me off, but he didn't succeed. Richard has tried hard to live as dangerously as he can for the last twelve years."

We carried on up the long, straggling street. "I worry about you, Rose."

"You always did." I shifted my basket to my other arm.

An edge of concern entered his voice "I know this is a brilliant match, but he sounds dangerous. Rose, you've lived here all your life. You can hardly be said to be experienced in the ways of the world, but Lord Strang is."

"I know," I said, not at all disturbed.

"By society's standards he's a brilliant match; one of the catches of London." Tom wasn't convinced; I heard it in his voice. I glanced sideways at him; his mouth was set in a hard line and he stared straight ahead at the church at the far end of the village. "You can't make a life with someone on a fancy."

When he'd heard of my betrothal to Lord Strang, Tom had declared himself delighted and embraced me warmly. He'd obviously been reading the newspapers since then. He stopped, pulling Trusty to stand behind him. Sighing, I turned to face him. He motioned his sister and Lizzie to walk ahead. "We'll catch up with you." Lizzie made a moue at me and kept walking.

Tom took my hand in his. "Lord Strang's had more women than I've ever met." He watched my face closely. I kept my expression bland. "He has a reputation as a setter of fashion, and a raiser of ten kinds of Hades."

There was a reason for Richard's wildness, but I couldn't betray him by telling anyone, not even Tom. "He's done that, yes."

"And you think you can reform him?" Tom jutted his jaw

forward. "Rose, sweet Rose, no one can reform anyone else, unless they want to be reformed. Are you sure Lord Strang isn't just looking for a mother for his children, someone to take care of his responsibilities while he rackets around London? I'd hate to see you reduced to that, however grand the setting."

I was taken aback—I'd never thought of Tom as the thoughtful type. Usually, if it wasn't thrust in front of his face, he never noticed anything. It was clear that he'd been considering this at some length and it touched me. "Thank you, Tom. I love your concern for me. But I'm sure, really I am. Besides," I added, in an effort to return to an everyday level, "I'd scandalise half society if I cried off now."

"I doubt it." He turned around and continued up the street. "They'd just think you'd come to your senses."

It was as well he didn't know I'd seduced Richard within a month of our first meeting.

"Wasn't there some scandal to do with his brother, as well?"

"Yes, there was, but it was over long ago." I skipped over a rut in the road almost without noticing it. The street was sadly in need of repair, but it had always been like that. I had no doubt it featured in James's plans for improvement.

Richard's brother had confided the nature of the scandal to me, but the details were not generally known. I couldn't tell Tom without Gervase's permission. It wasn't my secret to tell. "Gervase had to spend some time abroad, but he came back from India a rich nabob and all was forgiven."

"Well they sound like a pretty shaky family, rich or not." Since anyone not born in Devonshire seemed shaky to Tom and his family, it wasn't strange he should think that.

I watched Lizzie and Georgiana, still walking in front of us, and I thought how pretty and out of place they both looked. Lizzie had made sure her mourning clothes were good quality, and Georgiana was dressed in a bright cotton print gown, far more appropriate to this bright spring day than my shabby grey woollen one. I might have passed for a well-off villager, from a distance.

"They're all talking about you, rich and poor." I didn't need Tom to tell me that.

I thought I should try to explain about the Kerres, but then I knew I couldn't. The situation wasn't a simple one, not easily explained. "Let them talk," I gave up. "I don't care."

Tom stared at me in surprise. "That's not like you. You were always so afraid of gossip."

"Perhaps I've discovered other things are more important."

When we reached Mrs. Hoarty's, we parted. Georgiana elected to visit the old lady with us, and Tom promised to call back after his errand to collect her. We watched him walk by the side of the church, leading his horse. Then we went in.

Mrs. Hoarty lived in a comfortable house on the edge of the village, near the church. The land had belonged to her husband's family forever, but this house was a new one. After they married, her husband rebuilt the house completely to suit his new wife. Now it stood foursquare, a white stuccoed house set back from the road but in good sight of it, like a swan among the ducks of the village cottages, most of which harked back to another age. Our house, the Manor, was larger, but it and Mrs. Hoarty's house bracketed Darkwater like bookends supporting the frailer fabric of the little cottages.

Mrs. Hoarty was a kind lady, but a garrulous one. She had one son, a lawyer in Exeter, unmarried as yet, who visited her frequently. She led a comfortable life. Moreover, if there were anything to be known, she would know it; from the front parlour window of her fine house she could see everything that went on in the village.

The lady must have seen us as we approached, for her maid was at the door before we could knock.

Mrs. Hoarty was sitting in the large room at the front of the house, where she could watch the comings and goings in the village. "Why, my dears, how nice to see you." She didn't get up to greet us, because she suffered badly from arthritis. I bent down to kiss her papery cheek and gave her the basket. "Why how kind of Lady Hareton."

"How are you?" I asked.

"Very well, considering." She never complained of the pain she suffered, despite the illness that twisted her hands into disused claws.

We gave the maid the basket of treats Martha had prepared, and settled down to satisfy her curiosity for as long as it took Tom to get his horse shod.

"Such an excitement there's been, dear Miss Golightly! Your nuptials will be the talk of the county for years to come."

I knew it. "I'm glad I'll be away from all of it. I'm not used to being the centre of gossip."

"Will your Lord Strang be arriving soon?"

I sincerely hoped so. "He wrote that he would come soon, but there are guests at Eyton, and he can't get away yet." I stifled my sigh. It wouldn't be proper to reveal just how much I missed Richard and how much I looked forward to seeing him again.

The conversation was about my forthcoming nuptials, what I would wear, when Lord Strang would arrive, what we would do after the ceremony. I really tried to satisfy the old lady's curiosity without becoming too impatient, but waiting for Richard this last month had been hard, and my nerves were frayed.

Evidently, Tom didn't have to wait long at the blacksmith's, because he was back in good time. We saw him at the end of Mrs. Hoarty's front garden with his steed within the hour, so we began to take our leave.

Georgiana looked out of the window as she passed it. It had an excellent view of the main street in the village. "What's Tom staring at? He looks as if he's seen an apparition." We joined her at the window, but we couldn't see what he was gazing at so intently.

Mrs. Hoarty chose to walk with us to the end of the garden, to take some fresh air and incidentally to investigate the spectacle outside. I gave her my arm to lean on, and Georgiana supported her on the other side.

We stood by the gate, and looked in the same direction as Tom. His freshly shod horse stamped and jingled his harness beside him, but nobody took any notice.

Two figures walked up the street towards us at an easy pace. I knew them immediately. I waited, my throat tightening as I watched.

I felt stupid, behaving like a lovesick schoolgirl. I stood back a little to regain my composure, taking a few deep, steadying breaths. In any case, I wanted to see what impact the brothers would make on my friends. Separate, they were remarkable enough, but together they could stop the conversation in a room without effort.

As usual, the Kerres were dressed in the height of fashion. One wore impeccably cut, sober garments of the finest cloth, simple but full of quality, his natural fair hair held back in a plain queue. He walked with a confident stride, chatting casually to his brother. His twin brother.

The other man was the picture of fashion. He wore deep, rich, blue cut velvet today, a heavily embroidered waistcoat underneath, with an elaborately curled and tied wig. He carried a clouded Malacca cane at a precise angle. He looked like a visitor from a distant country. Taking his ease, he ignored the curious stares of the villagers, effortlessly picking his way through the ruts on the road. One woman stood at the door of her cottage and stared at them without any effort at subterfuge. She put her hand to her mouth as though suppressing a laugh, but then the brothers glanced in her direction. She turned her back and went indoors, the recipient of twin icy stares, the kind that depressed all pretension in their own milieu of fashionable London.

"A popinjay," breathed Tom in delight. "We don't get many of those here."

Georgiana, standing just in front of me, stared in unconcealed admiration at the vision. "They're beautiful."

Lizzie smiled.

I wondered which one my old friend would choose for me. "Which one is it then, Tom?"

"Oh, you wouldn't take up with a dandy. I can't see you at ease with the fashion plate, so it has to be the other. I must say he looks quite a pleasant man, for a great lord—and a rake."

I reluctantly tore my gaze away from the brothers to Tom. "He's not a great lord. His title's only a courtesy one."

But Tom didn't seem to be listening any more. He stared at me, his eyes wide. I frowned crossly. "What is it, Tom? Do I have a smut on my nose?"

"No, something about you—oh, I don't know!" He turned away in exasperation as at last, the brothers drew near.

It must have become obvious to Georgiana and Tom now that the Kerre brothers weren't just twins—they were identical twins. The only difference between them was Gervase's darker, rougher complexion, gained during his years in India. Their similarity was one of the reasons why they turned so many heads when together, something neither of them liked but had learned to live with in their separate ways.

Appreciatively I watched them make their bows, and allowed Lizzie to perform the introductions. Georgiana blushed and curtseyed prettily when Richard took her hand and kissed the back of it. She was eighteen, only just out, but she would do well, and she was the picture of rustic innocence today. Lizzie had also seen Tom's confusion, and mischievously, she introduced the twins together, so Tom wouldn't know which one was which. He bowed his head, and they bowed in return, but didn't add any extra flourishes.

Finally I came forward and gave my hand to Gervase. He bowed over it. "You're looking well, Rose."

"Thank you." I smiled, and passed on to Richard.

A smile flirted at the corners of Richard's mouth. His clear gaze met mine for the first time, and reminded me yet again how helpless I felt in his company. He took my hand and kissed it lightly, then offered me the support of his arm. "You, my dear delight, have just made me walk the length of that street. You could have met me halfway." He used a complaining tone, but with a softness underneath that told me he was teasing.

I smiled. "I wanted to see the spectacle."

"Witch." He smiled so warmly I had to look away, towards Tom. "It's the popinjay. You lose." Tom flushed and I was sorry at once for the tease.

"You thought my brother had cut me out, sir? He might be as rich as Croesus, but I do have some attractions of my own." I met Richard's eyes and I lost myself in them all over again, like the first time I had gazed into those blue depths.

I introduced the brothers to Mrs. Hoarty, who declared herself overcome by the honour. This would give her plenty of ammunition when she next met her particular friends. She took in every detail of Richard's appearance. Although aware of her scrutiny, he didn't give her any kind of set-down as he could so easily have done.

"Mrs. Hoarty has an invitation to our wedding. She was so kind to us as children. I used to use her house as sanctuary when the Manor got too crowded for me."

"Then I shall ensure she has the best of attention, as my meagre thanks for keeping you safe before I could do so," he said at once. I knew he meant it, and that he would remember. Mrs. Hoarty had been delighted to receive an invitation, but since the wedding was at Exeter Cathedral, it might have proved too much for her if she didn't have the best of care. Her health was too frail. The pampering Richard would make certain his people bestowed on her would guarantee her presence. I was sure she would enjoy herself much, which was more than I could say for myself.

The location of the wedding had been a matter of dispute between us. I wanted to be married in my local church, but Richard's mother, Lady Southwood, wanted the chapel at Eyton. However, she agreed to Richard's suggestion of Exeter Cathedral. She was so pleased to see her son take a wife at last that the venue for it lost its importance. At least this compromise meant I would be married from home.

We took our leave of Mrs. Hoarty and proceeded along the busy street. The villagers stopped to watch us pass, except the one who had received the icy stares earlier. She stayed indoors. Odd how many people found business to attend to at the front of their houses. The more respectable brought buckets and scrubbing brushes to clean the steps, the less respectable just stood, shoulders idly propped against the doorjamb, watching in silence.

Richard and Gervase, used to the stares of strangers, ignored them but the rest of us had to nod and acknowledge the greetings we received. "A raré show," Richard commented acidly to me. "It serves you right."

I was so happy nothing could spoil the day for me. "Well, now they've seen you in all your glory and they can be satisfied. When did you arrive?"

"Barely an hour ago. I couldn't bear my immolation in the coach any longer, especially on such a fine day, so I asked Lady Hareton where you were and came to meet you. Besides," he added simply in a low tone, turning his head to speak to me alone, "I've missed you. I couldn't wait to see you again."

I was touched by the honesty of his statement. Such confessions were hard for him, after so many years locking his feelings away. "It's only been a month."

"Has it? Well, I'll not make any foolish comments about it seeming like a year, but it does seem considerably longer than a month."

His tone was conversational. No one who wasn't within earshot would have realised he was not merely passing the time of day with me. I didn't think Tom, leading his horse behind us, heard. He had his hands full with the animal now the blacksmith had done his job. The horse champed at the bit, longing for something more exciting than a sedate walk.

At last, after what seemed like an age, we reached the end of the street and took the road to the Manor. We didn't live far from the village, a problem for James's development plans for the house, but the architect had promised to come up with a solution for him. The hill at the end of the street obscured the view to our house, and mature trees surrounded it, so at least we were not overlooked.

Georgiana had taken to Gervase, and he behaved with great gallantry towards her, indulging her desire to flirt. When he saw his sister's attempts, Tom snorted, and then tried to turn it into a cough. "She's trying her wings with every man who comes her way these days."

By mutual consent, Richard and I dropped back to walk with him. I let my hand fall from Richard's arm, to take his hand in a less formal pose. To touch him, skin to skin. He gripped it and threaded his fingers between mine. Tom saw the gesture, but didn't comment.

"It's natural to flirt at eighteen. And Georgiana has been sheltered. Most girls are out by seventeen at the latest."

"I don't remember you ever doing such things. Not until— oh, Lord—" Tom broke off when he remembered. The jingle of the harness filled the sudden silence.

"Drury." Richard's mouth set hard. Tom didn't know what Drury had tried to do to me at Hareton, but Richard had nearly killed him for it.

Tom was confused by his slip, his reference to my previous would-be lover. "I'm sorry, my lord, I shouldn't have said anything, but I've known Rose forever, and I told her it would come to no good."

"I wish she'd listened to you," Richard replied.

This accord seemed to put Tom more at his ease. "She never said what happened. Not properly." He gave the reins a little tug when his steed found an attractive patch of grass.

I didn't want to explain to him. I still felt that some of it was my fault.

Richard's hand tightened around mine. "He offered Rose behaviour that was far from acceptable."

Tom nodded. "I thought he might be that sort. He was the curate here, you know, and he seemed to spend all his time in the homes of eligible young women. I can only be thankful

Georgiana was too young for him."

"She's extremely fortunate in that." Richard turned his head to me, his concern evident in his eyes. "I'm afraid we might come across the Drurys again. Julia's father has forgiven her, and they are living in his house. They may wish to re-enter society. I thought I must tell you," he added, as he saw the dread in my expression, "but you are not to let that concern you. He will not be allowed near you."

I smiled tentatively in reply, but I was not entirely reassured, as I knew Steven was a schemer and I had every reason to suppose he held a grudge.

Tom made a sound of disgust in the back of his throat, and Richard turned to look at him, one eyebrow delicately arched. "Beg pardon, my lord. I'm glad the man is away from here, though. If you need any help dealing with him, I'm your man."

"Thank you," said Richard gravely. "I'll remember that." Some of the wariness they showed towards each other thawed in the grim smiles they exchanged.

Chapter Three

We parted at the house. Tom shook hands with Richard and Gervase. "My mother is having people to dinner tomorrow night. I'm sure she'd love it if you could come."

"Delighted," said Richard promptly.

Tom gestured vaguely across the fields. "We live at Peacock's, a mile or two over the hill. I usually walk, because it's longer by road."

"I think we might take the carriage." Richard swept a bow over Georgiana's hand, and she took her leave with her brother, after turning to bestow a winsome smile on Gervase.

We watched Tom and Georgiana walk up the hill towards their house, and then we turned to go in. The Manor stood in front of us, sturdily foursquare; the sort of house that brooked no dallying with fancy columns and curlicues. Its creamy stonework was clean and scrubbed, like everything and everyone inside. Martha was a good manager.

The front door opened and Martha came outside with the children to greet us. My sister Ruth, sweet sixteen and practising to be a heartbreaker, had not yet seen Richard, and although Lizzie had described him to her, it was nothing like experiencing the reality.

She gazed raptly into Richard's face as he bowed over her hand. He gave her the blinding smile he usually reserved for attractive females and entranced her. She wouldn't be out for a while, but she was forming well. Ruth was Lizzie's full sister, and it looked as if she would inherit her mother's blonde prettiness; the prettiness my mother hadn't possessed, and so I didn't have either. I exchanged a glance with Martha, who was watching the small performance with a cynical eye. She had her reservations about my choice of husband because of Richard's fearsome reputation in society as a philanderer. We read about it in the newspapers for years before we actually met him, and it would take some time for her to trust him.

I'd always thought of myself as an unremarkable brunette, too tall for beauty, too shy for flirting, until the startling events of the previous autumn disabused me of that notion. I still found it hard to believe, but here I was and here he was. Richard had signed one of the most punitive marriage settlements I had ever seen without a murmur, and declared himself perfectly content.

Richard left me to greet Martha, who had a few quiet words with him. Gervase moved to my side. "He missed you very much, you know."

I looked away, feeling my cheeks flush with heat. I was one of the only two people Richard allowed inside the barrier he'd built up for himself—Gervase because he couldn't hide anything from his twin and me because I had stormed barriers I never noticed at the time. But I was a newcomer, and although I loved Richard, I felt I didn't know him well.

"I missed him," I confessed. "I feel stupid really, because it's only been a month, but I can't be completely content without him."

"Don't worry. Soon the circus will be over and you'll have time to yourselves." Gervase smiled reassuringly at me, and I smiled back.

Not for the first time, I thought how strange it was that Richard should arouse such strong emotions in me, and his twin brother engendered nothing more than the sort of warmth I felt for Tom Skerrit.

"I'm not happy about all of it," I confided to Gervase now. "I don't suppose you understand because you've been in the public eye all your life, but I'm nervous. The only thing I'm sure about is Richard." It would have been difficult enough getting married to a local man in the local church, because I hated to be the centre of attention, but a public marriage to such a well known figure as Richard made me deeply apprehensive.

Half polite society had promised to attend the wedding and Lizzie was more excited than I was. I didn't know if Richard knew about my nervousness; I had tried hard not to show him.

"You just do as you are bid, look beautiful, and everyone will be satisfied," Gervase whispered to me. "Tell Richard how you feel; no one else will comfort you like he will." I laughed at him, foolish man, but at least he had made me forget for a time what was to come the next month, the thought of which made my stomach contract.

Richard came back to join us, and we let the others climb the steps to the front door before we followed them. To my surprise, instead of following the others going upstairs to the drawing room he turned aside, and took me into the breakfast parlour at the back of the house.

He closed the door behind us. "Your estimable sister-in-law has given us half an hour, and then she says I must go upstairs and meet the rest of your prodigious family. I need some sustenance to see me through that. So will you come and greet me properly?"

His smile made the warmth increase inside me. "With pleasure." I put my arms around him under his coat and turned my face up for his kiss.

The first touch of his lips on mine gave me the bliss I'd missed this past month, and I lost myself in him. He pressed me close, letting me feel how much he'd missed me, and I responded, trying to show him I'd missed him too, letting my hands roam over his body, holding him tight. After the first, tentative touch, he took my mouth like a man starved and I feasted along with him.

I was breathless by the time he drew away and looked down at me. "So you didn't miss me at all?"

"Not at all." When he looked at me with that warmth, he

made me wonder how I could wait another month before I gave him all he asked for and more. And all I wanted, too. Once, an afternoon out of time, he'd taken me in his arms, undressed me and loved me but since then, none of our diligent chaperones had given us the opportunity.

His eyes were a bright, cold blue, but I saw the warmth he reserved just for me.

"I didn't expect you so soon."

He smoothed his hands over my back. I felt his touch through the layers of clothes, through my stays, as though he was touching my bare skin. "Without you I found our guests too tedious for words. My mother doesn't approve of my choice, you know that, but she knows better than to quibble. I told her it was you or no one. She tried—" He broke off and took another kiss, effectively confusing my mind so I forgot he hadn't finished his sentence. "Lady Hareton volunteered to let us stay here, though where we'll sleep is a mystery to me. This house seems to be stuffed as full as it can get."

I laughed, too happy to worry about accommodation. "Oh, we have a couple of guest rooms. They may not be as grand as your usual rooms, but if you're prepared to put up with us, we'll try to manage with you." He smiled and kissed me again, lightly this time. "I'll enjoy it here," he murmured, his lips close to mine. "We don't have to be apart again, you know. Ever."

I caught my breath. He drew back, but kept one arm around my shoulders. "My family will arrive a week or two before the wedding, and then I'll move out to whatever house Gervase and I find for them, but I won't go further away from you than that. I can't imagine Lady Hareton will want me under her feet so close to the wedding."

"Martha is a hospitable woman. You never saw her to advantage at the Abbey, but she loves to entertain, and her powers of organisation are formidable. She has my trousseau organised, the wedding is well under way, and she's made James hold his alterations to the Manor back until May."

He caressed my back, letting his hands roam over the

fabric of my gown. "I saw the difference she made to the State Rooms at the Abbey in a mere few weeks. I wouldn't like to get in the way of any of her plans. Does she approve of me?"

I moved into his loving touch. "I don't think she entirely trusts you. She was pleased you signed the contract without demur, that went a long way to convince her, but—well, she cares for me, and she wants me to be happy."

"As do I. And I signed that contract because I haven't the least intention of breaking it." His voice softened to a caress. "And I, too, want you to be happy, so I had it made so you can break it off at any point you wish."

"Even if I didn't want you any more?"

"Even that. If you were unhappy with me, I couldn't bear it. I'm not sure it wouldn't be better to see you happy with someone else."

I lifted my head to look at him, into the depths of those startlingly blue eyes. "I've never met anyone like you. All this is new, the people, all the fuss. If I had married a year or two ago, only the county would have been remotely interested in me. Now fashionable society wants to beat a path to our door, and I seem to be the only one unable to cope with it all."

He pulled me close. "My poor love." He kissed my forehead. "All you have to remember is I love you, and I intend to take you away from this when it's over. Let my parents and your sisters have their day, and then we can have ours." He let me go, and dipped his hand in his coat pocket. "By the way, I thought you should have something to cheer up your mourning dress." He pulled out a long box and gave it to me.

Inside, gleaming with their own life, lay a string of perfectly matched pearls. Their bluish glow gave them a world of their own, serene in their own importance. I touched one, with the tip of a finger. It was cold. I looked back at him. He watched me, waiting for my reaction. "Oh Richard, they're beautiful."

"Here. Allow me."

He lifted the pearls out of the box. I felt the warmth of his hand when he clasped them around my neck Then he took me to the mirror over the sideboard, positioned me in front of it, and stood behind me, frowning while he judged the effect. "They look good against your skin. And you have dark hair. I've always thought pearls compliment brunettes best." I studied us both in the mirror. We were an incongruous couple.

He was so fashionable, so much of his class, dressed in expensive, exquisite perfection and I was of little consequence except locally until last year. He bore himself like a prince, unconsciously graceful.

My clothes were plain, dowdy mourning clothes. If I'd been expecting him to arrive that day, I would have put on one of the newer mourning gowns. He was every inch the man of fashion, at his ease in it as I thought I never would be. I didn't deserve him, and I might not be able to keep him. Fear and doubt filled me to overflowing. "Oh, Richard, are you sure?"

He met my gaze in the mirror. "Oh yes." He dropped his hands and took a step away from me so I could only see my own reflection. "What do you see?"

I shrugged, but tried to be honest. "An ordinary, not young woman, tired. The sort of woman you would have passed in the street and not looked at twice, if we hadn't found ourselves in the extraordinary situation we did last year." I avoided any self pity and tried to tell him the truth as I saw it.

"My turn." He came up behind me again and put his hands on my shoulders, turning me away from the mirror to face him. "Tired I would agree with, but nothing else, so I shall have to make sure you get more sleep. Five and twenty isn't on the shelf, my love." He regarded me steadily, his gaze sweeping my face. "The young don't appeal to me the way you do. You have far more about you than a seventeen-year-old, fresh from the schoolroom. You have a well-informed mind; no doubt that sickly brother of yours helped there." I remembered the hours I had spent keeping Ian company while he read, or I read to him in one of his many childhood illnesses, and was forced to agree. But I said nothing, just listened to him. "It gives you character. Your face is far more interesting than the blank canvasses presented to me season after season for the last ten years, as soon as I returned from the Grand Tour." He lifted his hand and caressed my cheek. "You have an elusive quality all your own, something I've never encountered before. Elegance, poise, serenity, and when I've finished with you, you'll have style. No one will ever pass you by, unless you wish it."

Did he mean to turn me into something I wasn't, something I was uncomfortable with? For him, I would do even that. Anything, for him.

He looked at me closely, no guile, no fashionable languor here, and his face relaxed. "But apart from all that, the first time I saw you I fell in love with you. I found it confusing, and I tried hard to combat it. When I got to know you a little better, I knew I had no reason to fight against it. So I surrendered, and I've not regretted it. If you were Miss Golightly of Devonshire, as, let me remind you, you were when I first saw you, I would still have moved everything in my path to win you. You know I'm not particularly handsome, not particularly special." He ignored my protests. "I've made myself something else because I wanted to. You know some of the reasons for that, and you'll probably get to know others but, my love, it's all in the mind. Take the fancy clothes, jewels and wigs away and what are you left with?"

"A remarkable man. Loyal, intelligent, handsome." He threw his head back and laughed at that. "And the man I love."

He folded his arms around me again, drawing me to his heat. "Enough philosophy. Kiss me once more, and then we'll go and join your excellent family." I did as he asked, satisfied for the present, happy to feel him close, to be loved as never before.

My previous suitor, Steven Drury, was far more handsome than Richard, but Richard had something Steven could never possess. Presence, self possession, confidence. Everyone looked at him when he entered a room. He had an energy people found exciting. I'd seen it operate almost without his knowledge, the way people turned to stare at him, as they had done earlier in the village.

The door to the breakfast parlour burst open, and I tried to break away in embarrassment, but he held me close and turned us both in his own time. He kept one arm about my waist, firm and sure.

It was the hope of the house, Martha and James's oldest son, Walter, at nine so full of confidence and bravado that even short doses of him were tiring. He had been dressed in his best breeches and waistcoat, probably when Richard and Gervase had come to the village to meet us, but his fair hair tumbled about his face in unruly curls, and a small smudge of indefinable dirt marred the soft cheek. Walter attracted dirt. "Oh, I beg your pardon. I should have knocked. Mama told me to knock." He didn't sound in the least sorry and I guessed the omission was deliberate.

"So you should." Richard's voice held a stern edge, but he wasn't really angry. I heard the softness beneath. "Did your mama send you to fetch us?"

"Yes. Are you Lord Strang, who's going to marry my Auntie Rose?"

"I should hope so. If I saw anyone else with his arm about her waist I would be severely displeased."

Walter laughed. "Even me?"

"*Can* you put your arm about her waist?"

"Oh yes." Walter had all the overweening confidence of the child. "Auntie Rose is tall for a woman, Mama says, but I'm getting tall too." He would have demonstrated, but Richard kept his arm firmly around me and wouldn't let him.

"Your Auntie Rose is not to be manhandled. Except by me." He glanced at me, his intimate smile warming me. "Now, shall we go upstairs?" He released me, took my hand instead, and we followed Walter out of the room and upstairs.

We went into the drawing room hand in hand, but he dropped mine to individually greet every member of my extensive family. I went to join Gervase who, having already made his bows, watched the performance from a seat by the window.

My Lord Strang was supremely accomplished in social

situations, but a family gathering like this presented a different challenge. However, the informality didn't upset his sangfroid, and one by one, he was presented to my family. First he met my brother Ian, tall, thin and ascetic, and then his opposites, my niece and my other nephew, Mary and Frederick. Martha always said Frederick was the noisiest child in the world, but we loved him dearly.

Richard accepted a glass of wine from Martha and set himself to charm them. I sat next to Gervase. "I hope they haven't tired you too much."

"Not at all," he replied, but I guessed this was not his preferred occupation. He watched the children warily. I don't think Gervase understood children, but many people don't, despite having spent several years as one.

It became clear that my sister Ruth admired Richard greatly. She hardly took her eyes off him, watching the gracefulness of his movements, taking in every detail of his dress. He pretended not to notice, and I was pleased and relieved at that. He was perfectly capable of taking Ruth apart, delicately dissecting admiration until it became hate or fear. I had seen it once during my visit to his parents, and it showed me a side of him I had not seen before, and was glad I'd not seen up to that point. It would have made me afraid of him.

Richard was perfectly capable of depressing Ruth's admiration more gently if it became irksome to him. However, I saw nothing but good humour when he raised his glass to me from across the room. I smiled back to show my amusement at his predicament. Noisy children surrounded him, children who until now had grown up in a not particularly remarkable house as well-loved children from a close-knit background. In any case, Martha would send them to the nursery soon. When I looked across at her I saw she was watching me closely while I watched him. I hoped she saw what she wanted to see.

Chapter Four

Increasingly nervous about the dinner Tom had invited us to, I spoke to Martha. This wouldn't be a normal occasion, when I could relax in the company of my peers. They wanted to meet Richard and assess him.

"I hope they won't think I'm putting myself above them. Flaunting my new found position in their faces. That would be unbelievably crass of me. Do you think they believe that?"

Martha looked up from her stitching. We were alone in the little parlour, because I needed her to speak her mind with no other person present. Her grey eyes were calm. "You know what the people here are like. There's nowhere better than Devonshire. They pity anyone who doesn't live here, and they think themselves the equal of anyone alive."

She made me laugh. "No one is good enough for a Devonshire girl."

"Precisely." Calmly, she set another stitch.

"I never thought of leaving here before. Or of going so far afield."

"You would do that whether you married or not. We'll go to London in the autumn while this house is rebuilding. Our world is growing larger."

I knew she was right. "Richard is my home now. If he'd been the son of a squire hereabouts, I would have taken him, and then I could have carried on almost the same."

"If he were the son of the squire he wouldn't be the person he is. He's a great lord, from one of the most distinguished families in the country. He frightens most people." She kept her attention on her work.

"Frightens?" I echoed, but then I understood. His flawless exterior intimidated, and it still awed me sometimes until he smiled at me. "He doesn't frighten you, does he, Martha?"

She lifted her head and met my gaze levelly. "Yes. Anyone who can hide their true nature as completely as he does is capable of anything."

I'd only known Richard for six months. I believed he'd let me in without reserve, but the only guarantee I had was the way I felt about him.

I dressed with some care that evening, knowing all eyes would be upon us. I'd done my best, but we were still in mourning, forbidden large gatherings and dancing for another week to come. I wore grey, as usual, but it was brocade, and I put it with a watered tabby petticoat, a white embroidered stomacher and of course, my new pearls.

Richard came down to the hall and bowed to me with a flourish and a gleam of amusement. "Will I do?"

He looked exquisite, as usual. His lilac coat and waistcoat were laced with silver and embroidered by fairies it seemed, so delicate was the stitching. The linen at his neck and the lace ruffles of his shirt were starched to perfection. He wore the latest in low-heeled shoes and everywhere lay the cold glitter of diamonds, from the single stone at his neck to the buckles on his knees and his shoes.

Gervase bowed to me, but his aspect was graver. He wore impeccable dark green brocade, trimmed with gold lace.

"You both look wonderful," I assured them. "You must know you do. Do you try to look different, or does it come naturally to you to demonstrate in as many ways as possible how a fashionable man can appear to advantage?"

They exchanged a laughing glance. Not many people would have dared ask them, but I was allowed into the world they shared, though it was not my birth which allowed me such a privilege.

Richard held his arm out for me. I rested my hand on it, enjoying the thrill I felt whenever I touched him. "You haven't powdered. It's charming."

"I tend to avoid it. My hair is so dark the powder never takes properly, and the dead white doesn't suit me. I have to put up with it for more formal occasions."

"In London more and more ladies in the younger set are leaving off powder. You should set a fashion." The idea I should be a leader of fashion made me laugh, but he gave me a mock severe frown. "As my wife, you will be looked to for a certain style. You will set it perfectly."

I had no patience with such things. "They'll have to take me as I am."

He laughed, his frown completely gone. "Then that, my sweet, will be your style."

Lizzie joined us. I was firmly convinced my sister could wear sacking and outshine everyone else in the room, but she took a keen interest in fashion. Tonight she appeared in spectacular black. She had lightened the colour with white, as we were in half mourning, but the dramatic effect only heightened her beauty, the fair skin and gleaming bright blonde hair, shining against the stark black of her gown.

Dinner was at four, so carriages were ordered for three. The Skerrits' house wasn't far from ours, and normally we walked, but we couldn't think of it on this occasion. We were far too grand to walk.

Fascination lit Gervase's handsome features when he saw Peacock's. It was nearer to the coast than our Manor house, and much older. Gervase studied every part of the frontage. "It must date back centuries." He didn't take his eager gaze off it for one minute.

Peacock's was one of the few half-timbered buildings in Devonshire, with stone mullioned windows, but I had known it since I was tiny. I was so used to it I didn't really notice its beauty any more.

The entrance led to the oldest part of the house. I went in leaning on Richard's arm, with Gervase on my other side. Gervase caught his breath. The Great Hall was old, the timbered roof soaring above our heads in stripes of light and dark. A large oriel window decorated the end wall, still bearing its stained glass, sending streams of bright colour on to the stone flagged floor. A fire had been set in the generous fireplace, so the hall was reasonably warm. I was thankful to see it, because beautiful though the hall was, it got cold at this time of year.

Most of the guests had already arrived and they watched us come in, giving us the kind of attention I still had to get used to. At one time I might have entered unobserved, and taken my place by Martha at one side of the room, but those days were gone.

Once we'd greeted Sir George and Lady Skerrit, Tom and Georgiana, I took Richard and Gervase around the hall, introducing them. Everyone looked at them, and none at me, but that was only to be expected, as they had known me always, but never on the arm of anyone as spectacular as Richard. I ignored the speculative stares, and I knew as if they were speaking what they must be thinking. Why was someone like Richard with someone like me? I was far from answering that myself.

Some of the girls here had even pitied me. Miss Eustacia Terry, the daughter of a squire a few miles off didn't like me, and sometimes went out of her way to taunt me. She looked pretty tonight, in a pale blue, low-cut gown, which suited her light colouring admirably. I had thought I would enjoy my triumph of attracting one of England's most eligible bachelors, but to my surprise I found it mattered little. Perhaps it was because Miss Terry's opinion had never meant much to me, so it didn't mean much now.

Richard bowed over her hand and to my surprise, Eustacia simpered. I'd never seen her do that before, so it must be a new trick. Miss Terry was accounted one of our local beauties and she tried to play all the new games she could find. I wanted to see her try her tricks out on Richard.

I moved back to stand with Lizzie, and together we sipped our wine and watched the show.

"La, sir, I was never as surprised as when I heard our Rose had caught you in her net," she said.

Richard shot a startled look at me, but I smiled beatifically at him. I saw him catch my amusement then, and he must have decided to play up to it. Perhaps he remembered my glancing references to her as my tormentor in the local assemblies and gatherings. When Lizzie made her debut in local society and put Eustacia's nose out, she never missed an opportunity to denigrate me, but I hadn't told Richard just how much she'd done this. Miss Terry had always despised me for having missed the opportunities to ensnare one of the young men who always passed me by, and she mocked me whenever the opportunity arose, but I had merely mentioned it to Richard in passing once.

I should have known better. Richard never forgot anything when it concerned me.

She took on a deliberately coquettish pose when she leant towards him, offering him a view of her charms, should he wish to take advantage of it.

"Indeed, madam?" He reached into his pocket and drew out his snuffbox. I had seen him take snuff before, an art complete in itself, but to my surprise this time, before he took some himself, he offered the box to Miss Terry. It was considered a privilege if one person offered another his snuff, but ladies rarely partook, and I knew that Miss Terry had never tried it. Gervase, standing nearby talking to Lady Skerrit, glanced at his brother, an eyebrow arched in surprise.

We watched Miss Terry gingerly take a small pinch, put it to her nose and sniff. Since she had not done this before, she did not accomplish the task with too much elegance and the surplus fell from her fingers on to her gown. Richard compounded her inelegance by pinching an infinitesimal amount himself and taking it in one swift, exquisite movement.

I suspected he disliked the stuff. He never took it in private, and a boxful seemed to last him a long time. He snapped the pretty box shut and replaced it in his pocket, but in an elegant flourishing way that showed off the lace on his sleeves and the jewellery on his hands to great advantage. The great emerald on his finger glittered, and I stared at it, wondering anew how this exquisite creature could ever be mine.

He put the box and his handkerchief away and moved back a little. Miss Terry's sneeze, when it came, was satisfyingly explosive and it stopped all conversation in the hall. She groped in her pocket for her handkerchief, and finally she had the presence of mind to spread her fan before her face while she recovered her composure.

"Dear me," said elegant Lord Strang, surprise in every inch of his form. "I do beg your pardon, madam. Do ladies here not take snuff? It's becoming quite the thing in London these days." I lifted an eyebrow at Gervase who shook his head slightly. Not the thing, then.

Miss Terry looked at her tormentor, her pale eyes doubtful. "Does Rose do it?"

"Sadly no." He shot a regretful glance to where I stood by Lizzie, his eyes glinting with banked-down delight. "She has expressed a positive dislike for it, but I may bring her round yet."

"No you won't," I told him, and I moved forward to join in again. Not being a saint, I had enjoyed Miss Terry's embarrassment, but enough was enough, at least for now.

"Nor," continued my love, pursuing his quarry, "have I ever heard her say 'la'. You should take it up, sweetheart, you could set quite a fashion." I frowned at him but he continued to smile at her, unperturbed, elegantly assured.

Miss Terry must have thought everyone in London used the term, but she should have realised that nothing is so dated as the jargon of a previous generation.

The shock of realisation jolted me. He'd called me "sweetheart"' in company. Richard wasn't demonstrative in public, and usually referred to me as "Rose" or "madam".

I knew, as clearly as if he'd told me, that he was letting Miss Terry know something about us, but I don't know if she'd noticed. She didn't know Richard well.

"You shall tell me what words I should use instead." She leaned forward confidentially to lay her hand on his arm.

He looked down at the hand, and then up at her face. Miss Terry had recovered her composure and seemed too dense to see that his smile had gone, or so sure of herself she didn't imagine he could resist her charms. He bowed his head. "Naturally, I would be delighted."

We moved on. He behaved himself impeccably with everyone else, but in a quiet moment said to me, "I would appreciate your opinion on these people some time. I don't know them from Adam. See if I won't try to bring them out."

I sighed. I'd seen the gleam in his eye, his enjoyment at baiting Miss Terry. "You won't get rid of Miss Terry for a while. She put it about you jilted Julia Cartwright for me—" He glanced at me, frowning. I continued hastily, "Oh, everyone knows the right of it, but she loves to make trouble, and she's been heard to say if you'll jilt one, then you'll jilt another. She imagines that every man who comes within her orbit will fall madly in love with her." Julia Cartwright had run off with my erstwhile suitor, Steven Drury, before Richard had formally asked for my hand in marriage. The fault lay with her and Richard had taken great pains to ensure no condemnation lay on me. He would not like Eustacia's gossip.

"Does she indeed?" He lifted a single delicate eyebrow in displeasure.

"She's stupid, you mustn't mind her."

"Oh, but I think I must." He would say nothing else, and Lady Skerrit was coming towards us, so he moved forward with his charming smile to greet her.

Dinner was served in the large dining room, at a huge table built there *in situ* by the original builders of the house. If this was not a formal occasion, I swear Gervase would have been under it, examining the timbers for signs of the long-dead carpenter's tools. He did ask Lady Skerrit if he might come another day with his sketchbook. "I find this building enchanting, and I'm sure it must hold many secrets."

"Gervase will ferret them all out," Richard warned her. "I've never seen such a passion for antiquities. I believe we have an old castle ourselves, Gervase."

Gervase turned in surprise. "Have we? I don't recall."

"Our Tudor ancestors virtually abandoned it. Our father takes no interest in it. You should go to see it. For all I know it's a complete ruin, but it might amuse you to restore it."

"It might indeed." Gervase's face brightened. He proceeded to ask Lady Skerrit many questions about the house, some of which she couldn't answer.

Tom had no idea either. "I didn't think anyone else would be interested in Peacock's. I love it, but then I would."

"It's a wonderful example of early Tudor, one of the finest I've seen." Several young ladies heard Gervase's comments, and I wondered how many would find a similar passion in the early Tudor style before Gervase left the district.

Richard, placed by my side at the table, set himself to charm Miss Terry, seated on his other side. I had some suspicion of what he was about, and I wasn't sure I approved. He told her she must be sure to come and see us later in the year, as he wished to go to London after our bride trip.

"Bride trip?" I hadn't thought about after the wedding.

"Yes, had you forgotten? Bride visits will have to wait until I've had you to myself for a while."

"Where are we going?"

"Everywhere and nowhere." He gave me a maddeningly enigmatic smile and would say no more, returning to Miss Terry instead. "You remind me of someone, ma'am. One of the Misses Gunning perhaps."

Eustacia lowered her eyelids and smiled up at him, a trick she practised on the local cavaliers, with excellent results. I had seen it many times in Exeter Assembly rooms, and it rarely failed in its effect. Richard smiled back at her, and Gervase, seated on my other side, choked. The Gunnings were great beauties, famed throughout society. It was an outrageous compliment, but Eustacia saw nothing amiss in it. "Or Miss Chudleigh," Richard continued, his quarry well in his sights. Miss Chudleigh's morals were known to be lax, to say the least.

Eustacia opened her eyes wide. "I cannot think I come up to their standards, sir." She unfurled her fan and made to tap him with it, but he moved his hand away.

"You need town polish, Miss Terry," Richard said. "Then you will astonish us all. Do you mean to come to town?"

Eustacia glanced at her parents, seated further up the table. Mrs. Terry watched her daughter carefully—little escaped her close regard. "We might plan a visit for the season next year, but we are unused to town ways and we will need someone like you to show us how to go on."

"I'm sure many people will rush to help you." That committed him to nothing.

Skilfully he worked on Miss Terry, enchanting her, winding a silken web of delight around her willing form. His compliments were flowery, insincere but delightful, the kind a society lady would dismiss out of hand, but which I feared Miss Terry took only too seriously. The other young ladies present eyed her enviously from time to time, and one or two glanced at me to see how I reacted. I stayed serene. Richard unobtrusively saw to my every comfort while holding the girl on his string, and I thought I had a good idea what he was about.

On my other side Gervase murmured, "Has the young lady offended you?"

"In the past she has done her best."

"Did you tell him?" I nodded. Gervase tsked. "That might not have been the wisest course."

Tom observed me with concern. He could see how much Richard flirted, but he didn't know him as well as Gervase did, and wasn't able to divine his purpose. It looked like I was being ignored, but this was far from the case. I knew the moment I asked for his attention, Richard would turn away from Miss Terry and back to me.

"Do you remember this table, Rose?" Tom asked.

"I remember it well." I knew what he meant. "Do you think the mark your tomahawk made will still be there?"

"Oh, it's still there all right," my childhood friend assured me with a boyish grin.

"Tomahawk?" Richard looked away from his target, the languid interest replaced by real curiosity.

Tom's grin broadened. "It's a weapon like an axe that the natives of America use. We used to have one, but Rose and I took to playing American natives under this table and when I pretended one of the legs was a tree and I wanted to cut it down, Father took it away."

"I threw it away that same morning." Sir George Skerrit smiled at the memory. "I thought the table might be worth keeping for a few more years, and I could certainly live without a tomahawk."

"Can it be I'm to marry a hoyden?" Richard's limpid blue gaze filled with astonishment, but I saw the humour lurking deep.

"Oh, I thought you'd worked that out for yourself at the Abbey. Did I not show you deeply hoydenish behaviour there, one afternoon in particular?" His eyes gleamed. I knew he was remembering something not to be repeated in polite society, but I met his gaze levelly. "Only I don't think the word hoyden came into it at the time."

His eyes caressed me with their warmth, reminding me of the time they had caressed my naked body—followed by his hands and his mouth. "No, it assuredly did not," he said slowly and turned back to Miss Terry. "I can't believe you, ma'am, would do anything of that nature."

"No indeed." she replied, even though she couldn't possibly know what we were discussing. She shot me a spark of triumph. "I wasn't allowed out of the nursery wing until I was seventeen."

"And you were always taught proper manners." Richard leaned back in his chair and picked up his wineglass. Twirling it idly, he watched the red liquid swirl around inside, a tiny turbulent sea.

"My mama thought it essential." Eustacia looked towards her mother once more. Mrs. Terry smiled indulgently back at her only child.

"Do you always follow the principles of good behaviour?" he asked.

"Oh yes, sir."

"Do you *never* deviate from them?" He caught her in his gaze, a silent challenge lurking there for her to answer.

Miss Terry put up her chin. "I might." She flushed a little. After a furtive glance towards her mother, she favoured Richard with a coquettish smile.

Richard watched her steadily. When he'd gained her full attention, he slowly let his regard move down, to her décolleté neckline, and back up to her face again. "I'm pleased to hear it." He returned to his wine. Miss Terry coloured, and looked away, then back at him, but he had turned away to speak to Sir George.

Gervase sighed. "He knows to a nicety how far she will go to attract him, but this is as far as he cares to take her tonight. He's preparing her for a mighty fall."

"I know."

Apparently blithely unaware of Miss Terry's blushes and simpers now, Richard spoke to our host. "Do you take your seat in Parliament, sir?"

"Not every year," Sir George replied.

"Very wise. Gervase is thinking of going into the House. Our father is delighted, for he's tried to persuade me for years, and I've always refused him."

"You would have to enter the Lords surely, my lord?" Sir George said.

Richard shook his head. "No. My title is a courtesy one; I could still enter the Commons. But I fear I might find it a dead bore."

"Really, Richard! The affairs of nations are settled there," Gervase protested.

"You know my sphere of influence, Gervase. It doesn't include the affairs of nations." He smiled at Sir George. "I take a particular interest in our justice system, and the way it is carried out." Sir George nodded, but a tinge of curiosity entered his expression. Perhaps he thought a man of fashion like Richard couldn't take an interest in anything outside his wardrobe. People often made that mistake. Richard addressed his brother. "Now you would make an excellent politician, Gervase, and you could remain in the Commons."

"You could be a new Pelham and Newcastle," said James, referring to our present leaders, also brothers, one in the Lords, the other in the Commons.

Richard's shudder was so pronounced it could have been seen right down at the other end of the table. "I thank you, no. If anything could persuade me to stay well out of political affairs, that reference could."

"Can it be you support the Tory cause, my lord?" asked Sir George with a sudden increased interest.

"I have no idea what that could be." Richard drained his glass and watched the servant refill it. "If I am anything, I must be Whig, but that doesn't encourage me to admire Newcastle. Pelham is a competent man, I think, but his brother seems to lack the resolve a good politician needs. He prefers sycophants to men of ability. I should like to think I'm too good for him, but I'll never know, since I don't intend to try."

"Is your father interested in politics?" asked James.

"He supports Henry Fox, but he doesn't aspire to high office. So, madam," he said, turning to me, "if you were hoping to be a political hostess I'm afraid I must disappoint you."

I smiled, relieved he had let Miss Terry alone for the time being. "I can live without it. But if I really wanted to, I could always become Gervase's hostess."

"Until he gets himself a wife of his own." Sir George smiled, and Miss Terry eyed Gervase speculatively. Of all the people at this table tonight only Richard, Lizzie and I knew Gervase's secret, that his scandalous elopement had been with another man, not the man's wife, as had been put about. I had confided in my sister, with Gervase's permission, and she had been a lot less censorious that I had supposed. Society suspected, but when he returned from India, his riches went a long way towards convincing society that he wouldn't cause such scandal again. He did seem to have learned his lesson, and he kept his affairs admirably discreet. Moreover, he was an amusing and much valued dinner guest, and would have been a sad loss to many hostesses, so most people let it be. I hoped there would be no scandals here in my home county. Surely the Kerre brothers would not be here long enough for that.

Chapter Five

The dinner ended. I stood with everyone else and watched the men drift apart from the women. Richard inclined his head and favoured me with a wink as he stood with the other gentlemen while we left the room. I lowered my head on a smile. It was like him to tease me in public, try to make me lose my composure while giving me every support. The perversity of his nature alarmed me sometimes.

Lady Skerrit twined her hand around my arm as if she had suddenly grown frail; an extraordinary accomplishment considering her sturdy form. She flicked out her fan and used it to direct me to the drawing room at the front of the house. I felt like the leader of a flock of brightly clad sheep walking along the candlelit corridor. Tall paintings of Skerrit ancestors peered down at us from either side.

The drawing room candles were already lit. Tea was laid out on the sideboards and the tables set up in the centre for card playing. Lady Skerrit's servants were most efficient, as always.

Lady Skerrit drew me aside, with a concerned expression, echoing that of her son. "A word, if you please, Rose."

We sat a little apart, and talked quietly while a maid brought us tea and cakes. I waited to hear what my dear friend's mama would have to say, but I feared I had guessed already. "My dear, I hope you don't mind if I speak out, but you and Tom have run together since you were children, and I almost look on you as one of my own. In fact, once I hoped—" She broke off and sighed. "But it was not to be."

"Lady Skerrit, I—" I hoped to head her off, but she held up her hand for me to cease. It was a gesture I remembered well from my childhood and I was quiet.

"Lord Strang is a personable man, but he is a man of the world, and you, despite your age, are an innocent. I've seen men like this before. They cause great misery to people and I don't want you to become one of them. My dear, are you sure about this?" Her regard was all earnest anxiety and because we had been so close, I didn't try to turn her concerns away lightly. She truly cared for me.

I sighed, and put my tea dish down, as I met her gaze with a frankness that matched her own. "Yes ma'am, I'm sure. I truly appreciate your concern, and I think, because you have known us for so long, I ought to tell you a little more. But please, don't let it be generally known." Lady Skerrit nodded and leaned towards me, so as not to be overheard.

I didn't want to tell her, but if I didn't try to explain, she would worry about me. "It's not something one looks for in marriage in the usual way, but Richard and I are deeply in love." I paused, searching for the right words. "Most people think he saw me as a better replacement for Julia Cartwright, but he'd already determined to be rid of her by the time we met. You remember Steven Drury, of course?" Lady Skerrit nodded. "She's like the female version of Steven. They're well suited." I paused again. It felt like a betrayal, but I could trust Lady Skerrit not to gossip. "We didn't look for this, but believe me it's there."

My best friend's mother frowned. "I could see little evidence of his affection for you tonight."

"You mean Miss Terry?" She nodded, tight-lipped. "I'm afraid I made a mistake. I told Richard about Miss Terry's behaviour to me in the past." I spread my fan and stared at the pattern, rather than meet her eyes. The cherubs painted on to the pleated surface stared back at me blankly.

"It seemed to me that this only attracted him to her, rather than repulsed him. He hardly took any notice of you at dinner."

Her voice sounded as fierce as a mother cat's, defending its young.

I tried again. "Lady Skerrit, did you notice how often my glass was empty, or if I'd had enough to eat?" She shook her head. "He saw to it I had everything I needed but in a way that didn't draw notice, because he knows I dislike that. If I had required his attention, believe me he would have given it."

"Why should he devote himself so much to Miss Terry?"

"Because he wishes to bring her down," I confessed. "He will entrance her, lead her on and then drop her."

"Why should he want to do that?"

It sounded far-fetched, if one didn't know Richard. I shrugged. "I told Richard about the slights she offered me in the past. I only mentioned them, but Richard has a fierce loyalty to those few people he allows into his confidence."

She bridled, her shoulders stiffening. "He won't do it here." After a pause, she continued, in a softer tone, "But really, my dear, everything I've seen here today only confirms the reputation he brings with him. He's a roué, a rake, a charming deceiver."

I looked up at her, smiling slightly. "Yes, it is quite a reputation, isn't it? But I cannot take credit for reforming him. He gave all that up before he met me. He told me he'd grown up."

"I've never seen a leopard change its spots that much," she commented acidly.

I couldn't tell her everything. Not the years of anguish he spent living down Gervase's scandal, furious with his parents for sending his brother away, angry at his mother's cold, calculating attempts to marry him off. "He created his own reputation and then it bored him." I hoped that would do. A thought occurred to me, how I could make her understand. "Lady Skerrit, do you trust Martha?"

"Lady Hareton? Of course I do."

"Then ask her how it is between Richard and me. She only saw the depth of affection we share once, but she's unlikely to have forgotten it." I had recourse to my fan once more. I continued to trace the pattern with my finger as I told her. "This must go no further, but if I can't trust you, I can't trust anyone."

No one could hear us. They were all sitting slightly apart, most of them listening to Eustacia Terry in full flow. Still, I spoke quietly. "Steven Drury attacked me at the Abbey—in a particular way, if you know what I mean." I met her eyes, and saw she was horrified, but in consideration of where we were, she didn't exclaim aloud. "He didn't succeed, but in order to escape him, I was forced to rouse the house with my screams. Martha and James saw Gervase stop Richard from killing Steven, and then he turned to me, and—well, they all saw what happened then." The kiss, the total attention to me, the way he picked me up and took me away to tend to my sprained ankle. His total absorption in me. I smiled when I remembered. They saw what I meant to him, and they were unlikely to forget, since it was so unlike anything they had seen in him before. Richard didn't allow people to see the man under the glittering exterior very often.

Lady Skerrit took a deep breath to steady herself, and let it out slowly. "I see. Well I would trust Lady Hareton's opinion as much as I trust my own. Thank you, I shall certainly speak to her."

"And when the gentlemen return, watch him closely, ma'am. I'll try to draw him out for you, just for a moment." She nodded, but I saw she was still sceptical, her lips pursed, a slight frown still creasing her forehead.

I got to my feet. "If you'll excuse me now, I'll try to limit the damage Richard is inflicting. Speak to Miss Terry, try to warn her away."

"I'm not sure that's wise, my dear. Perhaps, if things are as you say, you should speak quietly to him later. Persuade him not to lead Eustacia on."

I shook my head. "He won't be deterred from his purpose. Not after I made the mistake of telling him—what I have told him. But perhaps I can make Miss Terry listen. He will only persist if she encourages him."

"I doubt it," said Lady Skerrit, but she let me go.

I walked to where Miss Terry and her friends stood, to one side of the great fireplace, out of reach of the sparks that occasionally spat from the logs. They bowed civilly enough but a distinct chill lay in the air, as though they had been talking about me. I had become accustomed to that, in the past.

"Your cup must overflow," Miss Terry said acidly. "First the elevation in your fortunes, then you catch such a notable bachelor. Tell me, do you expect him to give up his wicked ways for you?"

"He gave them up some time ago," I said calmly. "I'm afraid I can't take the credit for that."

"It didn't seem like it over dinner," said one lady. Miss Terry hid behind her fan in pretended embarrassment.

I regarded her with cool hauteur. "That, in case you didn't recognise it, was flirting. Miss Terry, I came to warn you. Please be careful. Lord Strang is dangerous." With an inward groan I wished I'd put it differently. But how to explain Richard to someone who didn't know him? Someone who didn't want to listen?

She flushed and tossed her head disdainfully, her golden ringlets bouncing around her pretty shoulders. "Dangerous? I couldn't see any of that. I did think he was one of the most charming men I have ever met." She leant forward to me confidingly, not lowering her voice one jot. "Is it true he jilted his previous fiancée?"

"No, she jilted him."

She laughed. "I can hardly believe that. She married Steven Drury didn't she? Who would prefer Steven Drury over Lord Strang?" Her acolytes tittered in chorus.

"Miss Cartwright evidently did," I said. "She's a considerable heiress and used to getting her own way. She wanted him, so she took him."

"She sounds like a woman after my own heart—except she

chose the wrong man." Eustacia looked around for approval and her friends laughed again. "I wouldn't let Lord Strang go, once I had him. Though you'll have your work cut out to keep him."

It was a secret fear of mine, but I was determined not to let her see that. "It's true that you have more to redeem you than Miss Cartwright." Miss Terry's thoughtlessness and cruelty was drawn from her youth and inexperience, while Julia Cartwright's was calculated. Richard had always thought Julia stupid, but I wasn't so sure. Miss Terry showed a loyalty to her friends that would be alien to Julia. It was why I tried to help her now, but I feared I was too late.

Miss Terry bowed in mocking acknowledgement of the compliment. "Still, he may prove more fickle than you think. And that brother of his—is he attached to anyone?"

I replied in the negative. It might be as well if she was drawn to Gervase. He was kinder than his brother and she wouldn't come to any harm with him. With that in mind, I gave Eustacia a few hints. "He's so rich, even he doesn't know how much he's worth. Although he left the country in disgrace, he returned in triumph. Lord Strang sometimes says he's the poor relation, in comparison to his brother."

Miss Terry fluttered her fan. "I still prefer the elder brother, and the title. I'll get him off you, Rose, see if I don't. He'll marry me in Exeter, not you."

At that point, the gentlemen came in. Richard looked around the room and strode over to us when he saw me. "Such a charming sight." He fixed his prey again after a brief, reassuring glance at me. A vigorous fluttering of fans rewarded him. "May I show you ladies a trick or two?" He gently took my fan. "The ladies in London deploy their fans—so—if they wish to attract the attention of someone across the room." It was pretty to see all the girls as they copied him, like a chorus. "And so, and so," he continued, demonstrating. His gestures were exquisite, elegantly delineating hidden emotions and desires, showing how beautiful the language of the fan could be in the hands of a master, but at no time were his gestures anything but masculine. Richard exuded masculinity with every pore, his affectation of rich clothes only underlying the fact that he needed no props to prove his essential nature. A predator in the ballroom, a dangerous, untamed element always in his eyes, in every ripple of well-trained, sleek muscle.

He shot me a wicked glance and I realised one of the gestures he'd used was not at all proper. "This means 'would you like to dance with me?'" I knew it meant something far more risqué.

During my visit to Eyton, one of the guests at his parents' house kindly demonstrated some of the elegant gestures to me, and had shown me one or two of the ones to avoid. The one Richard just demonstrated was definitely one of those.

"My lord," I said in warning, but the expression he turned to me was one of angelic innocence.

"Madam?"

I sighed. "Never mind." This was mild, compared to what he could do. Perhaps that wickedness would satisfy him.

Lizzie came over to join us. "Martha says it would be quite proper if you should like to play for us, Rose, and Lady Skerrit says she would love you to play." I suspected they were colluding to get me away from the group, but then I realised how I could get Richard away from his game, and I agreed.

I went over to the harpsichord and searched for some music amongst the sheets piled on a little table next to the instrument. I soon found what I wanted—a fiendish piece which had taken me forever to master. I ran my hands over the keys to ensure the tuning was suitable. It was.

With Lizzie to turn the pages for me, I began to play, and soon the magic happened. I loved music, and spent much of my spare time practising, but Richard had never heard me play before. I had not thought it seemly in Derbyshire, being in deeper mourning, and in Yorkshire all the instruments were out of tune.

I forgot myself when I played. I tried hard to be worthy of the music, but this time I kept some of my attention on the gaggle by the fire. Richard had his back to me, but after a little while, a few minutes at most, I saw his back gradually straighten. He bowed to the ladies, turned, and came over to the harpsichord. Miss Terry shrugged her shoulders because she knew of my prowess on the keyboard which she disdainfully referred to as my gift. It was not a gift, because I had worked so hard for it.

Richard stood by me, his attention on my hands, and occasionally he glanced at my face, his expression inscrutable. He still held my fan, but he quietly laid it down.

I finished the piece to the usual smatter of applause, and requests for more, but I smiled and bowed, and left the instrument for somebody else. I picked up my fan and led Richard to a sofa where we could sit together, away from his admirers.

"I had no idea you played," he said.

"Everybody plays."

"Not like that they don't." There was no guile now, no elegant flirting.

I tried to explain. "In a house as crowded as the Manor, there's little privacy. With my music, even if there was someone else in the room I wouldn't have to talk to them, I could enter my own world. So, I practised a great deal. Do you like music?"

"It's one of my greatest pleasures. I, too, can enter a different world with its help, and believe me, I've needed to from time to time. I shan't give you any flowery compliments on your playing; it would be an insult. You must know how good you are. It stands alone, without any help from me."

"Do you play?"

"Everybody plays," he repeated with a smile, then got to his feet. "I'll get you something to drink. I confess I need something. My mouth is completely dry after that particular surprise."

He came back with two glasses of wine. I accepted mine, sipped and put it down. I glanced across the room and saw Lady Skerrit watching us, as I had asked her to. I picked up my fan and spread it. "I do love you," I said from behind it. It was enough.

For a brief moment the polite mask was dropped, and his face glowed when he lifted his glass to me. "To your eyes," he said, and drank. When he lowered his glass he was back to the socially adept Lord Strang again. I hoped Lady Skerrit had seen, but I dared not look across to where she sat.

"Do these ladies go to the local Assembly Rooms?" he asked easily.

"All the gentry around here does."

"You'll be out of mourning next week. Should you like to go?" At one point I would have dreamed of nothing better than to attend Exeter Assembly rooms with my own betrothed by my side. I used to sit by the wall with a fixed smile on my face and dream my time there away until it was time to go home. I hardly left my station at all the whole evening, but now, I was happy to leave it all behind me and go on.

"Do you want to flirt with those poor girls again? You shouldn't you know, Miss Terry has already put up a challenge to me."

He looked amused. "Will you take it?"

"Do I need to?"

He smiled at my response. "You know the answer to that. But I promise I won't overstep the mark. Will that satisfy you?"

I sighed. "It will have to."

"And I know of one or two people who will arrive in Exeter early for our wedding. Lord Thwaite expressed a wish to explore the area when I last spoke to him. London will be emptying and while many people will head straight for Bath, and only come here for a few days, there are others who will use our wedding as an opportunity to see something new. Society is constantly bored, you see. I'll see if I can muster any of them for the Assembly Rooms. The chances are, the young women here will be so taken with all the new people, they'll leave me alone."

The thought of that relieved my mind considerably. "In that case, I think it an excellent notion. It will also give Martha a chance to meet some of the people she'll be expected to mix with in future, but on her own territory."

"Then that's settled. When is the next one?"

"The end of next week, I think." I knew well when it was. It used to be our only distraction, and Lizzie's only chance to show off to all and sundry.

"I'll speak to Lady Hareton tomorrow," he promised.

Chapter Six

Martha had no objections to our attendance at the Assembly rooms the following week.

On the Sunday I watched with amusement Richard's and Gervase's reactions to the family preparing for church. We attended the local parish church, and although we usually walked there, in deference to our exalted visitors, today we took carriages.

Someone flung open the main door to the Manor and the air filled with the cacophony of small children. "Walter—where is your hat?" mingled with, "Lizzie—can you lend me some gloves?" from Ruth and "Where did I put my prayer book?" from James. All at high volume, all at once.

Martha dealt with all the demands and requests one by one, patiently and steadily. I ran upstairs a couple of times to fetch various items, including my own prayer book that I had forgotten, and soon enough everyone was ready.

I took Richard's arm and Lizzie took Gervase's when he offered it. "Is it always like this?" Richard murmured to me, bewilderment and amusement mingling in his voice.

I smiled up at him. "No, sometimes we're late. This is restrained compared to usual. They're being good because you're here."

He smiled broadly and turned to Gervase. "Could you see our mother putting up with this for long?"

Gervase responded with a grin that matched his brother's. "She would have the headache instantly."

"Our last day of mourning," Lizzie reminded me.

I had grown so used to seeing the subdued greys and blacks I'd forgotten how we must all appear, but next to Richard's scarlet cloth coat, our dowdiness became explicit. Gervase, in a soft brown, blended in with us, but Richard stood out without effort, perhaps without noticing—but I doubted it. "I'm glad this is ending. This is a travesty of when I really mourned before. I might throw my mourning gowns away and start again if and when I need them."

"You'd be well advised to," Richard said. "I don't mean to disparage you, my love, but whoever made these gowns for you did you no favours. They seem to have been made for somebody else."

"They were. Martha bought them in York readymade, and they were altered by a maid for me. I have some new gowns, and I shall wear one tomorrow. For you."

"I shall look forward to it." He smiled again and leant closer. "If it wasn't the Sabbath, I'd make a totally scandalous suggestion I have every intention of carrying out in the near future." I flushed, and he laughed and took me out to the carriage.

I felt foolish travelling down the high street of Darkwater village in such style, amongst the villagers who knew me so well, but I stuck it out and when we reached the old church at the end of the street, events were almost normal. I tried to forget Richard's murmured words to me.

I burned for him. I thought of that time at Hareton almost constantly now our wedding grew closer. I wanted him so much sleeping had become a problem for me, and now he slept only a few doors away from mine, the urge grew worse. Not the thoughts our vicar would encourage, but I was always honest with myself, and I knew the few weeks until our wedding would be the longest I ever experienced. I wasn't used to this intensity of yearning, and I had no idea that one experience of lovemaking would lead to this longing, until touching him blew me apart.

Richard and Gervase were used to stares, so they took no notice of the congregation, but once we were ensconced in our high-sided pew nobody but the Reverend Mr. Claverton from his high perch in the pulpit could see us.

James dozed as usual and the children behaved like little angels for a change. Even Ruth stopped scowling. The service continued on its soothing way, the familiar litanies and responses passed without pause and I let myself dream of what was to come, trying to keep my mind away from the more physical aspect of our relationship. I'm not sure what the sermon was about, but it wasn't long, only half an hour or so. I itched and burned with desire and shame, sitting next to the man I loved, feeling his presence.

We led the congregation out, and spent some time accepting felicitations from people. Richard was gracious, I tried to follow suit.

Afterwards we stopped to speak to the vicar. Mr. Claverton had the pleasure of Steven's assistance last year, and after the usual courtesies, Richard asked him about it. "Do you miss Drury's services?"

"Frankly, my lord, not at all," Mr. Claverton said. "I hardly knew he was gone. I did have my doubts before, but once he left, I realised how little he attended to church affairs."

"So you would oppose any attempts he might make to enter the church again?" Richard's voice was soft, but his gaze steady and firm. There was nothing of the society man, or the libertine about him today.

Mr. Claverton studied him carefully, his clever eyes assessing. "I do not think he would be suitable for church office, sir, especially in the light of recent events."

"I couldn't agree more," Richard agreed promptly. "I keep him under observation, and if he makes a move in that direction, I'll let you know. If he asks you for any favours, please contact me, and I'll deal with it if you wish."

"Thank you, my lord," said Mr. Claverton.

It was the first I had heard of it, that Richard was having

Steven watched.

"You mean he might try to continue his career in the church?" Knowing what I did about Steven, the thought appalled me. Not all churchmen were suitable for the office they occupied, but if I stood by and let Steven Drury apply for a bishopric, I would be the worst kind of villain. The one who stood back and did nothing.

I'd hoped Steven was out of our lives, but if Julia Drury's father had allowed her back into his affections, it gave Steven a way back to society. Unconsciously I moved closer to Richard. He put his free hand over mine. "You know some bishops and other churchmen?"

"We have a clutch of 'em in the family," Richard replied, his voice firm. "I'll certainly write to them."

"Steven has a vicious nature." My voice wasn't entirely steady, and Mr. Claverton turned a curious gaze on to me.

Richard pressed my hand and released it. "He will not approach you." I believed him.

Martha stopped us before we entered the carriage. "I wonder if you could visit poor Mrs. Hoarty again. She didn't seem at all well in church this morning, and I couldn't get close enough to her to ask."

"Yes of course," I said. Mrs. Hoarty lived close to the church, and it would be a short walk to her house. Richard offered to accompany me.

"I'll send the carriage for you in an hour," Martha said.

"We could walk home." It was an opportunity to spend some precious time alone with Richard.

Martha was firm in her refusal. "I'll send the coach."

We had an hour then, half an hour's courtesy visit to Mrs. Hoarty and half an hour for ourselves.

We watched the coach leave and Mr. Claverton go back into the church, then we turned to walk along the secluded path from the church to Mrs. Hoarty's house. Nobody else was walking that way and high hedges protected anyone from looking over into the houses beyond.

I laid my hand on Richard's arm, and walked sedately down the path with him until we were out of the cleric's sight. As soon as I was sure we couldn't be seen, I turned to him and at once he put his arms around me. Dragging me close he kissed me, his mouth hungry on mine, and I knew he had missed me, perhaps as much as I'd missed him. I pressed myself to him, felt his body hard and comforting at the same time, and I knew I would only find my solace in him.

"I don't know which is worse," he murmured, his lips against mine. "To be apart, or to have you near me, and not hold you like this."

"Soon," I breathed.

"Three weeks." He sighed. "Knowing what I know, having tasted what I have, makes this waiting time so much longer."

"Yes." But I would never regret what we had done.

He laughed. "I feel like a small boy with his nose pressed up against the sweet shop window and no money in his pocket."

"You don't look like one."

"I did once."

"You? I can't believe it." I ran my hand up the cloth of his impeccable red coat.

He tilted my chin with one curled finger and kissed me again, long and lingering. "Believe it," he said, his lips next to mine. He took my mouth again, taking his time, showing me his need in heated passion, firing me to respond with passion to match his own. He kissed me again, small, nibbling kisses on my throat and up to my forehead. I responded, pressing myself to him.

Eventually he loosened his hold. "I fear we must continue on our errand. If we're caught here, like two children experimenting, we'll lose all credibility."

I looked up at his face so dear, so desirable. Anything less like a child was hard to imagine.

I put my hand through the crook of his arm, and we strolled along the lane. "Will you play the harpsichord for me today?" he asked.

The idea was scandalous. "Richard, it's Sunday. There would be more scandal from that than if we were caught a moment ago. I'll play for you tomorrow."

"The provincial mind! It's as if the Puritans never lost control. I always thought music was a gift from God, so wouldn't it be appropriate on a Sunday? Still, I'll be satisfied if you'll promise to play tomorrow. It's an extra gift, my love, that you play so well."

"I may lose the gift, if I don't practice."

"Then I'll try to ensure there's a keyboard of sorts wherever we are. I'd hate to see such a gift die from thirst."

I found it hard to explain what music meant to me, but I had to try, for him. "When I practice, it's almost as if I'm on my own. It gives me a kind of solitude, even when there are other people in the room."

He paused and pressed his lips to my forehead. "The more I learn of you, the more there is to love." I glowed, basking in happiness.

We strolled in companionable silence, before I remembered something he had said to the vicar. "Richard?"

"Yes, my sweet?"

"You said back at the church you were watching Steven. You didn't tell me."

"I didn't want to bring his name up, since it upsets you, but I said at the time I wouldn't allow him to hurt you any more. I've indicated that in the future we'll accept no invitations if they are present, and most people know I disapprove of him. It won't stop everyone, but it will mean we won't meet."

"How are you having him watched?"

"I would say, 'my secret', but lamentably, I fear that won't stop you."

He didn't sound upset, so I persisted in my questions. "No, it won't. Richard." I stopped, and made him turn to face me. "I don't want any secrets between us. Will you promise me?"

He stared at me. "None at all?" He sounded appalled, his voice rising slightly at the end of the sentence.

"No important ones. If you have a mistress, I want to know about it from you. If you have any other secrets, I want to know." The thought of Richard taking a mistress after our marriage sometimes haunted me at night. "I can make the same promise in return." I put my hand up to his cheek.

His stricken expression reminded me he'd never trusted anyone else in his adult life. Since Gervase had gone abroad, he'd kept his own counsel. It might be too much for me to ask.

I let my hand fall, turning to continue to walk. "I'm sorry, I shouldn't have asked. It doesn't matter."

He laid a hand on my arm and drew me back. "You have every right. I promise. No secrets." He drew me to him and kissed me, softly, the sealing of our bargain, and we walked on together to Mrs. Hoarty's door.

We found both Mrs. Hoarty and her only son at home.

Mr. Hoarty spent most of the week in Exeter, where he was a well-to-do lawyer. He probably knew all the skeletons in the closets of the more prominent families in the district. He was five and forty, and had the confident demeanour of a man who knew his world and was content in it. Now he was past the first flush of youth, his figure had filled out and he had taken to wearing bob-wigs, as a reflection of his trade and station in life, instead of the elegant queued wigs Richard and his friends preferred.

A maid brought tea and small cakes in to us, and we sat in Mrs. Hoarty's comfortably upholstered chairs. Mrs. Hoarty's parlour wasn't the most fashionable I had ever been in, but it was one of the more pleasant ones. The furniture was unassuming, the fire blazing generously.

I hadn't seen Mr. Hoarty for a while, and his presence today unwittingly reminded me of something. I caught myself up on a laugh and blushed when they all looked at me. "Oh, I beg your pardon, but when I saw you again, sir, it reminded me of the time you caught us in your orchard. Tom Skerrit and me, do you remember?"

"I remember only too well," the gentleman replied gravely, but with a gleam in his eye. "I dragged you both indoors, and I found your pockets full of our apples."

I laughed when I remembered. "We were always hungry in those days. And your orchard was easier to scrump in than others, because it wasn't overlooked." It seemed so long ago now.

"Always hungry?" repeated Richard. "I wasn't aware your family kept you hungry."

I laughed. "Martha would be appalled if she thought that. It was only the natural hunger of childhood. And stolen apples always tasted so much better."

Mr. Hoarty chuckled. "Especially ours. But that was the last time you tried it, I believe."

"We were getting too old for such things." I met Richard's astonished blue gaze and burst into laughter. "I'm sorry, but you look so shocked. Did you never steal apples when you were young?"

"I can't say I did. Did I miss something?"

Mr. Hoarty smiled, his stern face relaxing. "I should think so. But those two were the best. They were the scourge of all orchards hereabouts until that day."

"Mr. Hoarty took us home," I told my astonished love. "And my father beat me and locked me in my room for a few days. Tom got the same treatment from his father. After that, we reasoned the punishment wasn't worth it, and we asked for our apples afterwards."

Richard laughed, too. "I said I was marrying a hoyden. Madam, will you never cease to surprise me?"

I was pleased to see Mrs. Hoarty had cheered up, as she thought of past times. She was in almost constant pain these days, and I was happy to bring her pleasure.

Richard sat facing the large sash windows at the front of the house. "You must see everything from here, ma'am."

"It helps on the days when I can't go out," she said. "To see other people as they go about their business. Sometimes, though I see too much."

"Oh?" Richard's ready curiosity was aroused by her words. He sat back at his ease, and watched the lady closely. "Does this have anything to do with free traders? I was at a dinner last week where someone mentioned there had been a run recently. Do you find a barrel of brandy by your back door occasionally?"

Mr. Hoarty gave a snort. "It sounds romantic, doesn't it, my lord? No, we don't find brandy by our door, because the community knows I don't approve."

"You're a rare lawyer indeed, sir, if you seek to uphold the law."

Mr. Hoarty shot Richard a sharp look, but it was apparent from his serious expression that he wasn't joking. "That's as may be, my lord. And I can't say everyone in my profession is a model of propriety, but that isn't the reason I oppose them. Smugglers are not groups of freethinking individuals as they would have people believe. They are oppressive, violent gangs who wield far too much influence in districts such as ours. They weaken the government and make a travesty of the law. They don't merrily import a few barrels of French brandy; smuggling is big business. There's a great deal of profit to be made, and when that is the case, inevitably the most ruthless rise to the top. They terrify many people hereabouts. It has undoubtedly worsened recently."

I remained quiet. I knew something about the trade, but like most of the families here, I'd chosen to stop my eyes and ears to it where Mr. Hoarty, to his credit, obviously had not.

He stood, and went over to the window. "Most people don't live as close as this to Darkwater, they don't see some of the things we've seen. They hold this village in thrall." He gazed out the large window at the front of the pleasant room. "Nothing goes on here without their permission."

"Who are 'they'?" Richard asked. Mr. Hoarty had gained his interest where many could not.

"There are groups of people up and down the coast who run the gangs," Mr. Hoarty said, his attention on something outside.

"Here, it's a family called Cawnton. They organise all the runs in these parts, and recruit from the villages from here to the coast. If they're refused, they exert pressure. I've seen women and children with missing fingers, or with an eye put out by these villains in an attempt to pressure the men of the family to help in the runs. And the level of violence has worsened in the last few years. The Cawntons always used to run their activities like a business. Their threats and violence were restricted. I assumed it was because of the example of other gangs. If their violence becomes impossible for the authorities to ignore, then they finally do something about it. The Cawntons didn't want to damage their lucrative business by drawing attention to it." His voice was bitter.

Richard was interested now; his relaxed pose was no indication of the tension I sensed beneath. I felt it like an added presence. "I had no idea. I was brought up in Derbyshire, not a county renowned for its smuggling activities. I should have realised, after some of the other things I've seen, but I'm afraid I looked on it as a kind of pastime, except in London. Aware of the damage smuggling does to the economy, but not really aware of what it does to everyday life. Can the authorities do nothing?"

"They haven't enough money, nor enough men." Mr. Hoarty turned to one side, so he could still keep an eye on whatever was happening outside, but politely face his mother's guests. "We thought, with the cessation of the war, they might send troops to help, but we've seen nothing."

"The war hasn't ceased," Richard said. "It has merely paused while the sides regroup."

Mr. Hoarty nodded, and glanced out of the window again. The war in Europe was much further away than this, the war on our doorstep. His voice sharpened. "Lord Strang, look at this."

Swiftly, Richard went over to the window, and stared out of it. "My God!"

"Two of Cawnton's people," said Mr. Hoarty.

I stood and would have gone to the window, but Richard spun around, his expression grim. "I will not stand by and witness this." He wrenched open the door and went out.

Mr. Hoarty ran after him. "My lord, don't do this, they'll likely kill you! They're no respecters of rank or privilege." The front door slammed and I ran to the window in time to see Richard stride up the village street towards the trouble.

Mrs. Hoarty joined me and not thinking what I was doing, I took her hand for comfort. I held my breath in fear.

Two men stood in the street, and with no attempt at subterfuge, viciously kicked a bundle on the floor, a bundle that writhed and tried to get out of the way of the booted feet. The attackers were tall and strong and they would hurt anyone who interfered with their business. Mr. Hoarty hurried after my lord, but he couldn't catch up with him.

Richard ripped off his coat as he went, and threw it carelessly over one arm. The street appeared to be deserted, but shadowy faces lurked at all the windows, if you looked closely at all the cottages fronting it.

From hearing about previous encounters, I knew no one would interfere, and if they were asked, no one would have seen anything.

Fear clutched at me. Richard, like most of his sort could probably use a sword, but only in the courtly, skillful way prescribed by his world. As usual, he wore his dress sword, which he'd left at the church door and retrieved after the service. He put his hand on the hilt as he strode up the street towards the bullies.

The men turned to stare at him, no alarm at all in their reactions, but perhaps a little surprise. One of them looked him up and down and laughed in derision. At least they stopped kicking the poor man on the ground.

Richard snapped something, curtly. We couldn't hear any sound through the window, but it was obvious he demanded they leave their victim alone. The second man stared at him, shrugged, and, without taking his eyes off Richard's face, kicked his prey once more, casually, as if his victim was nothing more than a sack of potatoes. The man crumpled in pain.

I couldn't see any expression on Richard's face, but in one sweeping movement, he drew his sword. I clutched Mrs. Hoarty's crippled hand and she gasped, but I didn't let go, forgetting the poor lady's pain in my fear. I was so agitated about the scene outside I didn't even notice, though I remembered the gasp later and was deeply ashamed I had caused it.

I thought Richard might assume the pose I'd seen fencers use—slightly crouched, one foot in front of the other, but he didn't bother. He stood still, holding his sword pointed at the ground in front of him, and said something. The man spat at his feet.

Without a pause Richard lifted his sword and drew it down the smuggler's arm. He didn't appear to use any force.

The weapon must have been sharp, for it went through the heavy coat and the shirt of his victim, and drew blood with little effort. It couldn't be a serious wound, but the man clapped a hand to the wound and let forth what I confidently assumed to be a stream of invective. Blood trickled down his arm. Now the other man made his move.

From Richard's other side, the bully lunged to Richard's left, away from the sharp sword. In a blink Richard threw his coat at him. The blanket of scarlet temporarily blinded and confused the man. I gasped again when Richard seemed to lose his balance, falling down on one knee and dropping his sword in the dust.

The first man came forward, on the attack again. Terrified, I watched from my station by the window. Mr. Hoarty stood by the fracas, shouting. Perhaps he was telling them the identity of this stranger, his rank. I knew it would do Richard no good. The smugglers could simply disappear if they killed him, evade justice by joining another gang further up the coast, or by going to ground in one of their many hideaways.

They were going to kill my love. I would have to watch him die, unable to prevent it. A moan escaped me and this time Mrs. Hoarty tightened her grip on my hand.

Something gleamed wickedly in Richard's left hand, the one he'd used to throw his coat. He tossed the object from his left hand to his right. The knife glittered in the pale sunshine. He sprang to his feet, kicking out with his left leg, and at the same time swept the new weapon in front of him. All gentility had gone. Only a fighter, strong and supple, remained.

The kick found its intended mark in the groin of the man in front of him, I could almost hear the shriek of pain from where I stood behind the plate glass.

Richard stood over his sword so they couldn't retrieve it. In the confusion caused by his kick reaching its mark, he swept it up again and stood, twitching the end of the sword, the knife in his left hand once more.

I could see what he was saying by the movement of his mouth, but I could hear nothing, trapped as I was behind the glass. "Come on, then!" One man held his groin, the other stood back. He said something to his injured colleague.

I held my breath as they turned, slowly. They began to walk up the long street away from us. They must have decided on discretion, at least for the time being.

With a cry, I was released from my spell, and forgetting all propriety, all concealment, I ran out the front door and up the street towards him. He caught me around my waist when I reached him. Incredibly, he was laughing, but he stopped when he saw the tears on my face. "What, you thought those two bullies were too much for me? Oh ye of little faith."

"Richard, they could have killed you." I couldn't stop crying; he pulled me close, giving me his warmth for comfort.

"Them?" He stared after them, and then turned his head against mine, let me rest on him. I didn't care who might be watching. "They're fools and praters. Easy pickings, my love."

"I fear you're right, Miss Golightly," said Mr. Hoarty heavily. "They may seek revenge. It's a matter of honour with them that their kind go unmolested."

"Unlike this poor devil," said Richard, as his attention went to the man on the ground.

Past my worst shock, I released Richard, and knelt in the dirt, to see if I could help the poor man. "He'd be better indoors," I said, my voice still shaky. "Does anyone know where he lives?"

I looked up to see a woman, not in her first youth. By the tears pouring down her face, it was obvious the victim belonged to her in some way. Richard dropped his weapons, knelt and lifted the victim without effort, leaving Mr. Hoarty to follow.

The woman, still in tears, led us to a cottage nearby. I didn't flinch at the animal stench within, although it turned my stomach with its intensity. Richard followed, and laid the man on the filthy bed, then stood back to let me examine him. He had reason to know I had some knowledge in that area.

I pulled up the poor man's shirt to examine his wounds, and examined him in silence, passing my hands over the wounds to feel for broken bones. I became convinced of one thing. "This was a punishment beating. There'll be no permanent injuries, but he has some nasty bruises and a couple of cracked ribs. He'll be in pain for a while."

"Was it skillfully done?" he asked.

I nodded. "These men knew what they were about."

"Less thugs, more hired help." Richard rubbed his chin. "I'll have to do something about this, otherwise I fear Mr. Hoarty may be right. They'll seek retribution."

I got to my feet and repeated my findings to the woman. She mopped up her tears with a filthy handkerchief. "Why would they have done this?"

"I'm sure I don't know, miss." I knew she was lying. The sight of her man brutalised in her presence was enough to ensure her silence. It was obvious to me that we could do nothing more here.

Richard took his belongings from Mr. Hoarty with a smile of thanks. He sheathed his sword and put on his coat, then he reached into his pocket and brought out a leather scabbard. Mr. Hoarty handed him the knife without comment, but I put out my hand for it, and after a moment's hesitation, Richard handed it to me.

It was a plain looking knife, beautifully balanced, with a fine, thin steel blade. "Do you always carry this?"

"I generally have one or two about me." He took it back and sheathed it, then returned it to his coat pocket.

I had a vision, of the time at the Abbey when Steven had attacked me. Richard had hit him with the hilt of his sword, and knocked him out, but then his hand had gone to his pocket. No wonder Gervase had been so quick to catch his arm. Richard must have been going for one of these vicious little knives. It shocked me that a gentleman should carry such an item as a matter of course and that he knew how to fight as street urchins did, although I would never cease to be thankful for it. He might be lying in the street, badly wounded or dead. I'd assumed Richard would fight like a gentleman, surrounded by rules and esoteric skills, but Richard had done what was needed in an economical and efficient way, with none of the showy about it, and none of the elaborate flourishes required of the expert swordsman. He fought like he knew what it was to fight for his life.

He watched me closely, waiting for my response. I met his stare with a steady one of my own. "More secrets?"

"Not any longer, I fear." He broke his scrutiny, and glanced down at his coat with a wry grin. "Carier will not be pleased." He tried to brush off the worst of the dirt, but knowing his valet, I didn't think Carier would mind too much, although he might pretend to.

Richard held out his arm for me to take in an imperious gesture. I couldn't gainsay him.

We left the cottage and returned to the large house at the end of the street, where the carriage waited to take us home. From behind the safety of windows, I felt the hard scrutiny of anonymous watchers on my back.

Mr. Hoarty tried to apologise, but Richard cut him off. "It might be wiser if you saw to your mother. This can't have been good for her."

Mr. Hoarty saw the sense in this, but lingered long enough to say, "Be careful, my lord. It was a brave thing you did today, but perhaps not a wise one. You have made some enemies, I fear."

"I'll add them to the list," Richard informed him, and handed me into the coach.

Once inside and past the hidden eyes in the village, I leaned on his shoulder and indulged in a hearty bout of tears, which much relieved my temper. His arms tightened about me. I felt blessedly safe. I knew it was an illusion, but I let myself believe it for now. He was as vulnerable as anyone else. "I thought they would kill you."

Busy drying my tears with his own handkerchief, he smiled and drew one finger along my cheek. "When I have so much to live for? They hadn't a chance."

"What is all this? Why do you carry extra weapons? Where did you learn to fight like that?"

"Shhhhh..." He drew me to rest on his shoulder. I smelled him, and felt content, breathing him in. "Did you think we always fought fair? How do you think the aristocracy got where they did in the first place?" He pressed his lips against my hair. "I learned to fight like that because I wanted to win. I carry extra weapons because a dress sword is of little use, although I do try to carry one of Toledo steel. The rest can wait. I will tell you. I made you a promise, but let that suffice for now."

"They'll come after you," I said from the safety of the folds of his coat.

"I'll do my best to ensure they don't."

When we got back to the Manor, he helped me down, took me upstairs, and gave me into the care of my maid. I partly resented his pampering, as though I were an invalid, and partly appreciated it. I'd never known anything like it before, this cherishing, this care.

Before I went into my room I heard what he said to Carier, who had appeared silently on the scene, waiting. "I became involved in a fracas with two representatives of the local band of thieves. The name of the leader is Cawnton. Get word to him I'm only here to be married, not to get Thompson's involved in their affairs." Carier nodded and left. Richard went to change his coat alone.

Chapter Seven

I must have been in shock because I slept until dinnertime. Martha sent word that I must stay upstairs and rest. After a short interval to eat the dinner sent up to me on a tray, I slept well that night, despite my worries.

I felt much better in the morning. My gown of yesterday had been ruined by its short visit to the mud, but I didn't care, because today was my first day out of mourning. I was glad to give my maid the order to throw away the ruined gown, and to lay out my new blue flowered silk.

When I looked over the banister on my way downstairs I saw Richard, waiting for me. Lizzie stood in the doorway of the breakfast parlour. She smiled back at me when I smiled my good morning. She looked lovely in a pale yellow striped gown. Richard took my hand, and openly studied at me, and I lowered my gaze, flushing when I saw the warm expression on his face. "So much better," he said.

I met his eyes. "You like it?" I turned a little to make my skirts move and heard the rustle of the new silk. For once, I felt equal to his magnificence. He was dressed simply today, but a master had fitted his country coat, and the attention to detail in the waistcoat embroidery, the arrangement of the folds of his neckcloth, spoke of the leader of fashion.

"Elegance personified." He kissed my hand. When his mouth brushed my knuckles a shiver passed through me. "Should you like some fresh air?"

"Yes please."

There was a shawl on the window seat by the front door, which Richard picked up and arranged over my shoulders. Even this simple gesture made me feel cherished. I glanced at Lizzie who hadn't spoken and I saw her smile again. She sighed as I turned away and put my hand on his arm. We walked past her to the garden and Richard bowed his head to her as we passed.

"I'm so glad to be out of mourning," I told him.

"I'm so glad to see you looking better."

"I needed the sleep."

"You must have done; I don't think it's just the blue gown making you look so much better."

It was a fine day today; the sky scattered with clouds with no rain in them. The flowers were beginning to come; buds on some early shrubs and the daffodils coming into full bloom. "Does it get better than this?" I said.

"Oh yes."

What I saw in his eyes, the promise of intimacies to come, made me blush. "I'll make it better for both of us," he said, twining his hand with mine.

"I'll do my best." Glancing behind to make sure we were unobserved, he drew me to him for a gentle kiss.

We went back in for breakfast to the usual cacophony of a family breakfast. Martha liked the children to join us for this less formal meal. Out of politeness Richard and Gervase agreed that this custom must continue while they were guests at the Manor, but I feared it might try their patience. They weren't used to living so close and having the boisterousness of small children intrude upon their daily lives.

I remembered a promise. "I said I would play the harpsichord for you."

"So you did." I had finished my meal, so he stood and pulled back my chair for me when I got to my feet.

Martha stared at Lizzie meaningfully. "Can I come?" Lizzie asked. Gervase asked if he could come too, and so our chaperones accompanied us.

We went upstairs to the music room, and I smiled at Richard. "You're doing well with the children. They're still in awe of you, but not as much as when you first arrived."

He smiled wryly in return. "I hope to keep a little distance between us." Richard was not yet comfortable with children. I hoped that one day he would be.

The music room was on the first floor, one of Martha's show rooms. Small sofas were spread about in the new informal style, and a large, decorative harp dominated the room. The harpsichord stood behind it. I walked to the instrument, and on my way drew my hand along the strings of the harp. I watched Gervase and Richard's faces contort in a reaction to the disharmony produced. "Nobody plays it," I explained. "Lizzie wanted to try, but she gave up after a while."

"I thought I would show to advantage, and give Eustacia Terry something to think about," my sister confessed. "But I couldn't come to terms with it."

Gervase grinned. "Several ladies have taken it up in that spirit. But I've rarely heard it played well."

Lizzie assumed her most coquettish expression, chin tilted, gazing up at Gervase through her abundant lashes. "Ah, but do they look elegant when they're playing it?"

Richard added his mite. "I always thought that the ear and the eye should be pleasured at the same time."

I sat at the harpsichord and sorted through the sheet music I kept on top. I chose favourites, so no one would be obliged to act as page-turner. Scarlatti and the German composer, Bach. Gervase saw Lizzie seated, and I watched her dispose her skirts elegantly about her and lay her fan by her side. Richard sat, equally elegantly, on a sofa opposite, and Gervase found himself a seat in the space Lizzie had left. In a presage of spring, sunshine streamed though the large window on to the despised harp, right across the room. I began to play.

Richard said little, but closed his eyes from time to time. Gervase and Lizzie were equally silent, but it was the harmony of tranquillity. I enjoyed playing, forgot myself in the music, a blessed time.

Unfortunately we weren't left alone for long.

A knock fell on the door and the butler brought in a salver with some ominous pieces of pasteboard resting on it. Visitors, marking the end of our peaceful morning.

Lizzie took up the cards and I brought the piece I was playing to rest.

"There's two groups of guests waiting to see us," Lizzie told us with a sigh. "Lady Skerrit and Georgiana, and Mrs. and Miss Terry." She looked up at the butler. "Show them up here, please."

"The beauteous Miss Eustacia Terry." Richard's voice was suspiciously cool. I gave him a suspicious look.

"We're out of mourning now," Lizzie observed wryly. "Fair game for visitors."

Gervase gave a short laugh. "And it looks as though we're being hunted. Richard, could you possibly behave yourself this time?"

"I? Whatever can you mean?" Not a trace of guile lurked in Richard's eyes.

Gervase threw up his hands in a gesture of submission. "I hear Frederick Brean is coming next week. I can only hope he succeeds in distracting local society. Rose, can't you prevail on Richard to stop his campaign?"

I shook my head. "No, but I have made him promise not to take it too far."

"That will have to do then." The door opened and the redoubtable Marsh announced Mrs. Terry and her daughter, with a ceremonious flourish. Mrs. Terry paused on the threshold. I noticed, not for the first time, her sheer size. She was often described by the kinder element as a "comfortable" woman, but the tight lacing she customarily used made her bulge at top and bottom like a generous hour glass. She loaded her person with fashionable ornament, throwing the more simple attire the rest of us affected into the shade. Her daughter was dressed to impress in crimson striped satin and garnets.

Perhaps not the best choice of colour for a pale blonde, but expensive items.

We stood and greeted them. Richard led Miss Terry to a window seat where he sat next to her. They all listened to me play another piece, but I kept this one simple and short.

I stopped when the servants brought refreshments. I closed the lid of the instrument, and went to sit next to Lizzie. Gervase had moved to occupy the place Richard vacated when he took Miss Terry to the window seat. "You play charmingly, Miss Golightly," Mrs. Terry said indulgently. She must have known some response was expected, but I suspected the lady of having cloth ears.

Richard corrected her. "She plays superbly."

Mrs. Terry stared at him in exaggerated surprise, her finely plucked brows nearly up in her hairline. She wasn't used to people correcting her opinions. Mrs. Terry considered herself one of the leaders of fashion in the county, and her opinions were usually accepted without demur. Discussions were not part of her nature. However, this time she evidently decided to let it pass, and smiled kindly at Richard. "I have an excellent ear for music. Miss Golightly's playing has always been welcome in my house. Do you know Devonshire at all, sir?"

I noticed the "sir", and winced a little bit. It was usual to use such forms of address when one knew the recipient for a time, not immediately after first acquaintance. They were planning to move in. We might see them in London before too long if we spent any time there. I saw myself becoming, "My dearest friend, Lady Strang," if I wasn't too careful.

"I can't say I do," Richard replied.

"No." Her voice held a pitying tone. "Then perhaps you have heard of my house, Penfold Hall?"

"Sadly not, ma'am." He didn't sound sorry.

"You really must come and see it." She addressed Gervase then. "I hear you are interested in old houses, sir."

"Only in antiquities. Many people think my interest amounts to an obsession." Gervase glanced meaningfully at this brother. "But everybody has an interest."

"Indeed so, sir," Mrs. Terry agreed. "My daughter has a great interest in painting, don't you, my dear?"

Eustacia started, her mind obviously on other things, but rose to the occasion with aplomb. "I paint in watercolours." She stole a glance from under her lashes at Richard, who smiled at her. Her mother watched with approval. Martha would have discouraged such flirting from us, especially with a nearly married man.

The door opened and Martha came in with Lady Skerrit. Remembering my last encounter with the lady, I hoped Lady Skerrit had taken my advice and asked Martha how it was between Richard and me. Lady Skerrit favoured us all with a pleasant smile until she saw Richard sitting next to Miss Terry on the window seat.

Martha busied herself pouring tea and passing round the various plates of this and that. When we were all hampered with tea dishes and little cakes, she took a seat.

Mrs. Terry had heard of the previous day's happenings in the village. "You were involved in an unseemly episode yesterday, my lord."

"Sadly, yes," Richard favoured them with a brief explanation. "Two bullies attacked another man. I made the odds a little more even, that's all."

"Did you know the men were Cawntons?" Lady Skerrit demanded.

"Not until afterwards," Richard admitted. "But it wouldn't have made any difference. I dislike injustice in any form, and I couldn't have stood by and watched."

"They could have killed you." Miss Terry was nearly breathless, apparently thrilled by the idea of such danger.

He smiled at her, a particularly warm smile for his society manner. "But they didn't. I sent them off, and they went quite willingly in the end."

"They may take it amiss, my lord," Lady Skerrit warned him.

Richard lifted his hands in the air in a gesture of despair, reminiscent of his brother's gesture earlier. "The whole county seems to be in thrall to these villains."

Gervase put his hand to his eyes and groaned. "Not another cause, Richard, please."

Richard looked across at him. "Not yet. I have other business first, but the matter should certainly be looked into." *Another cause?* What on earth did Gervase mean?

Lady Skerrit shook the heavy lace ruffles lying on her arms, drawing attention to their lavish splendour. "The gangs are large and well organised."

"And what is a little free trading?" Mrs. Terry queried. "I believe they run goods across our land, because we have found a barrel or two outside our door sometimes."

Richard frowned. "Apart from the fact that it's a violation of the law, these people create terror in the countryside. I cannot approve."

Miss Terry glowed, looking up at him, through her lashes. "You are a hero, my lord."

"You think I should take them on single-handed?" Amusement crept into his voice. "It might have been acceptable to knights of old, but then, they had armour to protect them. There's little I can do on my own, but I might ask some people I know to help me. But not yet." He glanced at me and smiled. I smiled back, an easy social smile, but I wasn't entirely at my ease. I glanced at Gervase. I smelled a secret, perhaps the same secret Richard had promised to enlighten me about the day before.

"We have nothing to do with them," Lady Skerrit said. "I love this county, but the smugglers are a slur on our good name. They don't pass over our land, to my knowledge."

Martha agreed. "Nor ours."

"You may find you have a little more influence with your change of fortune," Richard pointed out. "If Lord Hareton takes his seat in the Lords, he'll most likely find friends there."

Martha regarded him with interest. "I hadn't thought of

that. I shall certainly speak to him about it."

Mrs. Terry pursed her mouth. "Do you really think that's necessary? They do no harm, you know, and they do bring some prosperity to the county."

Richard leaned back in the window seat, every inch the man of leisure, not at all the sort of person who might run another through with his sword without hesitation. "Men can die on the beach as easily as they can die in the fields."

Martha's head turned sharply, but the Terrys didn't seem to notice anything amiss. Mrs. Terry never noticed anyone she chose not to, and that included everyone from servants down. Her perception was selective.

"I'm only glad Derbyshire has no such prosperity," Richard commented, apparently bored with the subject in hand. Mrs. Terry took his opening. "Derbyshire? Is your house near Chatsworth at all?"

"Quite near," he admitted.

"Do you see much of the dear duke?"

"You know him, then?" Gervase took the conversational baton, which gave Richard a chance to sit back and observe. The Kerres and the Cavendishes socialised, but were not close.

"We met him a little while ago." Mrs. Terry's tone turned to honey. "Such gracious manners." I couldn't think where they could have met. I'd certainly never met a duke in Exeter Assembly Rooms.

Gervase agreed without a tremor. "They spend most of their time in London. My father prefers the country, on the whole, so we see little of each other."

"I'll wager you prefer the excitement of the city, my lord. Mama says that we will pay Bath a visit this year. Shall we see you there?" Eustacia looked from one to the other of the twins eagerly. Either she had forgotten Richard's reason for being here, or she chose to ignore it.

Richard shook his head. "Probably not this year. Gervase, do you plan to go?"

"I hadn't planned it, but I might take a look. You'll have to tell me when you're to visit," Gervase added to Eustacia. They were playing the girl, passing her from one to another. The sport was mild, otherwise I would have stopped it, but in all honesty I had to admit she provided a tempting target.

"Oh yes," breathed Eustacia.

Richard stretched an arm along the back of the sofa, behind Eustacia's carefully curled hair. "Meantime, we may go a fair way towards making Exeter fashionable. You'll find Exeter Assembly rooms more populated than usual, at least for the next month or two." If I didn't know what he was doing, his arrogance would have appalled me. He was drawing Eustacia further into his trap, tempting her with the availability of fresh meat in the marriage mart.

Georgiana turned shining eyes to her mother. "May we go, Mama? Would that be possible?"

"We thought we might attend this Friday," Lady Skerrit admitted.

"Then we shall go too." Mrs. Terry beamed. "We have to uphold the county, don't we?" by "the county" she meant her sort, the few families that made up her social circle. I knew she would muster her friends. The whole of the Assembly Rooms would be packed and agog. Last year in the wilds of Yorkshire I had dreamed of showing off my betrothed at the Assembly Rooms, the scene of so many frustrations and humiliations for me in the past. Now I wasn't so sure, especially with the mischief I knew Richard was planning. I was suspicious of his motives, but also afraid I could do little to divert him from his purpose.

Morning visits were supposed to take half an hour. After that time Lady Skerrit stood, thus forcing the others to stand. "So good to see you out of mourning." She embraced Martha warmly. If the Terrys hadn't been there, she would have stayed longer, and been welcome. Martha left with them, to see the guests to the door.

Left alone with Gervase and Lizzie, I pleaded with Richard. "You won't drop Miss Terry in the middle of Friday's Assembly

Rooms, will you?"

"He's planning some game with that harpy?" Lizzie clapped her hands together in delight. "Famous!"

Richard smiled at her. "A woman with my own sense of justice." He gave her a bow. "I shall first see how far she is prepared to take matters. If she retreats, then so will I. On the other hand, if she chooses to flirt—"

"Richard!" from Gervase.

"Oh, my dear brother, not that. Granted, I have amused myself in the past, but not with a young innocent. In any case, anything more than flirting would hurt Rose. No, I'll not go that far. In fact, I'm not sure what I will do, exactly." He smiled at me. "I promise I won't let her down too badly, if she needs a set down. And, in any case, if you hadn't noticed, I didn't make most of the running." I had to admit that was true.

"She has all the tricks of the coquette," said Lizzie. "She doesn't need encouragement. It will do her good to receive a set down."

"Offer her a carte blanche," suggested Gervase. The idea that Richard should offer her his protection without his name made Lizzie gasp in appreciative delight.

Richard laughed. "Good God, I thought I had the reputation. If I did that, her father might well call me out."

Gervase agreed. "Once upon a time you would have done it."

Richard frowned. "Perhaps. But she's only silly, not malicious, and she doesn't deserve it. My natural inclination is to ruin her, at least in the eyes of society, but I will be magnanimous and merely set her down a trifle."

"Can it be Rose has taught you some humanity?"

"A little," he admitted. "But I shall strive to overcome it."

Chapter Eight

The following Wednesday we decided to go into Exeter. Richard and Gervase had an errand there, and Lizzie wanted to shop. It took us an hour and a half to get there in the carriage from Darkwater. Gervase, Lizzie, Richard and I went down the steps of the Manor to the new landau with the Hareton arms emblazoned on the shiny black painted doors. It was so unlike our previous all-purpose vehicle, it made me smile.

Richard helped me into the carriage, Gervase helped Lizzie and then the maid scrambled up after us. We felt the usual jolt as the horses stirred into action, and then we were away.

Richard pulled a note from his coat pocket. "Mother says she wants somewhere secluded. It shouldn't be too difficult. The agent says he has six properties in mind." They were to search for a house that the Earl and Countess could hire during their stay here for the wedding and a week or two beyond.

"I hope we don't have to look at them all," Gervase grumbled. "It would take all day."

I produced a similar note from my pocket. "With all these things we have to buy for Martha, we may have to separate." Gervase and Lizzie exchanged a fleeting glance, and a smile. I wondered what private joke they were sharing, but I didn't think about it too much. "Martha's glad to get us out of the house for a while. None of the things on her list are essential. It's all embroidery threads, ribbons and the like."

"Well now we're out of mourning," said my sister, "I'm beginning to realise how much I need to supplement my wardrobe."

That made me laugh. I looked over to my charming sister, not a golden hair out of place, dressed in a brand new light green silk gown. It was much more becoming to golden beauty than Miss Terry's crimson of the other day had been to hers. The maid sat between Lizzie and Gervase, pretty in her serviceable cotton print. She was a young girl, excited at the prospect of a trip to Exeter instead of her usual morning duties.

"You have so much," I said to my sister. "Surely you don't need any more."

"I must get a new fan for the Assembly on Friday. I have nothing to go with the gown I plan to wear."

It was an overcast morning, the sort of grey, drizzly weather that is so frequent when spring is trying to break through. The sun filtered through the early rain clouds when we arrived in town, but it began to clear up as the day went on.

We went straight to the house agents' and waited in the carriage while the keys were brought out to us, together with a note of the location of the houses. We declined the services of the agent, only too delighted to show us round, but busy. He brought the keys out to us himself.

We set out for the first house. "I think," said Gervase, "that we probably have the best of the bunch here. The agent is bound to know why his business has increased so rapidly the past month or two."

We went straight to the first house, but we didn't stay there long. It was a fine house, but too close to the main thoroughfares to afford any privacy, and the rooms at the front were too easy for any curious passerby to peer inside. We decided to leave the others until later. Lizzie and I directed the driver to take us around Exeter, mostly for Gervase's benefit, as the city contained many old buildings. I didn't care where we went. I was with Richard, and that was enough.

Exeter was a fine old town, with much evidence of its ancient past still extant, including several fine half-timbered buildings. I gave my guidebook to Gervase, who loved it all. The older the better for him. He drank in the history and told us much more than we needed to know, much more than the author of the guidebook seemed to know. It was as much as we could do to stop him getting out at each monument we passed. As it was we had to stop at the Cathedral Close for half an hour.

We stood on the path leading through the grass lawn to the great Cathedral. Gervase decided there and then to stay on after the wedding, to explore Exeter at his leisure. "I believe Mother has decided to go to Bath this year, so I can join them there later."

"If the young hopefuls hereabouts leave you alone," commented Richard.

Gervase grinned. "I can always go incognito. I wouldn't be the first member of the family to do that."

"Keep on dreaming," said Richard. "Once you came home any hope I had for passing unnoticed vanished, just as yours did."

"Separately we're unremarkable enough," Gervase replied. Twelve years apart had given each twin a sense of their own identity, although their faces were still so similar as to be remarkable.

"We're known. If they know you're here, they won't leave you alone."

"I can try." Gervase gazed in rapt wonder at the myriad statues ranked on every level outside the Cathedral. He dug his hands in the pockets of his serviceable but well cut brown coat, forgetting all fashionable poses in his trance.

Richard must have seen something in me because he turned to look at me properly and at once put his hand over mine. "What is it, my love?"

"This isn't for me, I can't get married here. It's too grand, too magnificent." I had a morbid dread of appearing foolish, something I had achieved more than once in my life, and once the dread arrived I found it hard to shift.

"You will marry me if I have to drag you here."

The thought of my wedding day made my stomach turn with nerves. I didn't think I would enjoy the wedding ceremony. I hated to stand out from the crowd. "Everybody will be looking at me."

I wasn't aware I'd spoken out loud, but Richard answered me. "So they will. And me too."

I took my attention away from the great church and looked at him instead. A much more reassuring sight. "Yes."

"Come, Gervase," Richard said abruptly. "We have much to do." Reluctantly, his twin turned away and we went back to the coach.

We went to the fashionable shops and after a great deal of pleasurable discussion, found Lizzie her fan. I bought one too, and then we bought one or two other trinkets, and did Martha's shopping. We saw a great many people we knew, some of whom we merely bowed to, while with others we stopped to pass the time of day.

Lizzie was in her element. Devonshire society considered her one of its beauties, and she was expected to make an excellent match even before our recent change of fortune. Even now, although she planned to make her come-out in London in the near future, some local swains still held high hopes. They stared at me with curiosity, the overlooked sister of the family, and then at Richard with frank astonishment and admiration. I must be getting used to his magnificence, because I thought he wasn't particularly grandly dressed today, but as usual everything he wore was of the best quality, and he held himself with elegance and style. His coat was a drab green, his waistcoat cream silk lightly but expertly embroidered. Waistcoats, he had informed me, were the epitome of a fashionable man's style, and his always reflected that. The only jewels he wore were a ring on his finger and the diamond solitaire pin at his throat. I wore my pearls, unexceptionable for day wear but finer than anything else I had, and another new gown, this time of deep soft pink silk, with a little cloak of a slightly deeper pink over the top.

Lizzie was captured by one of her more persistent swains, Mr. Humphrey Thomas, a short, well-upholstered man, who had paid her court ever since her Exeter come-out. He held her hand while he conversed with her, paying her compliments that became further and further divorced from reality.

A man, his head lowered and seemingly in a great hurry, pushed past Richard, jostling him in the process.

Gervase stared after him. "Good Lord, Was he a pickpocket?"

Richard felt in his pockets. "Nothing's missing." He shrugged and let the incident pass.

After we had made our purchases, we returned to the carriage and went to the second house on our list. This appeared much more promising, being on a quiet street in the midst of other, similar houses. It also looked slightly larger than the first.

Richard helped me down, and then turned back to help Lizzie, but she stumbled and fell, crying, "Oh, my ankle!"

Richard immediately lifted her back into the carriage and put her on one of the seats. I climbed up and drew her skirts back a little to see the nature of the injury. The maid followed and sat opposite, waiting for instructions. Lizzie bit her lip and winced when I touched her foot, but I couldn't see or feel any swelling. "I don't think there's any serious hurt."

"I ought to go home." To my surprise, she instantly turned to Gervase "Will you take me, sir?"

He opened his mouth, thought better of it, and closed it again, his expression an odd mix of fascination and amusement. Then he tried once more. "I would be honoured, ma'am."

"We'll send the carriage back for you when we reach home," Lizzie promised.

Richard touched my arm. Dazed by the speed of events I stepped back out the carriage with him and watched while the stairs were folded up and the carriage driven away. The whole thing happened so quickly, and I was so concerned to ensure my sister had suffered no serious injury I hadn't thought to question anything until I saw the vehicle roll away from us.

"Shall we?" said Richard, smiling, and we went up the stairs to the front door.

Richard closed the door behind us. The sound echoed through the empty house. As it faded away, silence fell, a stillness, as if anticipation itself awaited us. The noises of daily activity outside became more muted.

I took a couple of steps, very aware of the sound of my rustling skirts in the quiet. I felt the eeriness of an empty house for the first time. When Richard didn't follow me, I turned around to see what was wrong.

To my astonishment, I saw him leaning against the front door, helpless with silent laughter. As I turned, he made a small sound, and felt in his coat pocket for his handkerchief, still using the front door for support. He wiped his eyes and looked up to see my reaction.

I was curious to know what had amused him so much and not a little cross. If the vase on the pedestal nearby had been mine, I might have picked it up and threatened him with it.

He dabbed his eyes. "You should really tell your sister to remember which ankle she was supposed to have twisted." He put his handkerchief away and straightened, watching me, his eyes gleaming with amusement.

I put my hand to my mouth, realising what I had innocently walked into. "Oh!" Lizzie's subterfuge hit me like a brick on the back of the head, and with about as much subtlety. Relief surged through me. They'd taken the maid with them, when she should have remained behind as a rudimentary chaperone.

I wondered if Lizzie had contrived the whole scheme or if Gervase assisted her in her deceit. I stood alone, my hand against the heat of my face, waiting for us both to recover our composure.

When Richard stood away from the door, his smile changed subtly, from amusement to tenderness as he regarded me standing foolishly in the middle of the floor. I didn't know how to think or behave. His smile made me blush even more.

"Come here." He held out his arms. I didn't need a second invitation. I walked straight to him, instantly dismissing Lizzie and her schemes.

His kiss was more intense than he'd allowed himself recently. I emerged from it breathless. His cool blue gaze returned my regard, freely and without guile.

"We have two, maybe three hours." I took a quick breath, and seeing my doubt he added, "Of course, my love, if you want to survey the house and leave we can always hire a vehicle to take us home, but it is near enough to our wedding day for us to take a risk. If you wish it."

That would let me off the hook if I didn't want to do this, if I should wish to choose the safe way. "We ought to look at the house," I said steadily, still not decided on the course we should take. I yearned for him with an intensity I wouldn't have imagined possible, and his proximity to me only made matters worse. Exquisite torture. But now we had the opportunity to indulge in what we both longed to do, doubts assailed me. Could I really not wait a week or two?

We toured the house while my turbulent thoughts calmed. It was bright, well furnished, and seemed to be the kind of house where her ladyship and her family might comfortably spend a few weeks. The dust covers were removed in preparation for our viewing but unlike Hareton Abbey before Martha had taken control, everything was clean and in good condition.

He was a little surprised when I led the way to the kitchens. "Do we have to?"

"We must make sure the kitchens are clean and serviceable."

Grinning, he preceded me down the stairs. Martha's training in housewifery must have gone deep, if I could think of practicalities while the blood sang in my veins. Every time he touched me the hairs on my neck stood up. The tour gave me a little more time to make up my mind. I knew what we did here was my decision. I felt his tension as though it was my own, which in a way it was.

The kitchens were bright, clean and totally empty, the fire cold and comfortless. The copper pans hung clean and scrubbed in their proper places. I touched one and listened to the clang as it touched its neighbour. I had never in my life been in an empty house before. I found the experience strange, and not altogether pleasant.

We went to the first floor and examined the principal rooms where Richard declared himself satisfied. "This will do. I'm sure my mother will be content with this."

I had taken a couple of steps up the flight of stairs to the second floor before I realised what lay there and what it might mean. I turned back to him, my heart hammering. He smiled, and put his hand on mine where it lay on the banister. "We don't need to see any more if you don't want to," he assured me, his voice a soft, seductive purr. "I can wait three weeks."

His blue eyes gleamed with the desire he didn't have to articulate and then I knew what I wanted. I touched his cheek. "I need this as much as you do."

Before he could make a response, I turned and led the way upstairs. I knew I would have fallen to the floor with him then if he'd wanted it, all my training, my sense of social rightness gone.

This was not like our rash encounter at the Abbey. Most members of society would wink at this. Many affianced couples, given extra time and freedom to get to know each other, anticipated the wedding ceremony by a week or two. Several "premature" babies were born seven or eight months after the wedding. It was even considered desirable, a proof of the bride's fertility.

When we'd made love before, Richard was contracted to marry someone else with no prospect of being released from the contract. It had been a terrible risk to me and to my family. They would have been tainted, maybe ostracised by any scandal which involved me, but at the time I didn't care. I'd wanted to give him, free and clear, the only gift I owned which I thought worthy of him, and after some persuasion, he'd taken it in that spirit.

We'd been lucky.

The bedrooms were as charming and as bare as the other rooms, and we passed through them without comment.

We went into a large bedroom at the back of the house. "This will do for me," Richard said, no inflection, no emotion in his voice. That absence of expression told me he was apprehensive, too.

The windows were draped in some gauzy stuff, which afforded privacy. The large room was bright, as the sun had by now emerged from its cloud cover and did its best to indicate that summer was on its way. There was nothing personal about this room. The new-looking bed in the middle of the room had light draperies drawn back and tied against the mahogany bedposts. Fresh linen adorned the bed, and a light coverlet of blue quilted cotton. It was as though it silently waited for us to break its unoccupied spell.

I heard the click as he closed the door with a finality that made me shiver in anticipation. It had been so long. To hold him, touch him, talk to him and yet not engage in the ultimate intimacy had drawn me as tight as a drum. I had no idea this would mean so much to me, but it did.

Feeling the light pressure of his hands on my shoulders, I turned with unreserved joy into his arms. They closed hard around me and he kissed me, letting nothing hide his passion. I responded, eagerly trying to show him how much I needed him too. His tongue entered my mouth, taking possession, joining us in an imitation of what would follow. His kisses weren't those of the experienced lover, but born of an eager, frantic desire, each kiss devouring me as if he wanted to sate himself on me. We could have been new to the experience, both of us. It made me want him more until the yearning rose to an explosive demand that nothing could deny.

He loosened his hold to slip his hand between our bodies, at the buttons of his waistcoat. If I hadn't had my mouth on his, I would have smiled, for the first time we'd made love I'd been so eager and so nervous that when I had performed this office for him I'd pulled too hard, and showered the floor with waistcoat buttons. Obviously, he didn't want to take the risk this time.

He released me, but never took his gaze away from mine, his hunger apparent in his wide, blue eyes. If his society acquaintances could see him now all their preconceptions about the sophisticated man of fashion would fade into mist. He slid his coat and waistcoat off in one swift movement, the satin linings making it easy for them to slip to the floor. Then he returned to hold me and kiss me again, his heat tantalisingly closer. He pushed his tongue into my mouth, and my excitement lifted to fever pitch. I caressed his tongue with mine, letting him explore my mouth and meld his body to mine.

Even at this extreme of want, Richard didn't fumble; he knew exactly where a lady was hooked, pinned and laced. He put his nimble fingers to work on my gown, unhooking, unlacing with speedy efficiency, faster than I could have done. I helped as much as I could, eagerly tugging the cord of my side hoops free, so they fell to the floor with my gown and petticoat. My other petticoats followed in quick succession, and my stays had never come off so quickly before. I needed to feel his body next to mine, ached for it. I might stop breathing if I didn't touch him soon.

I was left in only my shift, and he went down on one knee and placed his hands either side of my legs, grasping my calves as if to steady himself. His breathing had become ragged, matching mine, the only sounds in this quiet room. He looked up at me, let me see the need in him. I stared back, hiding nothing, totally unable to. "You bring me to the level of a schoolboy with his first woman," he said, his voice as uneven as his breath. "I want you until I think I'll go blind from the need."

He drew his hands up the sides of my body, bringing my shift with them, and I lifted my arms so he could pull the garment over my head in one smooth movement. The feel of his hands as they ran all the way up my body quickened my desire and I gave a little "oh" of pleasure.

"Let me see you, love."

I stood unashamed in the middle of a discarded pool of multicoloured silk.

Quickly, efficiently, he stripped off his remaining clothes and tossed them to join the others on the floor, letting me see his hard, vigorous body while he gazed at me. It seemed we stood forever like that, the only sound being our breathing, ragged gasps. His slow smile could have stopped my heart.

Then, with an "Oh, my sweet life!" he surged forward and swept me into his arms so at last I felt his blessed warmth. He kissed me, bent to kiss the pulse on my throat that sent shivers up my spine, then he passed his hands over my back, a smooth river of caresses pouring unceasingly over me. His bare skin, his heat, his very presence intoxicated me and, as once before, I ceased to think about anything else.

There were only the two of us in the world. "Richard. I want you so much."

"Sweetheart, I didn't think it was possible, but I want you more than ever before." He put his hands under me and lifted me, taking a stride towards the bed but before he could do so, unable to wait any longer, I lifted my legs to wrap around his waist, and folded my arms around his shoulders. He laughed in surprise and delight and then gasped. I slid down to touch his erection against my entrance, aching to feel him there.

He was inside me before we reached the bed. When I felt him enter me, I knew my need as raw, instinctive passion, and felt his, ruthlessly reined back for my pleasure.

He sat on the bed, instead of laying me down as I expected him to and I thrilled with the realisation that this gave me control over our lovemaking. I took it eagerly. I'd never known this kind of power over a man before. The first time, I'd been so overwhelmed by the demands of my own body and of his, I'd let him guide me to pleasure. I hadn't questioned his control. Now he gave me this gift, the power to do what I wished.

I heard the sound like a mix between a chuckle and a low groan deep in his throat when I moved my body over him. The sound urged me to do more. I lifted up, using his shoulders as support and then sank down, opening my legs wide to take as much of him into me as I could.

He kissed me, moaned softly, murmured endearments, "Oh so beautiful, oh my dearest love." He nuzzled my breasts and I lowered my head to kiss him. I tried moving on him, shifting my body from side to side and he cried out, took my nipple in his mouth and sucked hard. Everything stopped, only this existed. When I froze, unable to do any more he pressed me close, lifted me to sink back down, slid his fingers between us and touched me in a place which made me explode. I held on tight, crying his name, my body racked by convulsions of ecstasy.

He waited until I opened my eyes again. His slow, loving smile touched my soul, and I whispered to him, "God, how I needed this."

"Sweet love. I need you as much as I need the air around us. Let me show you how much." He slid his arms around me, and lowered me on to the bed, moving on top of me without leaving my body. His movements were slow, smooth, making me feel every nuance, every touch, every kiss, going on forever. Time disappeared, life went away until there was only this time, such was the intensity of physical pleasure, the expression of love. When his movements quickened and his thrusts deepened, I cried his name and lifted my legs to pull him close, hearing his gasp. I thought he might have found his release then, but he continued to move, slowing to a languorous loving that reached to the deepest part of me. I didn't know how he held back his own climax. "I will not..." His teeth gritted and he pushed deeply. "You will come again, sweetheart, before I do. I want you trembling in my arms, helpless, as I've felt these past weeks."

It went on forever. I smiled into his blazing blue eyes, hiding nothing, letting him see everything.

His rhythmic movements brought a dreamy awareness of slow growth, but he smiled into my eyes. "Are you tired, my love? Shall we stop now?"

"No, no. Never stop, never!"

He laughed, the sound free of anything but delight, and I laughed too to hear him. He obeyed me, and let his body tell him what to do. His movements became ever more urgent, more demanding until with a wordless cry he stiffened and he shut his eyes tight. I felt a slight movement, as though he would withdraw, so I pulled him closer, letting him push hard inside me. He crowned his ecstasy in a series of shivers.

He sank down beside me on the bed. Our legs entwined, we lay together for a long time, still and overwhelmed.

I would have drifted off to a contented sleep, but I was brought back to our version of reality when he sat up, reached for the quilt we'd kicked aside and pulled it over us. It was only just April, and the house wasn't heated, though I couldn't say I'd noticed before. His movements roused me, and when I opened my eyes, I saw him propped up on one elbow, watching me with such warmth in his face it took my breath away. "You're an extraordinary woman."

I smiled up at him. "I've never thought of myself like that before."

"Few could have done some of the things you've just accomplished." He rested his free hand on my stomach. "You're supple, wanton, open and you have an inventive quality I can't wait to explore at some—considerable length. If I didn't love you already, I would still count myself lucky to have found you."

It sounded as though he was describing someone else. "I'm so glad I make you happy." I didn't think I'd done anything special, but unlike him, I had nothing to compare it to.

He lowered his head and kissed me long and sweetly, but then returned to his previous pose, leaning on one elbow, looking down at me. "You've made me promise something I might find hard, but I mean to keep." I quirked an eyebrow at him. "To keep no secrets." Normally I wouldn't need a reminder.

"Will you promise me something in return?"

"Anything."

He laughed at my instant response. "Truly? I might keep you to that. But for now, will you promise me you will never keep me from your bed? May we spend every possible night together?"

"That's easy." I reached up to touch his face. "I promise." He turned his head to kiss my palm. When he moved back, I saw the small curls of his close-cropped fair hair brightened into gold by the sun streaming through the windows behind him.

I was struck by a thought, and I felt relaxed enough to share it with him. "But you won't want me in a few months time, if I'm with child. I'll be fat and ugly."

It was one of my private fears, that while I grew large with his children he would revert to his previous ways, driven by his needs, and while I knew I had all his love, I couldn't bear to think of him like this with anyone else. A provincial attitude I know, but that's what I was at heart—a provincial. To share him might kill me. I kept my tone light, unwilling to let him know how much it meant to me.

"You'll be glowing, blooming and beautiful." He kissed me on each word. "I would only want you more if I knew you carried my child." His hand moved lightly over my stomach and I was placated for the present. I hooked my hand around his neck and pulled him down for another kiss.

I loved the warmth of him, the closeness of his body next to mine, and I lay back and luxuriated in the feeling. He caressed my breast, moved down to kiss it, then circled the other one with his hand. His hand moved lower, slipped between my intimate curls. His actions made me tremble. "Richard?"

"Shhh..." was his only reply. His kisses passed on to my stomach, long, lingering kisses on my breasts, my stomach, between my legs. I shivered, surprised and slightly afraid but I trusted him, and soon my body tingled all over in yet another new sensation. I gasped with surprise, thrilled to his touch, the feel of his exploratory fingers, his tongue delivering the intimate kisses that forced repeated shudders from me. He licked, kissed, tasted and then drove his tongue deep inside me.

I forgot who I was, where I was. My body arched of its own volition, so violent was the white-hot explosion that shook me through. I cried out, not knowing such intense feeling existed before this.

He came back up the bed to me. I reached for him blindly, and he entered me again, the sum of every part of me, all I could think of, all I wanted. He pushed me to the heights of pleasure, relentlessly drove me until I cried out over and over, losing all words except his name. He was all I wanted to be, all I wanted to have. He called out to me when he climaxed, accepting all I was giving to him.

Richard took his weight off me, but came back at once to take me closely into his arms. I breathed deeply, recovering, the scent of him surrounding me. I felt completely safe.

"What was that?" I still wasn't sure how he'd taken me so far out of my world.

He kissed the top of my head. "That, my sweet, was me, inadequately trying to show you how much I love you."

"It was wonderful." I couldn't believe the intensity of it.

He laughed, turned my face up to his with one hand, and kissed me in a gentle salute. "I love you. You're a constant delight."

"You're a constant surprise."

I felt the closeness; our hearts beat next to each other in time. I could have stayed there forever. When he released me I felt the loss keenly. I watched him throw the covers back and go to search amongst the discarded clothes on the floor.

I lazily watched him find his coat, and feel in the pocket. He brought out a small box, his watch and a piece of paper. He sat on the edge of the bed and read it. Then he handed it to me. "That should be good news. It was put into my pocket earlier, when I was jostled in the street." So that was why he hadn't made any fuss. It read:

Mr. Cawnton has received Mr. Thompson's account of the incident last Sunday. He accepts his explanation and assures him no further action will be taken, but warns him not to meddle in what does not concern him.

I was still afraid for him. I knew what these people were capable of. I handed back the note. "Who's Mr. Thompson?"

"Me." He tossed the paper on the nightstand. He lifted the quilt and slipped back into bed beside me. "Though most people think it's Carier. I hope these people do, and I'm supposed to be merely the messenger." He stopped when he saw the expression on my face. Secrets. "Yes, I know, it's a secret and I will tell you. But it would take longer than the time we have at our disposal now. Will you wait? I'll tell you when I can, I promise, but it's a long story."

I smiled, relaxed back into his arms. "That will do. I'm sorry I asked you to share everything. I had no right."

His lips touched my forehead, and when I looked up he kissed my lips. "You're wrong. I've asked you to put your life into my care, and you deserve to know it all. I don't want anything between us that might drive us apart. I will tell you everything, everything you ask, everything I can remember."

"Thank you. I don't deserve you."

"Wrong again." His arms were warm. I snuggled closer. "I've done some things I'm deeply ashamed of. I'm sure you haven't." He played his fingers in my hair. "All the women I've hurt, all the husbands I've wronged, I can't do anything to help them, but I can, through you, cause no more hurt. Only love."

"So I'm your salvation?"

"You're everything." Our lips met in a kiss that wasn't, for a change, charged with lust, but pure love, so sweet I almost wept with happiness. "And I have something else for you."

He reached back to the nightstand where he'd deposited the box. "You're out of mourning now, and it took some time to find this, or I would have given it you before. Wear this for me?"

I opened the box and my mouth dropped. It was my betrothal ring. He had chosen a ruby for me, enhanced by diamonds around the edge, but I had rarely seen a stone so full of life, so rich in colour. I remembered to close my mouth.

"It took me a while to find what I had in mind," he said, taking the ring out of the box. "Here, try it on." He lifted my hand and slipped the ring on my finger, then studied the effect critically. "If you don't like it, it can be changed, but I think it suits you."

I turned my hand to catch the rays of the sun to make it glint. "Thank you," I managed eventually.

"It's your right." He tilted my head up to him, and kissed me, long and slow, then released me with a sigh. "But now, my love, if I'm to make any kind of lady's maid, we have to make a move." He flung the quilt back, then turned around and came back to take me in his arms again. "How can I wait three more weeks?"

"How can I?" I smiled back at him and stretched my arms over my head, luxuriating in his loving gaze upon my body. "You don't have to wait. One more time, to tide us over?"

Chapter Nine

We got home just in time to dress for dinner, so I hurried upstairs and rushed into my clothes. Lizzie came into my room as the maid left it, and sat on the bed. There was no trace of a limp. "How's your foot?" I asked.

She grinned. "You know how it is."

I scrambled into my gown and began to hook it on to my stomacher. "Richard says if you bind it, you'll remember which one it is you're supposed to limp on."

"I'm obliged to him but Mr. Kerre already suggested that on the way home. I'm sure it will be perfectly all right tomorrow."

"I'm sure it will." I finished hooking the gown and went to the dressing table to find my hairbrush. She was still smiling, unashamed by her subterfuge. "Lizzie, how could you?"

"What?" Her innocent blue gaze met my more cynical expression. "Didn't you want some time alone with him?"

"It's not that, and indeed I'm grateful to you—" more than I could say, "—but it was so blatantly done!"

"Well, and how else was it to be done? I tired of coughing and rattling the handle of the door every time I went into a room. It's obvious to everyone here you needed some time alone together. You can hardly keep your hands off each other." She thought, tracing a pattern on the quilt with the tip of her finger. She looked up again, meeting my eyes shyly. "What's it like?"

I didn't pretend to misunderstand her, but my puritan heart was shocked she should think to ask. "Lizzie, how can you ask me that?"

She drew a delighted breath and a smiled broadly. "So you did it. I felt sure you wouldn't stop at kissing. Tell me, Rose, please, it might be *years* before I find out for myself."

She leaned forward, entreating me to tell her, looking alluring without even making the effort. I snorted. "I shouldn't think so for a minute. You'll find out soon enough. Lizzie. I have no intention of telling you anything." I was scandalised by her request, but as well, I wanted to keep the events of the day to myself, something to keep me warm at night. There were no words to describe the joy I'd felt that afternoon, and nothing would make me share it with anyone else.

Lizzie sat up, sniffed in an unladylike way and folded her arms. "Well it's the least you can do."

"No. But I will tell you something else." In truth, I felt I owed her something for the afternoon, and felt confident enough in her discretion to share my secret.

"All right." She still wasn't placated, but she folded her hands on her lap and prepared to listen.

"It wasn't the first time," I confessed, and I dropped my eyelids momentarily.

"What?" The heat rushed up to her face in a pretty rosy flush.

I smiled in triumph. "I became his mistress last October. That was the only time, before this afternoon."

"Dear God."

I had succeeded in shocking her, and my sister wasn't easily shocked. She couldn't speak for a while, and I was content to watch her in silence. Her changes of expression, from disbelief to horror ended in a gabble of words. "But you didn't know what he was like then, his reputation was fearsome. And he was betrothed to someone else."

"I was sure of him from the first day." As I said it, I realised somewhere inside me it was true. God knows I shouldn't have been so sure, but my naïveté had prevented me shunning what my heart felt, and I had won my heart's desire. Otherwise he might have left me, gone through with the disastrous marriage to Miss Cartwright and made both of us miserable.

I watched Lizzie, who now searched for words, stunned by what I had just told her. "You were fortunate not to quicken. How could you take such a risk?"

"I never thought of the risk. He did, immediately afterwards and he asked me to tell him the minute I knew."

"You were lucky."

I loved the new experience of having my gossip-loving younger sister lecturing me. "I know. I'm lucky in more ways than you know. I hope you have such good fortune."

She chuckled and stretched her pretty feet out before her. "Oh, I want someone of rank with lots of money and a pleasant personality, but if you'd involved us in that kind of scandal, what chance would there have been for me?"

"You could have survived it. And we would have made it possible for you to distance yourselves from us. But by that time Richard and I had committed ourselves to each other.

I stood and, linking arms with my sister, we went downstairs together to dinner.

When I saw Richard I blushed, and he laughed at me.

"Every time I look at you until I see you at the altar, I'll remember this afternoon," he murmured, leading me into the dining room.

Richard behaved in exactly the same way towards me as he had always done, and I took my cue from him. At first, I was shy in his presence, and sure everyone knew, or could see the difference in me. But I saw no change in anyone's behaviour and I felt easier as time went by.

The relaxed atmosphere persisted, as though our tension had pervaded the whole house before, and now had dissipated, only, I feared, to begin to rise again. Lust wasn't what I felt for Richard, but if I was totally honest with myself, it was part of it. I found him immensely attractive, and I knew I wasn't alone in that. His experience was diverse and plentiful before I had met him.

I looked forward to my wedding, and even more, what

would come afterwards.

That Friday we were due to go to the Assembly Rooms. Martha had asked the Skerrits to dine, and then we would all go to Exeter together. My brother Ian, as usual, cried off, feigning illness. He had suffered a lot in childhood but he had grown out of most of the illnesses that had made him a sickly child. Now he enjoyed all the benefits of the reputation and none of the inconveniences, using the excuse to avoid anything he didn't want to face. He preferred the company of his books to other people.

I dressed with care. I'd had a new gown made for when I came out of mourning, pink silk with flounces, fly braid and ruched trims, lightly embroidered with little flowers in silver around the hem and front opening, worn with one of the new smaller hoops. When I was dressed, I stood in front of the large mirror in my room and for once, smiled at what I saw. I looked frivolous, something I hadn't been able to achieve for months. Mourning precluded that. The pearls Richard had given me were the finest jewellery I possessed, so I put them on.

When I went downstairs to the drawing room, Richard complimented me, before his attention went to my necklace, and he frowned.

"Lovely though they are, I'm not sure the pearls are set off by that gown. You look beautiful, as always, but don't you think this would be better?"

Out of the corner of my eye, I saw Gervase watching me closely, and I wondered what Richard was about.

Richard drew a glittering string out of his pocket. Diamonds, a delicately worked necklace of flowers and foliage entwined together in a fiery chain. Everyone in the room including me drew a breath as the chain twisted in his hand, flashing dazzling sparks in the candlelight.

He came towards me, smiling. "Forgive the subterfuge. My mother had them when she was first married, and now they're yours. I sent to Derbyshire for them last week, when the trip to the Assembly Rooms was first planned."

I couldn't speak. I could see the mirror above the fireplace from where I stood, and silently I looked into it while he unclasped the pearls and fastened the diamond necklace about my neck instead. The jewels flashed every time I breathed.

"It's part of a set." He handed me a box, which had lain unnoticed on a side table. Inside, on a bed of blue velvet, lay matching earrings, a bracelet and several brooches to fasten to my stomacher. I touched them wonderingly with one finger, watching them glitter, then Richard spoke and I looked at him instead.

He gazed at me as though we were the only people in that room, openly loving, openly proud "I wish the whole of the Assembly tonight to know you are the future Countess of Southwood. And my chosen bride."

He'd known what this meant to me, to show me as his in that place. I groped in my mind for the words to show him how I felt, but couldn't find any.

Then Tom laughed, and broke the spell. "I've never known you lost for words before, Rose."

The rest of the room burst with expressions of delight, admiration and amazement. Richard stepped back, allowing Lizzie and Georgiana to come forward to examine my new jewels.

I hooked the earrings in the piercings in my ears. Although they were girandoles, three pendants from one central stone, they were light and easy to wear. The cold gold setting fell against my neck when I swung my head. Georgiana Skerrit took a deep breath of admiration while Lizzie pinned the brooches to my stomacher, and then made me sit down while she fixed one in my hair. It was set *en tremblant,* so it quivered every time I moved my head, and sent flashes of light about the room.

I lent the pearls to Lizzie for the evening, which delighted her, and then I touched the necklace, still cold around my neck. "Thank you."

Richard took my hand, and kissed it. "It's your triumph

tonight. Mine will come later, when I present you in town. They'll all hate that I saw you first, and seized the prize."

We had dinner, and then the carriages arrived at the door. Richard and I shared a carriage with Martha, James, Lizzie and Gervase. It was fortunate fashionable hoops had decreased in size recently, because there wouldn't have been room for us all with the wide, oblong hoops of the previous decade, but as it was we had to overlap our skirts to fit in. The skirts of Richard's rich, blue coat were full behind, pleated into two great jewelled buttons at the back, but were much easier to handle.

We drove to the Assembly rooms in high excitement, although I tried hard to calm my nerves. I wanted to look serene and happy, not as excited as an ingénue, and I'd managed to steady my breathing and smooth my excitement to some extent by the time we arrived.

When Richard handed me out of the carriage I looked with new eyes at the building, the scene of so many of my disappointments and humiliations. As usual on an Assembly night, it glowed with light in the growing dusk, and some local people were gathered around, curious to see the great and the not-so-good (but rich) of the county as they arrived.

We moved into the light of the flaming torches set outside the front door, and the crowd drew its collective breath. It was sweet to hear. I put my hand on Richard's arm and we passed inside, to be greeted by the master of ceremonies.

Chapter Ten

The master of ceremonies had never bowed so low to me before. I adored it, the man who used to favour me with a polite but brief nod, now giving me all his attention. I accepted his congratulations with a gracious inclination of my head, and slowly ascended the stairs, leaning on Richard's arm. Richard took his most intimidating form; stunningly adorned in gleaming blue satin, exquisite French lace foaming over the backs of his elegantly disposed hands and at his neck. Diamonds glittered at his throat and his knee, and he wore an expression of hauteur on his handsome face, the fashionable society appearance I should try to cultivate. But I knew him now, and he didn't intimidate me.

James and Martha walked in front of us. Martha showed to advantage tonight. She had powdered her hair, while I had daringly left mine bare, but the effect gave her more gravitas somehow, more dignity. A smile hovered under my self-control as I allowed Richard to escort me into the ballroom. I wanted to enter it as grandly as he did.

When James and Martha were announced a hush fell in the room beyond, previously humming with voices. We couldn't see them yet, but I knew every eye must be turned to the door. This was the first time James and Martha had attended the Assembly since they inherited the title of Lord and Lady Hareton. We gave them their pause at the door, and Martha smiled and nodded. She had taken her new fortune in her stride, although she hadn't wished for it, and she deserved every second of this, her grand entrance.

Then it was our turn. When we were announced the few voices quietly murmuring paused. A sudden hush stilled the voices, almost like a gasp for air.

I crested the top of the stairs. The room blazed with light from the dozens of candles set in the great chandelier and the wall brackets. Every face turned up to us. I hoped Richard could feel my happiness and thought then how shy and fearful I might have been without him, how I might still have been passed over, despite my new status. After all, a spinster aunt was a spinster aunt, whether the sister of an earl or the distant cousin of one. But the affianced wife of a viscount, the heir to a great earldom, was a different prospect entirely. Especially on the arm of the handsomest man in the room, and wearing diamonds.

I nodded graciously to the gaggle of girls gathered together by the large fireplace; their usual spot. They were my erstwhile tormentors. I tasted my triumph, felt the sweetness of revenge in my mouth. Petty, I know, but at that moment it felt like the greatest public triumph of my life.

We descended the stairs into the room at a leisurely pace and I heard Lizzie's and Gervase's names called out.

Her arrival filled the room with a buzz—it always did, and the sight of Gervase, closely following his twin, created a sensation. I stopped when we were clear of the stairs to glance back. Lizzie was having a wonderful time. She smiled and bowed to her acquaintances as she descended the stairs on Gervase's arm. Gervase, suave in brown velvet, glanced at me and I saw the gleam of amusement in his eyes.

Richard smiled to see my pleasure. "Happy with your reception?"

"It makes up for a lot," I confessed.

Richard surveyed the room, taking his time, ignoring those people who were ill-mannered enough to stare at us. "I see someone I know. May I make you known to him? He's a particular friend of mine."

He took me to a man who stood with one or two others by the side of the room. From their dress and demeanour, I assumed they were from Richard's circle of friends. They were elegantly attired in the height of fashion, jewels casually winking on their clothes and in their hair. When we approached, they all bowed. It was a pretty sight; the precious jewels and gold and silver embroidery gleamed and flashed in the candlelight. "Richard," the man said.

"Freddy," he acknowledged, then he introduced me.

I curtseyed, they bowed and I found "Freddy" was Sir Frederick Brean, Baron Thwaite, who seemed to be on good terms with my betrothed.

"So this is the *latest* future Lady Strang."

I looked at him, startled, but to my surprise Richard didn't take offence. "Indeed. And if I have anything to do with it, the last future Lady Strang of this generation, at least."

Lord Thwaite laughed, his pleasant features showing only amusement. "Delighted to meet you, ma'am. A great improvement on the last one." He glanced at Richard meaningfully, a challenge in his dark stare.

I smiled and inclined my head.

"I don't want to hear ill of Miss Drury. She did me a great service, when she ran off as she did."

"What did she do it for, hey? Did you frighten her off?"

Richard grinned. "I tried, but she wasn't to be frightened. She found a stray cleric and decided to throw in her lot with him when matters finally came to a head. She'll no doubt find him more to her taste. Easier to control."

"How angry was your father?"

"Furious." Richard was the only person not afraid of his father's violent temper. "But then he met Rose, and he came to see it was all for the best."

"Met them, have you?" Lord Thwaite cast me a quizzical glance that almost made me laugh. As it was, he raised a smile and I decided I liked him. He didn't make me feel in the least shy or awkward, despite the fact that I had never met him before and I disliked meeting strangers. His dark, indolent good looks and his voice carved out of velvet would make him a favourite with the ladies, and I hoped Gervase had been right when he'd said Freddy would cut Richard out with Eustacia Terry.

"I paid them a short visit after Christmas. I was still in mourning then, so I couldn't stay too long."

"Rum lot, don't you think, Miss Golightly? I'm allowed to say because I'm a distant cousin, so Lady Southwood is by the way of being my aunt."

I didn't want to give my opinion of the haughty Southwoods. "I've met rummer. The previous Earls of Hareton were the strangest people I ever met."

"Ye-es." Lord Thwaite raised his glass and took a thoughtful sip. "Strang told me something about that. Of course, it must have had its advantages, a big, empty house like that. Wish I could have the same advantage when I start my courting."

I blushed, but Richard smiled, perhaps at the memory of that small nursemaid's room and what we did there. "You're not married, my lord?" I managed, trying to turn the conversation. He was too near the mark for my comfort.

"No," he said triumphantly. "Although I turned thirty last week, and my mother's begun to increase her hints. Don't think I'll be able to hold off much longer though, now Strang's made his arrangements. Mind, if I had met you before Strang, ma'am, I might well have tried to cut him out."

I smiled, easy with his compliment. I didn't take Lord Thwaite seriously, but I liked him and I felt comfortable with him. I realised that could be a devastating weapon in the hands of the right man, that ability to put people at their ease.

"Can you introduce us to any of the lovelies across the room, Strang?" one of the other gentlemen asked.

"Look at them, George, and you're a dead man," the lady next to him said. "How do you do, ma'am? I'm this reprobate's wife, Caroline Fleming."

I curtseyed. She looked to be about the same age as me,

and she had a pleasant, open countenance.

I had been so used to reading about these people in the popular press that I had looked on them as some sort of supra beings, above ordinary living. When I looked at them now, I could believe they suffered from the same trials and tribulations as the rest of us. I felt at home, a strange feeling, surprising to me. I'd never felt at home in company before.

Lady Fleming admired my diamonds, although she wore a beautiful parure of emeralds herself. "I believe they're a family treasure. Richard gave them to me a few weeks early. He knows I spent my youth in these rooms, and he wanted them all to see me now."

"Oh I know that feeling," Lady Fleming exclaimed. "Sitting out dance after dance as the young men go after the latest sensational beauty. Who was your particular bugbear?"

"The young lady across the room in green," I said, without turning around.

She peered over my shoulder. "I see her."

"I see her too." Richard excused himself and crossed the room to greet Miss Terry and her friends.

Lady Fleming watched him with curiosity. "What is he up to?"

Although I had never met her before, I liked her. "I made the mistake of telling Richard she had afforded me several slights in the past."

Lord Thwaite saw the implications first, and let out a crack of laughter. "Well it's clear he's not attracted to her—he never went in for that sort of insipid beauty. Only peerless diamonds for Strang. Setting her up for a fall, is he?"

"I wish he wouldn't," I confessed.

Lord Thwaite watched Richard amuse the local girls on the other side of the room. "It's hard to deflect Strang from his purpose, once he's made his mind up to it. I remember when he took a bet that he could paint a red cross on every house in St. James' Square in ten minutes. He did it, too. Mind you, we were all devilish drunk at the time. George here tried to stop him, and almost got knifed for his pains, but it was fine to see when he finally took the pot of paint from behind the charley's box. He can move fast when he wants to, can Strang."

I imagined Richard would take it on, not for the bet, but for the dare. Lord Thwaite seemed an easy sort of man, so different to Richard and yet so much a part of his world. He would be indifferent to the sort of gossip that had crippled me for so many years and while I despised myself for my social cowardice, I still felt that tension every time I entered a room containing strangers. I would have to work hard to overcome that particular aspect. It would look like a lack of breeding to the ton.

Richard sauntered back across the floor towards us, and saw my amused expression.

"Blackening my reputation, Freddy?" He shot his lordship a look of diverted malice.

"Who, me?" his lordship said, the picture of hurt innocence. "Enhancing it, more like. Remember St. James' Square?"

Richard groaned and put his hand to his eyes. "I was drunk."

"I know," came the reply. "I was there."

I turned to Richard, struck by a sudden realisation. "I don't think I've ever seen you drunk."

"You might well have done, ma'am, without actually knowing it," Lord Thwaite told me. "You can't tell from his manner, except perhaps a look about the eye. More his behaviour. His recklessness is a joy to behold."

"Were you drunk when you asked me to marry you?" I demanded of him, smiling.

"Never more sober." He took my hand and placed it on his arm. "I'm sorry but I'm afraid I must take you away. There are some people you should meet."

We bowed to Lord Thwaite and the Flemings, and he bore me away to some more sedate strangers, more of his circle, and I was duly introduced. These people were older, and Richard watched me curtsey and saw them smile in welcome. We talked about the wedding, the weather and the beauties of Exeter, then the orchestra struck up, and he led me on to the floor for the first minuet, the formal opening to the proceedings. The first dance was always the minuet, and classed as such, while the ones that followed, the lesser minuets, were not as formal. I had never taken the floor for that first dance before and I quelled my trembling muscles in an effort to do this properly.

He danced beautifully, gracefully, but I was forced to concentrate. His attempts at conversation met with monosyllabic responses while I focused on my steps and my bearing for this supremely elegant dance of courtship. I met his gaze and he smiled reassuringly when he recognised my plight, but after that he helped me all he could, and didn't talk too much. I needed all my concentration to get me through it.

"I thought you would be a natural dancer," he commented, when the dance mercifully finished. "I shall make you practise."

"I spent too long holding up the wall." I flicked my fan open and used it to cover my blushes at having to confess this to him.

"You need not fear that any longer." He led me off the floor, found us some wine and we crossed the room to the group of girls who stood by the fire.

"I promised to introduce these charming ladies to Lord Thwaite. He has asked if he might meet them." He lifted a questioning brow to where Mr. and Mrs. Terry sat within earshot.

Mrs. Terry nodded graciously. "Take care of her."

"Ladies?" Richard bowed.

Eustacia's attention was on my neck, not my face, and her eyes widened. "What a beautiful necklace."

"One of the family treasures," Richard replied lightly. "My mother had them reset when she was Lady Strang, but the larger diamonds were always supposed to have been presented to an ancestor by Queen Elizabeth. He must have performed some signal service for her, but we've never been sure what it was."

"Can't you guess?" I asked.

He gave me a mock frown. "You shouldn't impugn the reputation of the Virgin Queen, madam." Miss Terry looked suitably disapproving.

"Not all virgins are virgins," I reminded him cruelly and was rewarded by a crack of laughter.

"True enough."

Miss Terry exchanged a speaking glance with her friends and then turned back to Richard, spread her fan, looked at him over its rim, and then lowered it again. He watched her appreciatively. "Your skills are developing well, ma'am."

"Thank you, sir. Won't you introduce us to your friends?"

"Yes, of course," he replied.

He crossed the room, bearing a lady on each arm, Miss Terry and her friend Miss Sturman. Behind his back, Miss Terry stared over her shoulder at me with a triumphant expression, as though she had won him, could always win anyone she wanted from me. But she had lost the power to hurt me, and I followed them with a serene expression and a black thought.

Introductions were made, and Richard stood back with me, taking no part in the ensuing conversation. Miss Terry said, "La, my lord," once, and I watched Lord Thwaite's quick expression of blank astonishment. He glanced over the lady's head at Richard, his eyes full of delighted amusement.

Then Miss Terry dared to try out her new techniques with the fan that Richard had taught her. At her first pass Lord Thwaite's eyes widened. Mistaking it for admiration, she tried another.

Lord Thwaite managed a quavering, "Goodness!" before he regained his composure and bowed low. I thought I saw his shoulders shake, but I couldn't be sure. "Well after that, I have to ask you if you could spare me a dance." Eustacia smiled, lowered her eyes, and said she would be glad to. He led her off, and left the company nonplussed.

Lady Fleming confronted Richard. "Did you teach her that?"

Richard turned his innocent blue gaze to her. "What would that be?"

"You know quite well what." Lady Fleming smiled. "She'll make a lot of conquests with that trick." Amusement brimmed over in her voice. Then she addressed me. "Was she *very* cruel to you?"

"Sometimes," I admitted. "I didn't take, you see. My sister was a sensation when she came out, and I'm afraid I was overlooked after that."

"You didn't take?" Lady Fleming repeated with incredulity, and then looked from me to Richard and back again. "You were lucky," she told him.

"I know it," he replied calmly.

"I've seen your sister," she said. "Mr. Kerre introduced us. She is lovely, isn't she? She'll be a great hit in town."

"I wouldn't be surprised if she ends up a duchess," Richard commented.

Much to my surprise, I found I was enjoying myself. These people were pleasant, and I could converse with them easier than with some of the people I'd grown up with. Tom joined us and found a great deal in common with Sir George, a hunting man, and soon the two groups of younger people mingled in an amiable way.

Tom claimed his dance from me when we got to the country-dances, as he always did. I could always rely on Tom to help me in the old days.

"They're all talking about you," he said as we passed down the line.

"What are they saying?"

"Well, Miss Terry told her friends she didn't know how you, and not your sister, had trapped Lord Strang, and she said it quite loudly, too, but she's the only one who doesn't seem to be happy for you. You never got on with her, did you?"

Tom knew our history. "No."

"Mama wanted me to get to know her better at one point, but I found her too stupid." He glanced to where she danced with Lord Thwaite. She smiled and glanced about the room to make sure everyone saw her great victory. Tom sighed. "She'll make her own downfall, that one."

We followed the rounds of the dance, and when we came together again he complimented me on my appearance. "You look beautiful tonight." I accepted this compliment with pleasure, since I knew he was not in the least in love with me and wouldn't have hesitated to tell me if my hair was out of place, or if the colour I wore made me look ill. "You're glowing, you know, and those diamonds have set the room alight."

"Lady Fleming has a fine set of emeralds."

"Yes, but she's a member of high society, she's the sort of person wears that sort of jewellery. You're Miss Golightly, the girl we've known all our lives, and that's what caused the sensation. They finally realise you've gone away from them, you're part of something they can't join."

"You can, though," I said quickly. "I'd hate to lose your friendship, Tom. Do you think your mother would allow you and Georgiana to visit us when we're married?"

"She'd jump at it. Do you know where you'll live? Will you live in Derbyshire?"

I smiled. We parted again, only to come together at the end of the dance. I continued to try to answer his question. "Richard says he can't live in the same house as his parents for too long. He says we'll decide after the bride trip." I dropped my head, at that reminder. When I thought of that, I wanted him again. I was turning into a dreadful wanton. Tom was too much of a gentleman to notice, and as the dance had now ended, and Richard was taking the floor with Miss Sturman, he took me back to James and Martha, who also seemed to be enjoying themselves hugely.

The older generation, too, seemed to mix well, my old world and my new one. I hoped Martha was feeling as relieved as I was. She too had been feeling a little apprehensive before the evening began, not being naturally happy in company, but now she looked much more at her ease, as she chatted to a lady she hadn't met before in a relaxed manner.

My hand was claimed for some of the other dances, and I managed quite well. Richard danced with Miss Terry, and whispered a few words to her, at which she first looked startled and then smiled, and nodded. More flirting, I supposed, and I wondered if he would be as brutal with her as I knew he could be. I wished I hadn't mentioned anything to him about Miss Terry's disdain for me, but the damage was done. Perhaps the fan trick had been all he would do. I could only hope so.

Chapter Eleven

I was finishing my second glass of wine when I faltered and was forced to put my hand down on the nearest chair for support. Richard was by my side instantly. "Are you all right, my love?"

"Just a little dizzy. A combination of the wine and the heat. I'll be fine."

"Come with me."

He took me out the main room, into the corridor that led to the card rooms. At the end of the passage he opened a door. We entered an empty room, where the fire hadn't been lit, so it was much cooler in here. He took me to a sofa set in front of the window and sat me down.

"I like to explore my terrain a little, and I discovered this room earlier. Stay here. I'll see if I can get you some lemonade or something equally innocuous." He left the room, returning in a few moments with a glass of lemonade for me and a glass of wine for himself.

I took a few deep breaths and smiled reassuringly at him. "That's much better. I drank too much at dinner because I was nervous, then it was so hot in the main room..."

He slipped an arm around my shoulders, and I sank gratefully into its protection, against his shoulder. "I should have noticed before. You're more accustomed to watching, aren't you? Are you enjoying yourself?"

"Astonishingly, yes." I sipped the lemonade, and put the glass to my forehead to cool the headache forming. "Recently, these Assemblies had become torture for me, but I had to go, to let Lizzie think I was content. I was relegated to sitting by the wall with the other forgotten women."

He snorted. "They don't seem to appreciate quality here. You saw how surprised Caroline was when you said you hadn't taken?"

"Yes." I sipped again.

"Do you believe me now?"

"In what way?"

"That you're a lovely woman and any man would be glad of you? You would have taken in London with or without me?" He took my fan from me and spread it out with a crack any woman would be glad to produce. He fanned my face, and I sighed contentedly. I began to feel my strength return and the budding headache fade away, though whether it was his care or the respite I couldn't say.

"It's hard to readjust to the idea. But I'm trying to."

"I should think so. And here's a secret worth knowing." He put the fan down and took a sip of his wine, then took up the fan again afterwards. "If you believe in your own beauty, other people will believe it too. Have you ever seen a portrait of an accredited beauty, and thought it must be a poor likeness because she isn't a beauty at all?"

"Frequently."

"Sometimes they are considered beautiful because they think so, and everybody else has been told so."

"Were the Gunnings truly beautiful, then?" I asked him, in a reference to the three beauties who had taken London by storm two years before.

"Oh yes, truly beautiful. But the whole circus became too much. People followed them about, once even a shoe was displayed in a cobbler's as belonging to Miss Maria Gunning, and it drew crowds of spectators. She got herself her duke in the end but I prefer a few brains with my beauty, and the Gunnings were as feather-headed as they come." He gave me a private sweet smile. "I'm so pleased I didn't join in with the general hysteria. I might have missed you, my sweet life."

I smiled back at him, and he gave me a lingering kiss. He made to close my fan, but studied it before he gave it back to me. It was the one I had bought on the previous Wednesday, not particularly special, but he seemed to need something to focus on.

"When I saw you falter in there, I thought—well I thought the most ridiculous things."

"What kind of ridiculous things?"

"Well, now." He spoke carefully, taking his time, "The first intimation my mother had of being with child with Maria was when she fainted at a ball. She wasn't the fainting kind, you see, and—"

I was forced to laugh. "Oh, Richard, after two days?"

"It was just my anxiety left over from last October. I worried desperately that you had quickened for weeks afterwards. I lost my head completely on that afternoon, didn't even try to protect you. I didn't want to hurry you into marriage, or cast any kind of scandal on our union. We made love twice. That was sheer madness." He shook his head at the memory. "But such sweet madness, as I heard someone say once." He tilted my chin up, studied my face, and kissed me, long and slow. I relaxed into his arms and felt completely happy there. I knew his reputation, I knew the dangers of marrying a rake, but this feeling, this bliss, couldn't be mine anywhere else but in his arms. "You were so brave to seduce me like that. Would you have told me, if you had quickened?"

"Like a shot," I assured him. He kissed me again.

"I'm glad to hear it." He put down his glass and touched my stomach with the edge of his hand, brushing the point of my stomacher. "Do you think we might have put a babe there this time?"

"I have no idea. Do you mind?"

"No, though I'd prefer a little time alone with you first. My parents would be delighted. An eight months' child would make my father bow down and worship you. Do you know he despaired of either of us ever producing an heir?"

"Even if Gervase couldn't, he must have known from your reputation that you were capable of it," I commented, in an oblique reference to Gervase and his preferences.

"Oh yes, but to my knowledge I never produced a child, you know. I was extremely careful." He picked up his glass and took a reflective sip before replacing it on the side table. "I could have been infertile, for all he knew."

"Do you think you are?"

"Not for a moment." He turned his head to meet my eyes. "You're the only person I've completely lost control with." I hugged the thought to myself, overjoyed at this proof that I was different to him, and drank the rest of my lemonade.

"Richard, you know you agreed to no secrets?"

"Yes?" A frown creased his brow.

"The bride trip?"

His brow cleared. "Everywhere and nowhere?" He laughed. "I know, my sweet, but I couldn't resist the tease. In any case, I don't think I can keep it a secret much longer, since so many of my friends have guessed. One of them is bound to tell you." He sighed, and looked at me, his gaze softening. "But I would have loved to have seen your face when you saw it for yourself. I have a yacht. I thought we might set sail for Leghorn. A good long journey and no one can come near us. Just us for a week or two. Does that appeal to you?"

I caught my breath. "Oh yes."

We lost a few moments then, as he kissed me more passionately than before. "I may at last have the chance to show you exactly how much I love you. With time, and only ourselves, it might just be possible."

"You said once you'd like to take me to Venice."

"I haven't forgotten. I will take you there one day. You'll like it."

"With you, even the Exeter Assembly Rooms are bearable."

He laughed and kissed me lightly again. "Do you feel better now? We should get back."

"Much better. I was too hot, that's all."

He stood up and helped me to my feet. "And one more thing," I said.

"Yes, my sweet life?"

"Will you leave Eustacia Terry alone now? I saw Lord Thwaite's face when she made that pass with her fan. What on earth did she say?"

"Well she thought she said 'I like you', but in fact, she said, 'Come to my bed tonight' or something a little more risqué."

"Richard!"

"Rose! But there's no harm done." He shrugged. "But you see I owed Freddy too, and to see his face—" He broke off, laughing.

"So she'll be doing that for the next six months?"

"No. I said I'd meet her in the first of these rooms. I'm certain she thought of it as an assignation, and a chance to spite you. But there will be other people there by now, and I'll tell her she hadn't got that pass with her fan quite right, and change it into something more innocent. She's probably waiting there now. Your pleas prevailed, you see, sweetheart. I was going to cut her dead tonight and kill her prospects for some time to come, but I didn't want to spoil your evening. The fan trick will do, although it doesn't go far enough to pay for the insults she has dealt you over the years."

A sneeze came from behind the heavily draped window behind our sofa.

Richard strode across the room and tore back the drapes. Miss Terry sat in the alcove, pale with shock, her eyes bright with tears.

"Really!" said Richard, exasperated. "I said the first door, not the last!"

He would have left her there, but I took her arm and made her sit on the sofa we had just vacated. She glared at Richard, but said nothing. I sat next to her. "I told you to take care. He can be far more dangerous than this."

Her regard went to me, wondering, speculative. "He loves

you?"

"Why else would I seek to break a perfectly serviceable marriage contract with someone else?" Richard snapped. He picked up the half glass of wine he had abandoned on the side table. "You had better drink this. You can't go back like that."

Eustacia was crying properly now, tears falling unhindered down her face. She shook her head, but I took the glass from Richard and made her hold it. "Indeed you should, Eustacia. It will help you restore yourself."

The liquid shook in the glass. "I can't face them in there. Not after—the fan—"

"Oh you can carry that off." Richard's face was tight and hard. He was exasperated with her, but he was trying hard to keep his temper. "No one will mention it again, and my friends will be gone soon enough." His face cleared and he smiled. "But to see the look on Freddy's face!" He saw my frown, but wasn't contrite. "Oh, it was two birds with one stone, my sweet. I owed him for a small trick he played on me in town."

Miss Terry looked up at me, her eyes still misty but a new expression settling on her face, one I was familiar with. Calculation. "Miss Golightly, he said—you said—two days..."

"Dear God, couldn't you at least pretend you hadn't heard that part? Have you no discretion?"

She studied him for the first time, never having seen him like this, irritated and angry. "You sat in front of me and I couldn't avoid hearing it."

Richard threw up his hands in exasperation and went to the cold fire. He put his hands on the mantelpiece for a minute or two, gripping it until his knuckles turned white.

Richard found it difficult to share his feelings and kept his private life fiercely close. He hated any intrusion into his private world where only his brother and I had places. This might put him over the edge; drive him to take the vicious retaliation I'd pleaded with him to forgo.

Miss Terry turned questioningly to me. She sat up straighter, and I could see her regaining her self-control, her mind beginning to whirr again. "I feel I should inform Lady Hareton of this. My mama would never allow—"

I prayed he wouldn't turn around. "So what is Martha going to do?" I said. "Make us marry? Eustacia, it isn't unusual, you must know that, and you know more than you should about our feelings for each other."

Miss Terry caught her bottom lip between her teeth, as she saw the truth of this. "Mama says men don't marry their mistresses."

Richard spun around, the heavy skirts of his dress coat swirling around him. His eyes rivalled the diamond at his throat, glittering icily as he glared at her; his pose, his attitude, everything displayed the offended aristocrat. There was no way through that hard shell, not even for me. "I'm obliged to you, ma'am. I had never looked upon Miss Golightly as merely my mistress before. I'm afraid I must inform you that your mother might be mistaken on this point. I can think of many men who have made wives of their mistresses. It depends entirely on the quality of the woman."

He crossed the room with measured grace, lifted my hand and placed it firmly on his arm. "If a man should unfortunately find himself shackled to a woman like yourself, with no refinement, no conversation, no discretion, then he may be forced to look elsewhere for friendship and companionship."

He moved, and I had to walk with him, and leave the room.

In the corridor, I didn't speak, and he stood still. An expression of polite indifference masked his anger from anyone who might see us. He breathed deeply, then he looked at me and his face cleared. His eyes had lost that icy, cold edge. I breathed a sigh of relief. "I'm all right now. I'm sorry she overheard, but there's no harm done. If she does spread any rumours, it will be to her own detriment, I'll see to it. Otherwise, you mustn't let this little incident spoil your enjoyment of the whole evening. Promise me?" He took my hand to his lips, while he looked at my face, waiting for my promise.

I could do little else. I promised, and did my best to forget, but when we saw Miss Terry later, it was only as she was leaving with her parents, after she had declared she had a headache. I couldn't say anything. I'd always disliked her, and if I came out with any excuses for her they would have sounded as hollow as they really were. Besides, Miss Terry was part of the world I was leaving behind. In three weeks I would be alone with my new husband and my new life. I longed for that day.

Chapter Twelve

The following Monday it dawned bright and clear, so we decided to ride down to the coast, a large group of us as it turned out. Richard, Gervase, Lizzie, Ruth and I, and Tom and Georgiana volunteered to come on the expedition. When I went down to the hall, I found Richard waiting for me.

He frowned when he saw my new riding habit. "Brown isn't your colour. If you'll allow me, I'll order one for you from town. In any case, I owe you a riding habit." I didn't understand at first, but when he saw my look of puzzlement, he enlightened me. "The day of the accident," he prompted.

I closed my eyes and I saw it all. The blood, all of it Richard's, and I remembered the rust-coloured stains on the riding habit I'd worn. I shuddered at the memory, but opened my eyes when I felt his touch on my arm. "I'm fine. I remembered your accident and what I might have lost."

"I wouldn't have brought it up if I knew it still upset you."

"It doesn't, not really." I managed a smile. "And yes, you do owe me a riding habit." I put my hand through the crook of his arm and we went off to the stables.

James always kept a fine stable, as befitted a country gentleman and the building here rivalled the Manor itself for floor space. Richard and Gervase's horses had arrived, and settled down well, so Bennett, Richard's groom, told him. The stables formed an angular u-shape around the cobbled yard, and everything was orderly and clean. James wouldn't have it any other way. The horses stood, saddled, with a groom at the head of each, all patiently waiting for us, except for one.

Richard's horse was, of course, a thoroughbred, a pretty chestnut, but Gervase's was a monster, a great bay animal called Nighthawk, which only Gervase could control. I'd seen him mounted on Nighthawk before, and thought then that he must have wrists of steel. Mine looked as though it came from a different race of creature, a dainty mare, but she was nervous in Nighthawk's presence, skittering to the side to avoid the great bay. The groom led her to the other side of the yard, and Richard accompanied me, helping me into the side-saddle himself before he went back to the centre of the yard and mounted his own horse. His touch was strong and sure, better than any groom.

I was forced to keep my mare away from Nighthawk until she became more accustomed to his presence, but Gervase's control over his mount was absolute, and she was in no danger. Lizzie always rode placid animals, and the one she rode today was no exception. It wasn't that she didn't have a good seat; on the contrary, but she liked a mount on which she could display herself to advantage, without worrying about the animal's reliability.

We rode the short distance to Peacock's, a journey I'd made countless times before. Tom and his sister Georgiana waited in the courtyard for us, already mounted, so we went off straightaway.

Tom, who considered himself a connoisseur of horseflesh, admired Gervase's mount immensely. "I was lucky to get him," Gervase told Tom. "I had to bid way above the usual price for him, but I saw we were meant for each other, so I had him."

Sometimes I forgot exactly how rich Gervase was. I don't think even he knew precisely, but as far as I could gather, he'd taken many risks for it and deserved every penny.

I wondered how to deter Georgiana, who admired both of the brothers, but I decided the best way would probably be to let matters take their course. She was no Miss Terry, and wouldn't bear a grudge, as I feared Eustacia might do, once she discovered Gervase's lack of interest in females.

I avoided thinking about Eustacia. Richard had not spoken of the incident again, but I knew it hurt him to know someone unauthorised had seen him in an unguarded moment. Even though that person could do us little harm, he still resented it. He might still choose to take some form of revenge of his own, something far more vicious than he had done before. The best I could do was try to forget the whole thing and trust in Richard's good sense.

Once in open country, I could give my horse its head for ten minutes, always something that helped to clear my head of unpleasant thoughts. I'd been forced to resort to it many times over the years, and the concentration required, together with the physical control of the horse, gave my whole body and mind something to do, and let me forget my troubles.

The familiar route and the feel of the animal under me gave me a slip in time. It was as if the events of the past few months had not happened. As though we'd visited Hareton Abbey, returned and resumed our ordinary lives, and I expected to remain the spinster aunt for the rest of my days. It all seemed unreal until I slowed and waited for the others to catch up. Then I saw Lizzie's new glowing happiness, which she carried around for most of the time these days, and Richard, the once-stranger who was now as familiar to me as I was to myself.

We reached the coast after a comfortable ride through the verdant Devonshire countryside that lasted a couple of hours. Tom was the first one to see the sea, and he swung round in the saddle, crying, "My sea, my sea!" as we always did when we were children. It stretched out to the horizon; grey, white tipped, never still. My surge of joy when I saw it was entirely visceral, a response I'd felt ever since I could remember. It represented freedom to me, and pastures new, places no one would know me, where I could start again.

When we arrived, we dismounted and crept as far as we dared to the cliff edge. I was used to the height, and went right to the edge, but Lizzie and Georgiana went only so far and no further. They didn't want to look over the edge, down the dizzying drop to where the sea swept up the small beach in the cove below us.

We stood together in silence, Tom, Richard, Gervase and I, and watched the foamy waves, the yellow sand, the curved shape of the bay around us, tried to see the horizon where blue-grey changed to celestial blue. Then Tom glanced at me and winked. I knew what he meant, and decided to join him in a trick we hadn't used for years. It was irresistible.

Tom seized my hand and, both of us ran. We roared and shouted as we rushed to the cliff edge, and—with no more than a glance—jumped. We heard alarmed cries, male cries, then the twins' heads appeared over the cliff edge, only the shapes of their behatted heads visible when we squinted up into the sun.

"I think," said Gervase gravely, "that to play the trick properly, you shouldn't laugh *quite* so much while you wait for us."

It was too late for gravity. Tom and I leaned against each other, helplessly overcome with laughter, not just because of the action itself, but because of the release it had afforded, and the fact we had not done this for years. I felt like a child again.

Richard jumped down to join us. He waited patiently for us to recover our senses, staring out at the view afforded by such a high perch. It was quite safe. We stood on a broad ledge and another one lay not far below it.

Eventually Tom and I wiped our streaming eyes and took a few deep breaths. "Oh, Lord! The number of times we did that."

"A lifetime ago." I thought of all the times we had managed to escape to this bay, when the adults were busy at their own games.

"We found the ledge by accident," I told Richard, "when Tom lost his dog and we found him here. It's not just our secret, though, we have good reason to believe it's popular with local lovers."

"Spy on them, did you?" Amusement curved his lips. "Then this place must be equivalent to the little cupboard in the music room at Eyton where there was room enough for two small boys. Why lovers should choose music rooms to do their courting always escaped me—until recently." He smiled at me.

Conscious I didn't present the figure of the ideal lover, I found my handkerchief and rubbed it over my face to rid it of the worst stains gained by my tears of laughter, and tried to distract his attention to the sea. "The smugglers use these cliffs as a look-out. You can see right to the end of the bay, and a little further on a clear day."

He obligingly gazed out to the sea, hands in his breeches' pockets, and leaned against the cliff face behind us, perfectly at his ease. No one would have guessed from his appearance today that he was one of the kings of the ballrooms of Europe when he chose. "It must be useful to them."

"This small cove is part of Lyme bay which stretches all the way from Exmouth to Weymouth," Tom told him. "We used to run away on our ponies here when we were small, and play games we weren't allowed anywhere else. We stopped being a young lady and gentleman when we came here, and became a little boy and girl with our dogs and ponies."

I smiled at him, the memory fresh in my mind. "I don't know what I would have done without those days if I hadn't escaped from time to time."

Tom took my hand and we stood together while we remembered our childhood and enjoyed the fine day, looking out at the blue sea and the sandy beach far below us. That I could behave with such freedom in front of my future husband only seemed to emphasise the trust we had in each other. Richard let us dream for a few moments and then said, "Well, I'm sorry to interrupt the reverie, but we should get back to the others, don't you think?"

We climbed back the easy way, at the far end of the ledge where it sloped gradually up to the cliff, but before we made the final ascent, Richard caught my arm and pulled me back. "Local lovers, eh?" he murmured, lips against mine before he let me go with a teasing smile. Tom had discreetly left us, but he must have seen me in Richard's arms before he went to join the others.

Lizzie, Georgiana and Gervase had tired of waiting for us, and unpacked the food that Martha had provided. Gervase had found one of the roasted chickens, and he was tucking into a leg with evident relish as we approached them. They had tethered the horses to some trees, a little way off. Gervase had found a separate place for Nighthawk. He stood contentedly cropping the grass, waiting until Gervase should be ready for him again.

Ever careful for the welfare of her guests, Martha had provided us with a much richer repast than Tom and I had managed to filch from the kitchens in the old days, and there were cloths we could use to sit on, to protect us from the damp grass. Martha used to despair at the number of times I arrived home with grass stains on my skirts, but somehow, even in his country clothes and relaxed mood, I couldn't imagine Richard ever doing such a thing. I said something to that effect and was surprised when Gervase laughed at me.

"Comes of seeing the finished product only, ma'am," he chortled. "My brother got through more pairs of breeches in a week than you could ever imagine. Two pairs a day sometimes, as I recall. He could lose himself in the grounds like nobody else; even the gamekeepers didn't know the places he discovered."

Richard grinned at his brother. "As if you didn't come with me."

We all laughed, remembering what we had been, and what we had become or would become.

We stayed there as long as we could, but all too soon, we realised if we didn't return we would be late for dinner, so we remounted and set off, away from the coast. The sky was more overcast now, but the exertion kept us warm.

We had just entered the squire's land when we saw something on the grass ahead. As we got closer it looked less like a fallen branch I'd thought it at first and more like a bundle of rags. With a sickening, sinking feeling, I realised what it must be.

Richard and Tom must have realised in the same moment, for they both kicked up their steeds to get there before us. They had dismounted by the time we arrived at the scene, and were bending over the figure, looking for signs of life. Richard found an arm and felt for a pulse in the wrist, but then Tom uncovered the man's head and breast, and we saw why he wouldn't find one.

Ugly welts marred all the bare flesh visible. The man had been stripped and beaten, no thoughts of punishment here, only murder. I stared at the welts, raised and red, and the blue bruise marks, which told me the man had been beaten for some time before he died. The back of his head was one large crater, leaving only a bloody, sticky mess of crushed bone and hair. Richard closed the staring eyes with a gentle hand.

At the first sign of what this was, Gervase took Lizzie and Georgiana well away from the scene. I was deeply grateful for his prompt action. Lizzie never went to visit the sick, her squeamishness more trouble than it was worth. While I was sympathetic, it was the last thing we needed here. In contrast to Lizzie's distress, I had discovered I gained satisfaction from helping with such injuries as they came my way. I liked to have the ability to help rather than to stand helplessly by.

However, I could do nothing here, other than go and fetch a cloth from my saddlebag, and throw it to them to wipe the mess from their hands. My horse skittered again when she got the scent of blood, and I was forced to move her upwind.

Richard waited until I had settled my mare once more and left her with the others, now waiting some distance away, and returned to him. "We came here the same way, didn't we? So he wasn't here earlier."

"No, my lord," Tom agreed, his face white with shock. He leant back on his haunches and stared at the man wide eyed as though he wanted to take in every part of his appearance, never forget what he looked like.

Richard observed his reaction. "You know him?"

"H—He's one of our servants, a gamekeeper," Tom stammered. "I've known him since I was a boy."

Richard looked sharply at him, and then he searched in his coat pocket and found his flask. He handed it to Tom without a word. The younger man took it, unscrewed the top, and drank deeply from the contents. Richard pulled up the rags they had tossed aside and re-covered the man's body. He stared down at the unedifying scene. "All right?"

I nodded. "I'm fine. His name was Fursey. He was a good man. He has—had—a wife and children in one of the cottages on the estate." I felt the spring breeze ruffle the hair on my neck and I shivered. Fursey would never feel cold or spring breezes again. I groped in my pocket for my handkerchief. Tears sprang to my eyes unbidden when I thought about this man and what someone had done to him.

Richard lifted his arms to hold me. This time he was careless of who saw us. He wanted to comfort me, and I needed to be comforted.

"I'm all right," I said into the warm folds of his coat. "It was the shock, that's all."

He tilted my face up and studied me. "I know." He let me go and went to Tom, to take his flask back. He shook it to see how much was left, then returned and gave it to me. "Just a little."

I lifted the flask and obediently drank some of the brandy, which burned a fiery trail down my throat. He stoppered the flask and put it back into his pocket, keeping his eyes on me, seemingly satisfied when I managed a wan smile. He looked back at Tom where he sat on the ground. No thoughts now about wet grass staining our clothes.

"Tom?"

Tom stared up, shaking his head in bewilderment.

"Who did this?" Richard demanded.

"He had no enemies," Tom said. "Poachers wouldn't have done this, they would have shot him, but—oh!" He turned and vomited into the grass behind him, as the shock caught up with him. We looked away, to give him his privacy while he regained control of himself.

"He was tortured," I told Richard, quietly so Tom couldn't hear me. "Then he was killed. That's right, isn't it?" He nodded in confirmation of my suspicions. "Then it could only be one group of people, and you've come across them before."

"Why only them?"

"Anyone else would have killed him outright, not done that and then left him for us to find."

"So you noticed they'd put him in our way, did you?"

"It must be the case. They saw us go, and laid him there for us to find. I don't think it was deliberately aimed at you—you were a bonus—but at Tom. His father won't give them access across his land, and you've seen how convenient it would be to them. Sir George sets people to watch on nights when there are runs, and they have to go the long way around. This is probably some form of coercion." I put my hand on Richard's arm. "What should we do?"

"What can we do? I've sent word to them I'll leave them alone," he said bitterly.

"Why should they care about you? What can you do?" I knew one man could achieve nothing against these villains, even if that man was Richard.

He smiled wryly, and covered my hand with his. "The time has come when I have to tell you about Thompson's. I'll consult my partner, and tell you tomorrow. It's not my secret alone, you see, or I would have told you before."

That was good enough for me.

He took my hand and led me back to where my horse patiently stood, and then he helped me get back up into the saddle. "For now," he said, as he looked up at me, "we go and tell Sir George, and see what he wants to do. If you join the others, I'll bring Tom across when he feels more the thing. Can you do that, my love? Will you trust me until tomorrow?" I nodded, and rode to where the others waited and he went back to Tom.

I broke the news to them and watched Georgiana closely.

She hadn't seen the reality of it as her brother had, and I didn't go into unnecessary detail, so she took it better than her brother had done.

Gervase said little but exchanged a glance with Richard. He must know we would tell him later. Lizzie suggested she should ride ahead to tell Sir George, but I persuaded her against it. There wasn't much point. The man was dead, not injured, and nothing would alter that.

We watched Richard and Tom remount and come over to join us. I was glad to see Tom had regained some colour in his face, but he was grim, and rode the rest of the way to his home in silence.

As luck would have it, Sir George was at home and Richard and Tom went immediately to see him, leaving the rest of us with Lady Skerrit, who did her best with tea and cakes.

They returned with Sir George, who informed us he'd sent some men for Fursey's body, and someone had gone to tell his wife, but in the circumstances, they would bring the body here to Peacock's. Lady Skerrit was extremely shocked, even though we didn't tell her the whole.

Tom's initial shock had changed to anger. His face was set and he murmured to me, "I mean to do something about this."

"I wouldn't if I were you," Richard said. "You can't do anything on your own against these people."

"You did, my lord," Tom said defiantly.

Richard sighed. "That was to save a life, not to avenge one. No, leave it alone, Tom."

He put his hand on Tom's sleeve, but Tom shook him off. "This was a man I've known all my life. I can't let it lie, it's not in me. These filthy villains, they're never brought to justice. Well, I'll make them pay."

"If you do, you'll likely start something you won't stop." Tom's temper was fearsome, like his father's, readily roused by injustice. I prayed he would listen to Richard and leave it to the authorities.

We went through the Great Hall on our way back to our

horses, and I thought of that dinner when Richard had teased Miss Terry for the first time. A lighter time, it seemed to me now. We bid the Skerrits good day and went out, remounting and riding away.

We rode quickly, for we were late now. Lizzie and I knew the terrain so well we were confident of the speed we had to make, so we exchanged little conversation on the way home. Richard stayed close to me all the way.

Martha and James were sad but not altogether surprised to hear the news. "The village has been on edge today," Martha told us. "There's been a lot of activity. We think there's a big run coming, and it must be fairly soon."

"Do you think they will try to intimidate you?" Richard asked.

"I don't think so," James said. "Our land isn't as useful to them as Sir George's, and we seemed to have achieved some sort of truce recently. I've sent a note to the Excise at Exeter, but I don't think anything will come of it." He sighed resignedly. "The smugglers pay them off, anyway."

"I wouldn't be in the least surprised," said Richard dryly. "They're not particularly well paid, and the smugglers make great profits in the trade, making their silence cheaper to buy. It would probably cost more to use violence against them, and cause more trouble."

"Exactly," James agreed heavily.

Lizzie was wide eyed, never having considered the possibility before. "Do you mean that the smugglers pay the authorities?"

"It's highly likely," Richard told her. "It's a sad world, isn't it?"

I felt guilty that I couldn't be entirely depressed by this turn of events, but I kept my thoughts to myself.

Chapter Thirteen

Richard remembered his promise to me, about this name that had cropped up: Thompson. He had said he would tell me the following day and accordingly, he asked for the use of the music room for an hour after breakfast. Martha assumed he wished me to play for him again, so she grudgingly gave her permission. I waited for him there.

Richard came in carrying a plain wooden box, about the size of a tea caddy. The maid stood by the door and curtseyed to him. I waved her out and, after casting one doubtful look in his direction, she obeyed and pulled the door closed behind her. I knew she must have received instructions from Martha not to leave us alone together. I must make matters right with my sister-in-law on the maid's behalf later.

Richard put the box down on the small table by the window, before he came to take me in his arms and kiss me good morning. "One day closer," I said, when I could.

"So it is." He seemed so sanguine about it. I still had doubts, not about my feelings for him, but his for me. I still wondered why he should have fallen in love with me, but I could say nothing. It would have been tantamount to asking him for compliments. Perhaps it was that I couldn't believe my good fortune.

He led me to a chair by the little table, helped me sit and then took a chair and sat down opposite me. He leaned one elbow on the table and gazed at me. I smiled back at him. "Thompson's," he said, with a smile.

"Yes, please. I've imagined all kinds of things. Are you a gang leader perhaps?"

He laughed, genuine amusement showing through his naturally serene expression. "With a highwayman's mask and a musket?"

I smiled too, as I had a ridiculous vision of him in all his court finery with a filthy scarf wrapped around his mouth, holding up a carriage on the road to Exeter.

"No, my love," he said eventually, "nothing so exciting, I fear. But let me tell it in my own way, and you'll know it all. There is one thing—"

"Yes?" I lifted my head to meet his gaze.

He caught his breath in an audible gasp. "Sometimes... You look so trusting there, sitting with the sun lighting your hair, and that look in your eyes..." He leaned forward, caught my hand in his, and gazed at me until I became embarrassed by what I saw in his face and looked down, blushing.

"How did you know what I was thinking?" he asked, amused.

"I recognised something in your eyes, and when I've seen it before."

He kissed my hand and released it. "Two weeks," he reminded me softly, and then took a deep breath and reminded us both, "Thompson's."

"Thompson's."

He took another breath and smiled at me. "When I was eighteen, Gervase left to go abroad, and the Strang family was in turmoil. Preparations were already under way for Gervase and I to go on the Grand Tour when the scandal broke and he left. My father insisted I go on my own. When I lost Gervase, it was like a betrayal, that Gervase had done this without telling me anything. I felt I could trust no one." Gervase had eloped with a married man. It had taken a great deal of money from his parents and courage from Richard to live the scandal down. To do Gervase justice, I know he wanted to remain in the country and face the critics himself, but his parents hadn't allowed it and packed him off abroad. At eighteen, he had little choice.

"We had been together always, and I never imagined it any other way. I hadn't considered a wife an impediment to that, you see. She was a necessity, a means of continuing the line, because that's the way my father saw it and at that time he was God to me." He smiled at me apologetically. "As you can see, I have changed." I smiled back to reassure him, but I didn't interrupt.

"This was a scandal of the worst kind, and at all times it was emphasised to me I must hold my head high and face the world proudly, so I did my best. That's when I started to wear the heavy maquillage, in effect a mask to conceal my face, and the clothes, to make myself something else, something new. Servants were procured for me and to my everlasting gratitude Carier arrived in my life. He'd served generals in the army, but was tired of army life, so he came on the Tour as my valet and bodyguard. I believe the pay was better, too, at least that's what he always told me when I asked him why he preferred to stay with me." He smiled reminiscently, but didn't pause his narrative for long. "I was on my own for the first time in my life. Only Carier saw what that solitude meant to me. I kept my mourning for private moments, but a good valet must always see some of that."

He stopped. A troubled frown crossed his features when he remembered a time that had tested his character to the full. He was left alone to face a scandal not of his making. I could only imagine how hard that must have been. I reached my hand across the table to take his, and he looked up and smiled, recalled to the present.

"Carier brought his army pension and a small inheritance with him. He's a resourceful person—he even contrived a meeting between Gervase and me in Rome. My father had set other persons to watch me when I went to Rome, to see that I didn't come under Gervase's baleful influence, but Carier helped me to give them the slip one afternoon." He stopped again. This was so painful for him, I could see that, but I knew I must let him tell it in his own way, and I said nothing. I let my hand rest in his.

"The meeting is not one of my favourite memories. Gervase's lover had left him, and he had nothing left. But Carier showed his loyalty to me many times during that terrible tour. His discretion then and afterwards has been absolute.

"By the time I returned to England I had formed and honed my new personality. I'd been away two years, and no one expected what they saw, but my older friends still recognised and supported me. You've met one of them, Freddy Thwaite." I nodded. He caressed my hand, rubbing his thumb over the palm. I wasn't sure he knew he was doing it. "I locked myself away, and gave myself over to hedonism. Cards and gambling I never cared for overmuch, although I tried for a season, until my father cut my allowance. I found myself so destitute then, and the humble apology I had to make to my father so humiliating, I decided to make my own money, independent of the estate."

He stopped. "Don't think I did as well as Gervase, because he could buy me ten times over and still have change."

I released his hand, and crossed the room to the small table where the decanters were kept. I poured two glasses of madeira. He was thirsty, for he accepted his glass with a smile and drained most of it before he continued.

"One of Carier's inheritances was a building in the City. We went to see it together. I made a business proposal to him, one I'd been considering for some time. At that time, my mother was always looking for a lady's maid, never able to find one, and her friends seemed to be in the same difficulties. I'm assured that a good lady's maid is hard to train and hard to find. My mother and her friends were exacting in their requirements, but the pay was good for the right person, and I couldn't see why they had difficulties until I visited a Registry Office with my mother.

"The records were sparse, and the future employer was expected to take up the references given for herself, which many of them failed to do. They could have been forged. Anyone could inveigle themselves into a place of trust in a wealthy household on the strength of a few pieces of paper. The building was in a small side street, run down and uncomfortable, not at all the kind of place my mother was used to visiting. If she hadn't been so desperate for a good maid I doubt she would have undertaken the errand herself.

"I observed all this and it sparked an idea. I proposed that Carier and I set up an office for high quality servants, at a price. Our offices would be spacious and comfortable and our servants the best available." I started to laugh, and he arched a patrician eyebrow. "What can I have said to amuse you?"

"Oh, I'm sorry," I gurgled through my hands. "So that's Thompson's? Oh, you can't imagine what I've been thinking."

He smiled at that. "Tell me."

"Well I knew of your—reputation for pursuing beautiful women. I lay in bed at night imagining all kinds of things!"

It was his turn to laugh. "You thought it was a brothel? Now what would a well-brought-up young lady know about that?"

"You'd be surprised," I managed, still laughing. It was such a relief, when I had imagined all kinds of sinister things, to find it was just a normal business, the laughter was as much a release as genuine amusement.

"You frequently surprise me," he admitted with a smile. "It's one of your many charms. No, Thompson's started as a simple registry office for servants. Nothing else was on offer, I do assure you."

He waited until I had recovered, and then he went to the decanter and replenished both our glasses, returning to sit down again. "There's more?" I asked.

"A little. Are you ready, or would you like the rest to wait?"

I remembered I had still not found out what the box was for, and I touched it with one hand.

"Yes," he said. "The box. There are only two of these. One is kept at the office, in the safe, and Carier and I have the other. It never leaves us. In it are names, directions, and areas of expertise."

"Expertise?"

"Listen, my love. Who knows all the secrets of the house? Who knows where, who, when?"

At once I saw where he was heading. "Servants."

"Perfectly correct. We provide lady's maids, housekeepers, butlers, valets, first and second footmen. Higher servants in positions of trust. Some of our people indicate to us for an extra fee and total discretion they—" he tapped the box, "—will help us if it doesn't compromise their position, or if we discover illegal activity. Sometimes a husband finds his wife has pawned the family jewels, and he needs to know where they are, to quietly recover them. He can come to Thompson's and we will do our best to help. Perhaps there's a mysterious death. They won't go to the authorities, that would mean far too much scandal and upset, but we can provide them with a solution on which they can then base a decision. Mysterious deaths are not always murder, and above all things my peers rely on discretion and reputation." He sighed. "I have long advocated a civilian force to administer and regulate the law, but public opinion is against it, although the matter has been brought up time and again in Parliament. If a man wishes to prosecute a burglar, he must instigate the investigation himself and provide the proof to the magistrate. We help with all that. Either we have one of our special people in place, or we seek permission to place one."

"So at the Abbey—" I began. He'd helped my family with a similar "little problem" there.

"Strangely, no. It was the first time I'd come across a great house without one Thompson's employee in it. I did that all on my own. With a little help, of course," he added, grinning.

"So when there's a problem, you're asked to stay?"

"Well, actually, it's not me they want. You see—nobody knows about my involvement except you, Mrs. Thompson, Gervase and Carier."

"Mrs. Thompson?" I'd wondered where the name had come from.

"Alicia Thompson, the third component of the unholy

triumvirate." I watched him closely for any signs of emotion, but there were none, so I imagined Mrs. Thompson as a comfortable widow of advanced years. It seemed I was right.

"Carier knew her in the army. After her husband died she needed a position, so we gave her one, running the office and the day to day management. After all, Thompson's is one of the best staff agencies in London these days. We take up all references before anyone is put on the books, and provide comfortable, if not luxurious surroundings where our clients may interview prospective servants if they wish to. Mrs. Thompson knows about all the other activities, and I couldn't ask for a more efficient manager. However, only these people know of my active involvement. Most people think I have invested in the company to give Carier a pension and that was, after all, how it started out.

"We thought it would be better to keep my involvement quiet." He paused to take another sip of his wine. "Of course, many people have guessed, but nobody knows for sure. The records of my investment in the business are well tucked away, and when we decide to retire, as I am considering now, the business will still be there for the others."

"You're thinking of retiring?" I echoed in surprise.

"My purpose was to make me some private income, so I wasn't so dependent on my father, but most importantly, to keep me busy, to stop me from becoming too bored. Everything seemed to bore me at one point, and eventually even the women—I'm sorry, my sweet, have I gone too far?" He broke off as he remembered whom he was talking to, but I knew his past, I knew his reputation. He had never tried to hide any of that from me. It had worried me since I had first met him. I still worried. He had proved his attractiveness to other women, how long could I hope to keep him?

When I'd first met him, he was a distant figure who had troubled me. His sardonic humour meant I could never tell when he was laughing at me. As it turned out, he never had, but that hadn't stopped me imagining it in the early days. His fine clothes were the most astounding I had ever seen, and if it had not been for the accident, he might well have remained that way, distant and unapproachable, but it had happened, I had been there, and now here we were.

I smiled and shook my head. "I know some of that part, and I'm beginning to understand better. It's the women in your future I worry about, not the ones in your past."

He took my hand and looked straight into my eyes, warm blue holding me, as always. "There's only one woman in my future. There's no reason why I should ever want anyone else," he said earnestly. "You're everything I ever looked for in a woman, and I'm so fortunate I can have you to myself for as long as I take care of you and love you. If you believe nothing else, believe that."

I was taken aback by the sincerity of his reply, and his lack of any kind of flattery or humour. I had to believe he really meant it, and put my trust in him. Today, he'd told me more than he'd told anyone else. I knew it, by the halting way he'd spoken, and by the total sincerity and lack of guile.

I answered in the same way, with sincerity, without flummery. "I'll love you anyway. I don't know what happened to me on that road in the dirt, but my world moved into yours then. Even if you had turned me away, married Miss Cartwright, produced your heirs, I would have loved you."

He stood up from his side of the table then and drew me into his arms. He held me close so I could feel the warmth of his body underneath those fabulous clothes. After a moment he slid his hand up under my hair at the back and kissed me for a long time. I returned it, savouring the warmth, the love I found only with him. "Two weeks."

"Two weeks," I repeated, smiling.

It was some time before we sat down, and then we knew we would have to join the world again soon. I was so grateful to him, he had told so much and had been so honest with me, so much so I wished I had a secret to tell him, but my life had always been open and tedious in the extreme. There was one thing I wanted to tackle before we left the room. "Richard, do you really wish to retire?"

"I'd like to devote more time to you than I could if Thompson's was still running its extra services," he replied.

"What if I helped?"

He shook his head. "There's no need."

But I started to see this as something else, something for me. "Does it make you happy, when you help with these problems, have that sort of power?"

He studied my face, and then sighed. "You know me too well already, love. Yes, it gave me a kind of contentment, a fulfilment."

"I would hate to take that from you. And it sounds so exciting, I should love to help. Just don't say you'll retire immediately, please."

He smiled. "If you insist, I'll leave it open, but I'll not make any promises."

I would get no more out of him that day. He looked tired, probably from revealing so much of himself, more than he'd done for years. I left him on a sofa by the fire, and went to the harpsichord. I found my music and I played for him, deliberately choosing the pieces I knew best, so he wouldn't have to come and turn pages for me, or do anything else except sit back with his eyes closed and relax. As I played, I glanced at him. I thought the cloud lifted from him, and I was thankful I could do something for him, that I had a gift to bestow.

Soon the magic took hold of me, and I felt the protective cocoon fold around me, the shield music always gave to me, and yet I still felt his presence. He was inside with me. Just with me.

The door opened once or twice, but people tended to look in and go away again, when they saw us so tranquil. It couldn't go on forever. I knew it after I heard the doorknocker sound.

Soon, a maid came in to inform us the Terrys had called, and Martha would appreciate it if I came to the drawing room. Richard opened his eyes and smiled when his eyes met mine. I got up, closed the lid and went to him.

Before we left the room he pulled me against him once more for a kiss, not as sweet as last time, an edge of passion to it. I responded, though the need made me ache. Whatever was I turning into?

I turned to leave, but he drew me against him, one arm around my waist. He kissed my neck. "May I come to you tonight?"

"What?" I almost turned to face him, but his arms held me tightly.

"Please?" Did I imagine the edge of desperation to his voice? If so it only echoed mine.

"How can we?"

"Easily. I'm only a few doors away."

"Won't someone hear?"

"Not if we're quiet. Rose, I've never needed anyone like I need you. I'd be happy—well, happier—" He gave a derisive laugh. "If I could hold you, be with you."

"You are, for most of the day."

He nuzzled my ear and murmured, "Skin to skin, my love. Touching, kissing, holding. Loving."

What could I say against that, especially when I needed it too? "Yes."

"Later, sweetheart, later." It was a promise.

We went together to the drawing room. Richard took the little box and gave it into Carier's hands in the hall. "Five of us know for sure now, Carier."

The manservant nodded and bowed. "That is as it should be, my lord," he said and took the box away. I took this as approval from him, and although this kind of comment would not normally be expected from a servant, I knew Carier was much more than that to Lord Strang.

We went upstairs to the drawing room. Richard must have felt my hand stiffen on his arm when I recalled the last time we had seen them. "Miss Terry knows more than she has a right to, and she might well have told her mother, but I don't think we should repine. What's done is done. I have nothing to be ashamed of, and if anyone maligns you, they'll answer to me personally."

Mrs. Terry faced the door, and she stared at us as we went in, so I thought it highly likely she knew the gist of the conversation her daughter had overheard. Her look was hard, her pale eyes narrowed in speculation.

I was surprised to see that her husband, Mr. Norrice Terry, had decided to accompany her. Perhaps he knew, too. Mr. Terry was a large man, tall and broad. He always reminded me of the later portraits of King Henry VIII, with his small eyes and harsh expression. He could be hard on his servants and his family, and with my new knowledge, I wondered if anyone from Thompson's was employed there. A maid from London would appeal to Mrs. Terry's pretentious nature. Upper servants knew everything their employers did, and if they put their knowledge together, they would probably know considerably more. I would have to ask Richard if we had any Thompson's servants in the Manor.

Richard made an elaborate bow and I curtseyed to our guests. I promised myself, as I always did when confronted with his social graces, to practise mine so he would have no need to be ashamed of me in company. Martha smiled at us, an edge of desperation in her face as we entered the room. Richard and I sat side by side on a small sofa. Richard allowed his hand to rest on mine, an indication of our status he rarely allowed himself even in public, but since we had to assume most of the company knew our devotion to each other, it seemed foolish to deny this small pleasure of contact.

Mrs. Terry's pointed gaze went straight to our hands, and then up to our faces, where Richard's expression of tranquil innocence confounded her, and she looked away again.

Her capacious bosom heaved a couple of times. "While it is of course charming to meet you again, my lord, we came to find out what the truth was about these dreadful rumours we have been hearing." She addressed us rather than spoke to us, as though she was speaking at a public meeting.

"I don't like rumour," boomed Mr. Terry from his seat on one of Martha's best spindle-legged chairs. "It is not a healthy state of affairs."

"What exactly did you hear, ma'am?" asked Richard.

I noticed Miss Terry then, uncharacteristically subdued, but watching Richard's hand on mine like a rabbit watches a snake. I felt uncomfortable under her regard, but since Richard had, I thought, noticed but refused to acknowledge it, I let my hand rest under his.

"That on an expedition to the coast—" Mrs. Terry turned to Martha momentarily, "—and why, dear Lady Hareton, people would rush to the sea quite so eagerly, when it is acres of nothing I have never understood—" then back to the company in general. "That on an expedition to the coast, you discovered the body of a poor unfortunate gamekeeper who had been brutally done away with. It is a most distressing thing, and I cannot think it the proper subject for the drawing room, but I felt it my duty to come, so my husband and I can put the minds of our employees at ease. As you know, we employ four gamekeepers on our land, and they are all most distressed by the rumours."

"You have four gamekeepers?" Richard said in some surprise, for the Terry's land was not particularly extensive.

"My husband likes to hunt and shoot in the summer," Mrs. Terry replied haughtily, "I would have thought you, my lord, might sympathise with his preferences."

Richard smiled. "I find one gamekeeper and several men under him sufficient. My father may employ a few more, but that is not my concern."

"You have your own establishment, my lord?" asked the lady.

"I have one or two places." He stiffened, defensive about his fiercely protected private life. "The main estate is in Oxfordshire. I've not up to now spent much time there, but I have sent for it to be put in order, for Rose to inspect when we return from the continent." At least Mrs. Terry had the good sense not to ask about the honeymoon, but she put her eyebrows up at his fond use of my first name, something he rarely did in company.

He pressed my hand, and I smiled. The promise of the night ahead had sharpened my senses. I felt his nearness, smelled the citrus scent he used, mingled with hot, hard man, and my appetite for him sharpened. "Do you intend to open the house, then, my lord?" asked Mrs. Terry, her eagerness open for everybody to see. She was probably thinking of invitations to come.

"It's entirely up to my future wife." He looked at me and smiled, an intimate smile saying more than words could do. "If she doesn't like it, we'll buy somewhere else."

"I'm sure it's charming." To be honest, I'd never thought of where we would settle when we came home. I was too taken up with preparations for the wedding and what lay immediately beyond it. Greatly daring, I added, "You know where I want to be."

"Yes," he replied, accepting it.

Martha cleared her throat. "As to the rumours you've heard, you'll find they're greatly exaggerated. I was not there myself but I understand only one body was found. While that is tragic enough, it's not as terrible as the rumours you've heard."

It was a cue meant for Richard and he took it. "No indeed." His face became graver as he looked away from me, back to Mr. and Mrs. Terry. "We only discovered one body. One too many, but only one. We believe it was put there on purpose for us to find on our return."

"What makes you think that, my lord?" demanded Mr. Terry.

"We all thought it," Richard informed him. "It wasn't there when we took the same route earlier in the day, so someone saw the route we took, and assumed we would return the same way. They placed the unfortunate victim there for us to find. Also, the man had been barbarously used. I don't intend to go into details when there are ladies present."

Mrs. and Miss Terry shuddered, and in that moment, the

resemblance between them was clearly marked. I saw what Eustacia could become in twenty years' time, her prettiness absorbed in flesh, her attitude matronly and autocratic.

"Who would do such a thing?" Eustacia's eyes gleamed with the inner cruelty she had shown me so often in the past. I hoped it was shallowness and not prurience that had caused her *frisson* of excitement. My dislike of her had sprung from her cruelty to me, but perhaps that masked an essential cruelty born of her inner nature.

"We believe it must have been free traders." Richard studied her, likely seeing what I had seen when her eyes had gleamed. "The squire doesn't allow the smugglers to cross his land, and this must be inconvenient for them. He posts sentries, and calls out the land-riders, or so he has told me, so they must be anxious to secure his co-operation. Somehow," he added with a gleam in his eye, "I don't think this will stop him. He seems determined on it."

"I can't see what he has against it," Mrs. Terry said. "There's little we can do about it."

"I would agree, ma'am," Richard said smoothly, and Mr. Terry shot him an appraising glance. "I don't think anything can be done here on the coast. It must be tackled in Parliament."

"What do you suggest?" Mr. Terry leaned forward. His chair creaked.

Richard leaned back so he could see me and answer Mr. Terry. "Cutting duties. The government would then receive much more revenue from all the goods passing through, as I believe many of the recipients would much prefer to receive their tea, tobacco and liquor honestly, at a fair price."

Mr. Terry sighed. "That would seem to be a long way off." He passed his tea-dish to Martha for another helping.

"It would indeed," Richard replied. "The brutality, however, should not be allowed to flourish unchecked. There was a Sussex gang broken up, was there not?"

"The Hawkhurst gang." I found it surprising that Mr. Terry

should know such things. We were a long way from Sussex.

"Just so. It was when their brutality became too much to stomach that the authorities found a way in to break it up."

Mr. Terry put a hand to his chin—at least one of them. "You seem well informed, my lord."

"Not really, but the case was a famous one, and I remember reading about it. I was under the curious misapprehension at the time that these things had a glamour they lack in real life. Pirates and highwaymen close up, are equally reprehensible."

"Not having met any, I don't think any of us can say for sure," said Martha tartly. She created a natural pause by pouring the tea, and then talk turned to the wedding and how far the plans had advanced. Despite the fact that it was my wedding, I took little part in the conversation. Martha and the Countess of Southwood had made most of the plans. They corresponded almost daily now. "The countess writes me she will arrive next week," Martha said. "I've heard so much from her, but I'm looking forward immensely to meeting her."

"She says the same thing about you," Richard assured her. "But when my family arrives, I fear I must take my leave."

"Yes indeed," agreed Martha. "We've enjoyed your visit much, especially one of us—" and she cast a significant look at me, "—but it wouldn't do for you to be married from this house."

Richard gave her one of his most charming smiles. "You've been an excellent hostess, and I hope you might still receive me from time to time."

"Every day if you should wish it." Martha smiled, and I knew then for certain that she approved of his devotion to me, and looked on it with kindness. Not every guardian would have approved of such open displays of affection as Richard had offered me, but Martha loved James, and had done since she had met him, in her case after the marriage was arranged. In fact, there was only ten years between Martha and me, but she had such a motherly way about her, she was so comfortable, that when she had taken the reins of the household we all welcomed it with relief. We were still overcrowded and to a certain extent still chaotic, but the important structures had been put in place; mealtimes, social visits, as a skeleton for us to exist around. Even the ascetic Ian had appreciated the more regular habits we slipped into after Martha had arrived.

This recent incident, so close to home, had upset Martha considerably, and she abruptly returned to the subject. "I do hope they catch the perpetrators." She looked more anxious than I had seen her for some time. "I don't like the idea of murderers running free hereabouts."

"I wouldn't concern yourself, ma'am," said Mr. Terry, "you should be quite safe here. The free traders have no interest in crossing your land, although, I believe you plan to expand your property, do you not? But you will be safe enough."

Richard leaned back, regarding Mr. Terry with an indolent expression. Of the people in the room only I knew Richard was at his most dangerous when he seemed most languorous. "You seem to be sure. Can it be, sir, you know some of these villains?"

"No more than most people hereabouts," said the gentleman.

Richard pursued the topic. "Most people hereabouts seem to know them. A great deal of the local wealth comes from smuggling, I think."

"You may be right, sir." Mr. Terry cleared his throat noisily.

Richard let the matter drop, but he was interested. Unlike the squire, Mr. Terry did let the smugglers run their goods through his land, and I thought he might have even turned his back a few times while his more outlying barns were used overnight to store contraband. He probably knew some of them, and where he could contact them.

James had always taken the view that the less he knew about it all the better, but others were not quite so sanguine. The squire took his position seriously and had always been concerned about the proliferation of smuggling. We received many goods from the Channel Islands, run across from France but I had never seen a run, and I never wanted to. We could make little difference. Richard was right. The matter needed addressing in Parliament.

Chapter Fourteen

It seemed an age until bedtime. I felt like a naughty child planning some clandestine activity such as raiding the pantry at midnight. I wondered if I had risked too much, if I was heading for a fall, even if Richard would come. Perhaps it had been a mere impulse, engendered by our unusual intimacy earlier in the day, but I didn't think so. I had never known him so needy and vulnerable, and after telling me his secrets, perhaps Richard needed me as much as I needed him.

Richard seemed his usual self, unruffled and serene, but his eyes held an extra gleam. I decided to pay him back in his own coin.

For the rest of the day, every time I went close to him I touched him. Touched his hand, brushed my fingers against his cheek, then when he moved to kiss them, took them away. All without anyone seeing. When we went into dinner, I caressed his delicious backside, tucked my hand under his coat and brushed my fingers against it. I felt the flinch before I moved my hand away and heard his self-deprecating chuckle. "Take care, my lady. I shall throw you down on the dining table if you continue."

I called his bluff. Throughout dinner I touched him when I didn't need to, brushed my fingers against his when he handed me a glass of wine, smiled my thanks, taking too long. He knew. And I took care that no one else should.

He joined me in the drawing room almost immediately after the meal, and I soon found out why. He wanted to retaliate.

Stretching his arm along the back of the sofa where I sat conversing with Ian, he tickled the back of my neck, lightly, warmly. I laughed at the wrong moment, and Ian frowned. I had to beg his pardon.

I got my own back when I stood to play for the family, and found the opportunity to trail my hand over his thigh. He leaned back, inviting the touch, raising an eyebrow in an unspoken challenge. For two pins I would have touched him further, but not under Martha's censorious eye. This was as far as I wanted to go. Or dared, for that matter.

Playing the harpsichord kept me out of trouble. At least I thought so until Richard came up behind me to turn the pages of the music. As if by accident, his hand trailed over me when he leaned forward. Under the cover of the flaring skirts of his coat, he touched the upper part of my breast. Then he was gone.

There was only one thing left for me to do. I played for a while, and then got to my feet. Instead of getting off the stool towards the room, I got off towards him, and if by accident, moved too close. For a second, I touched the bulge on the front of his breeches, and heard his indrawn breath. "Your game," he murmured to me, "but wait, just you wait."

As a result, when eleven o'clock came and I could finally excuse myself, pleading tiredness, I was drawn as taut as a bowstring. The maid I shared with my sisters helped me get ready for bed, and then all I had to do was sit and wait, with the door slightly open so he wouldn't have to knock.

I waited for some time. I'd been too eager to go, and the household had to retire before I could hope for him joining me. I thought of going to bed and getting some sleep, but decided I was too tense. Still it didn't make sense to sit and wait, so I climbed into bed and lay down, thoughts racing through my head.

A breath on my ear woke me, and I spun around, startled awake. I sighed with relief when I saw who it was. "Richard."

"Hush, love."

I put my hand to my mouth, to quieten myself. He leaned across the bed to me. "Aren't you going to ask me in?"

"Have you locked the door?"

"*Naturellement.*"

I threw back the covers, while he stripped off his robe and got in. He was naked, but he got into bed so quickly I didn't see him properly. Immediately he drew me close, and I felt at home and safe. His chuckle bewildered me until I felt his hands on my braids. "I couldn't stop Fraser doing them for me."

"While I'm sure they are extremely practical," he said, his hands busy unravelling, "I prefer it when your hair is loose. I like to feel it flowing over my hands, winding me in its web."

"So I'm a spider?"

He kissed my forehead, his lips just brushing the skin. "Arachne was a beautiful woman, turned into a spider for boasting and being right about it. You never boast, my love. Perhaps you should."

"It's not in my nature."

"Then I shall boast for you. I'm lucky to get you, sweetheart."

I laughed. "So you keep telling me."

He finished undoing the braids and thrust his fingers into my hair, combing them through the locks to untangle them. "Much better." He looked down at my face. "And if I keep telling you, you might believe it one day."

"I'll do my best. I have to promise to obey you soon, don't I?"

He grinned. "So you do."

Lifting up on one elbow, he leaned over me, and smoothed the hair back from my face. He'd brought a branch of candles in with him, and it stood on the nightstand by the bed, casting a light on his gleaming hair and his fine-drawn features. Looking intently down at me he said, "This is almost enough. Almost." He bent his head to kiss me.

What began as a gentle kiss of welcome soon deepened into

something more, his tongue reaching into my mouth, his desire searing through my entire body. I arched and felt his hands on me, pulling up my voluminous nightgown.

Eagerly I helped him, undoing the little buttons at the cuffs and neck, sitting up so he could pull it off over my head. Casting it aside, heedless of where it fell, he gazed at me, only me.

He touched my breast, traced the swell below and then cupped it, testing its weight. I closed my eyes and drew a breath. I was so sensitive to his touch.

"Every time," he murmured, "every time I touch you it feels like a miracle. That you want me, that you, so lovely, could have lain like Sleeping Beauty, waiting for me." He kissed the nipple, pushing with his hand to take more into his mouth.

His tongue curved, caressing me, and I touched his back, partly for support, partly for the sheer joy of contact. His touch made me weak and soft, his need for me made me want to give him everything without stint.

He drew back, only to fold his arms around me and seek my mouth with his. He gave me a long, penetrating kiss, his hands smoothing, caressing, rousing my body to a peak of need.

He smelled like no one else. Under the citrus perfume he preferred lurked an even sharper edge. Him. I'd know him anywhere now, in the dark, the light, in the middle of a crowded ballroom by scent alone. He surrounded me with his essence, held me fast, held me close. I moved my hands over the muscles of his back, feeling his reined-in athletic strength.

When he broke the kiss he was smiling. "I love you." He laid me down and moved over me to enter me.

When I opened my mouth to cry out, he covered it with his own, taking up the kiss he'd broken earlier, plunging into me with two parts of his body, tongue and hard, driving erection. I broke apart. My peak came quickly, taking me by surprise, raging through my body. I screamed and he swallowed my cries.

He held me down when I jerked, unable to control my

body's reaction to his loving, then pulled me against him to drive harder, closer. This loving had no gentleness about it. The teasing earlier in the evening had driven us both to this, serving as courtship and foreplay, making our bodies hungry for each other.

My peak came and went, driven by him, no quarter given, none asked for. He lifted his mouth from mine, gasping for breath, never stopping that demanding rhythm that had become the centre of my existence.

Before I knew it I was in the middle of another climax, coming up hard on the heels of the last. I arched my back, but Richard held on, his hands on my hips holding me tight and close. There were no words; not for this primitive drive powering both of us on. My heart pounded in time to his thrusts, to my drive, and I ceased to care about anything else.

Climax built on climax, rising to a fiery apex that somehow, Richard managed to sustain for me. I'd thought something this rarefied was impossible to keep up for long, but I lingered there, cried out. It was as well I was out of breath, or I might have roused the household, but what emerged wasn't the lusty shout I imagined but a half stifled, breathless whimper.

At the same time Richard fell over my body and buried his face in the pillow beside me to hide his own cry of fulfilment. I felt his body pulse and jerk as he'd made mine do earlier, and then we lay still, the only sound our breathing, harsh and ragged.

Turning his head on the pillow, still inside me, he laughed shakily. "Every time." I could only smile and lift my hand to cup his cheek and we stayed like that for a while, until he found enough strength to slide to one side of me. "Thank you, sweetheart. Why on earth didn't we do this earlier, when I first came to Devonshire?"

"I can't think," I replied. "Unless we were both trying to be good."

He smiled, reaching for me, and I went to him and rested my head on his shoulder. "That must have been it. I can't think of any other reason. So close to our wedding, we're not risking what we did when we first made love." He kissed my forehead. "I haven't broken any of the promises I made to your brother, you know. He didn't think to make me promise to keep out of your bed."

I turned my head to meet his eyes. "James made you promise things?"

"Oh yes. He cares a great deal for you. As do I." He touched his lips to mine. "I had to promise to take care of you, to be faithful to you and not to hurt you."

I knew James loved me, but I didn't know he would force such strictures on my future husband. It was most unusual to demand personal assurances outside the marriage contract. "Goodness."

"I'd already made those promises to myself."

I knew what that would mean to him, and to me. I turned my head and kissed his shoulder, tasting the sharp, salty sweat. "I can make those promises, too."

"Then when we make the promises in the Cathedral, they are implied. Yes?"

"Yes." We kissed to seal the bargain, sweet and loving, desire assuaged for the present.

"Richard?"

"Yes, sweetheart?"

"Why the Cathedral? Why not a private ceremony in a chapel somewhere like most people do?" I'd gone along with the plans but such a public wedding was unusual in his class.

He smiled. "I wondered when you'd ask. Because, my love, I want everyone to know I'm committing myself to you. All of them, the women, their husbands, and the rest of the world. If we'd married at Eyton in the chapel, or here in your village, it would have been a family affair. But there are people I particularly wish to know, and they couldn't come to a private ceremony." A public ceremony, marking his new life, and his new resolve.

Now he'd explained, I no longer worried about it. I knew it

would be a nerve-racking experience for me, as I hated to be the centre of attention, but it didn't matter. The reward far outweighed the temporary discomfort.

"We're having the wedding breakfast at Peacock's," I told him.

"Yes, I remember Martha mentioning it. That was the part I found a little puzzling."

"We have nowhere at the Manor where we can entertain all those guests so we're using the plans for rebuilding as an excuse. The wedding breakfast is James's responsibility and he's determined to meet the magnificence of the Cathedral. The Great Hall at Peacock's could have been made for such an occasion."

He lifted my face to his. "And we'll be that much nearer to the coast, and escape." He touched his lips to mine. "I shall lay my plans. I want you to myself as soon as it can be arranged. And no bedding ceremony, either."

I shuddered. "Good Lord, no." I couldn't bear the thought of being put in my nightgown and put to bed, to wait for him accompanied by friends and family. In the old days they used to watch the marriage being consummated. That would have been terrible, especially for a young virgin, already having to cope with the idea of marital intimacy. I was neither young nor a virgin, and I found the prospect unbearable.

"Our first night as man and wife will be on the yacht. And then we'll be at sea, out of the reach of any well-wishers, or ill-wishers for that matter." He looked at me, his gaze a caress. "If I lose you that will be enough for me. I've had many things I cared for taken from me, but no more. You would be the last."

Everything else forgotten, he kissed me again, sweet and long. When he tasted my mouth, invited me to taste him, it was more languorous, less needy. He caressed me, sampling, tasting, moving his hands over me in a leisurely stimulation. I returned his caresses, felt the smoothness of relaxed muscle, and then below, to caress his manhood, now far from relaxed. I began to discover the sweetness of mutual stimulation in well-known, well-loved bodies, instead of the excitement of discovery. We still had a long way to go. I prayed the time would be given to us.

Richard drew back, eyes half-closed, and rolled to lie on his back, pulling me with him. We kissed, touched, and enjoyed the sensuality of loving, all at a slower pace than before. He touched me between my legs. "You want me again."

"I could say the same," I answered, curling my hand around him.

"Indeed you could. Will you ride me this time, love?"

"What? How?" I still had a lot to learn.

"On top. Remember Exeter?" Richard put his hands under my armpits and pulled me up to a kneeling position, astride him. His hands moved to cup my breasts, thumbs brushing over my nipples. I smiled at him. "You'll have to help."

"All the time, sweetheart."

I took hold of his erection and went up on my knees, slowly sinking down until he touched me. I closed my eyes to feel his entrance into my body, and listen to him talking to me. "That feels so good, so right. That's it, oh, God. Perfect, perfect."

I opened my eyes and saw him, hungrily gazing at me, taking me with every sense he possessed. "To see you like this, so open to me, so inviting, all I ever want, all I ever need. Tell me what it feels like, Rose. What does it feel like to have me inside you, watching you?"

I moaned when I felt how deeply he was embedded inside me. "It's everything to know you want me. You think I'm beautiful,"

"Yes."

"So I am. I'll be anything you want." I paused when he thrust, and I moved again to meet him.

"Don't stop." I don't know who said it. It could have been both of us.

"Oh it feels so good, Richard. You're so deep inside me, you're touching parts I never knew existed before I met you. You're part of me, I'm part of you. That's how it feels, my love, when you're inside me."

I began to move in a rhythm reminding me of being on horseback, and I realised why Richard had asked me to ride him. "Can we do this on a horse?"

He laughed, and his breath caught. "I've never tried. I think we should try one day, don't you? Riding for real?" He timed his thrusts to meet mine; effortlessly settling into a mutual rhythm as natural as breathing, but far more exciting. The warmth inside me grew, but I'd forgotten something made possible by this position. He touched me, his hand warmly caressing my wetness, and the jolt nearly sent me through the bed canopy.

I remembered, in time, to hold my breath to stop myself screaming.

I lost control, or rather, I let it go, driving him as ruthlessly as he'd driven me a short time before. He rested his fingers where I would ride over them when I pushed forward, held one hip with his free hand to steady me. My knees gripping his sides, I surged on, bringing joy to both of us, my hair wild about me, in my eyes and my mouth. I was totally lost.

Until, with a stifled cry of "Oh love!" Richard exploded inside me, helpless beneath me.

I knew the power of having brought this to someone I loved by my own efforts, and I, too, felt ecstasy wash over me, as helpless as he'd been a moment before.

I collapsed on to his chest. His arms held me close. With Richard murmuring endearments, with him still sunk inside me, I slept.

Chapter Fifteen

I woke up with a start. I saw Richard lying next to me, his chest peacefully rising and falling in sleep. It was daylight.

Sitting up in bed, I reached for my watch, the one I usually kept on the nightstand, and to my horror realised we'd slept too long. The household would be awake. There was no chance of us hiding what we'd done.

Turning, I saw his look of loving amusement. "Good morning, sweetheart."

"Richard, it's seven o'clock!"

"Come here and put that thing down." He pulled me close and I dropped the watch. "First things first," he murmured, and kissed me.

I couldn't help but move to him, feel his warmth. He gentled me with the kiss, using his tongue and hands to soothe my agitation until I relaxed in his arms. "Sweetheart, I've been in worse situations, and I'm sure we can brush through this one. I can't regret this and I don't intend to try. What's the worst thing that can happen?"

My initial panic had gone. "Martha gets to hear of it."

"Quite. She'll ask me to leave, which I must do anyway in a few days, and she gives you a lecture. Now how bad does that sound?"

I snuggled against him. "Not too bad at all."

"Well worth the bliss of spending my first night with you, I'd say." He pushed the hair back off my face, ran his fingers through it. "I can't remember when I last slept so well."

I chuckled, burrowing into his warmth. "Can we really do this all the time? It scarcely seems possible."

"Believe it. It's a certainty."

We lay together until I came to my senses again. "Richard, what shall we do? Wait for the maid to come and find us?"

"Carier will work it out. I have no doubt he'll arrive shortly."

I lifted my head. "You've done this before, haven't you?"

He grimaced. "Once or twice." He curved his leg around me, touching my bottom with his thigh. It felt good. Too good.

"Richard!"

"We might have time to say good morning properly." He captured my mouth in a deep, consuming kiss.

There was a soft knock on the door. "Madam?" I recognised Carier's voice.

With a great deal of regret in his eyes, Richard released me. "Later, my sweet."

"A moment!" I called to the manservant.

Richard flung back the covers and got out of bed. I watched him search for his robe, his beautiful, athletic body gleaming in the light filtering through the shutters. Finding his robe he flung it on and fastened it before fixing me with a gaze that burned into my soul. "You look so beautiful like that. Tousled hair, that sweet flush on your face—I won't rest until I see you like this again." He sat on the side of the bed and took my hand. "I have to go into Exeter today. I meant to tell you last night, but something took it right out of my mind." He lifted my hand to his lips. "I need to see that the house is ready for my parents and Maria. They'll be arriving in a day or two. I won't stay, I'll be back as soon as I can."

He kissed me, then left. I waited, holding my breath until I heard the quiet click of a door closing further up the corridor. He was right. It wouldn't have been so bad had anyone saw, but I was glad not to have to suffer one of Martha's lectures.

When Richard and Gervase went to Exeter, I decided to

walk to the village with some things for Mrs. Hoarty. I would miss her when I didn't live here any more—she had been so kind to me over the years. She also provided a sanctuary for me when I was a child, letting me sit quietly with her instead of having to face the chaos of the manor.

I took a basket of flowers from our gardens, early crocuses and narcissi, so I was particularly keen to make speed so they should arrive fresh. I set myself quite a pace by the time I reached the main street.

People went about their business, and some of them wished me good day as I passed. I might never have gone away, except for the great ruby winking on my finger. Richard had done a great deal for my feeling of self worth, and I could hold my head high in any company these days, whereas before I would have shrunk to the background in my own drawing room. I wondered how I would have managed in polite society without his support, and supposed I would have been at the back there as well, too set in my ways to change.

Halfway along the long street, I passed a house where everybody knew smugglers lived. Most of the inhabitants had conventional positions in the farms or on the estates and lent a hand—for a price—on the nights when runs took place, but the people here belonged to the hard core of the gang, if at a humble level. The Cawntons had, however, not been foolish enough to employ these men when carrying out the beating Richard had broken up, but brought strangers in from another village to carry out the task, people I'd never seen before. Presumably, these men were called on when other inhabitants of other villages proved recalcitrant.

With an explosion of splintering wood, from the front door of the smuggler's cottage burst a large man, one of the inhabitants of the cottage. He yelled and cursed, his meaty fists uplifted.

I crossed the street, but slowed to see what was going on before I became involved in the melée. I could have justified myself by claiming to be a member of one of the largest houses hereabouts, with a vested interest in seeing law and order was not breached, but in truth I was as curious as the next villager. I didn't think to flee.

A second man backed out of the door, now only attached to its frame by one hinge, and deciding it was a mere drunken dispute, I decided to ignore it and pass by. That was until another figure advanced at a rush out of the same door.

When I recognised Tom Skerrit, I picked up my skirts, ran back across the street, and deposited my basket of flowers out of the way. Tom's friend Theodore Livingstone and two brawny footmen followed him. They raced down the path after the first man, who promptly took to his toes.

"Tom!"

He hailed his hurtling pursuit, and spun around on his heel when he heard my voice.

"What do you think you're doing?"

"Go home, Rose."

Fury and haunting guilt shadowed his dark eyes. "Tom, leave them alone."

"Someone has to pay for Fursey's death. We can't let that pass without some sort of warning."

"But, Tom, don't take these people on. For God's sake, wait!" Tom had run off in pursuit. I hoped the man would get away, for everybody's sake, but as the villagers and I watched, the first man reached him and lifted him off his feet. He yelled and fought while they hauled him back up the street.

I raced to where they had dragged him, hoping to remonstrate with them, perhaps shame them into stopping by my presence, but it was no good. The man stood, protecting his head with his arms, and they punched and kicked him, trying to drag him down to make him completely at their mercy. The blows landed with repetitive, dull thuds, followed by shouts to leave him alone before Cawnton saw to them. I didn't care to have such villains in our village, but I didn't see what good could come of this.

Such was the commotion my voice couldn't be heard at all, and I knew if I tried to intervene, I would most likely be hurt.

I did the only thing I could think of that would help. I lifted my skirts and ran for home, thankful I wore comfortable clothes and sturdy shoes, the easier to run in.

I'd never reached the Manor so speedily before. When I reached the front of the house I was thankful to see James, mounted, on his way out by the side gate. "Rose, whatever is wrong? What's happened?"

I leaned against the gatepost, pulling in breaths with great heaves. As soon as I could speak, I gasped, "James, Tom is in the village with Theo Livingstone and two servants. They're beating the hell out of a villager. One of the smugglers. You must do something, please, James."

James wheeled his horse around, calling to the grooms to mount quickly and follow him. Then he turned and called out to me, "Go inside. I'll do what I can."

Once I'd recovered my breath, I disobeyed him, and followed him back to the village, ignoring my aching feet. I passed my pattens on the way back, discarded in my mad dash to the house. The heavy overshoes had been hindering my speed, and I could easily survive wet feet. I was weary from the running, and had to slow down, only arriving at the village when it seemed to be all over.

The grooms passed me as I walked, but they didn't stop to take me up, being more intent in obeying their master and seeing what the trouble was. One of them looked back as he passed me, frowned, and waved at me to return to the manor, but my friend was involved, and I couldn't leave him alone, whatever he'd done, so I continued until I reached the main street again.

Tom and his companions stood to one side. A man lay on the road, ominously motionless. James had dismounted and stood over him. He only looked up when I approached. "I thought I told you to go inside."

"Be quiet, James, I'm perfectly safe." I knelt to examine the man, feeling for a pulse on his wrist.

There was none. I felt his neck at the base but nothing beat there either. He'd been badly beaten, his face and head a mass of blood, but what must have been the cause of death was the knife jutting out of his chest, a rough looking knife with a repaired hilt, not the sort of thing Tom or his companions would carry.

I looked up at James and shook my head, while Tom started forward. "It was an accident, truly."

Tom continued to talk, seemed unable to stop the flow of words in his panic. "We wanted to teach them a lesson, that's all, so we came to find him because everybody knows he's a Cawnton man, and when he ran out we ran after him, then he drew his knife and..." His voice was raising in pitch, getting faster and I recognised the signs of hysteria. I slapped Tom full across his face. He stopped abruptly.

Tom stared at me, his face white. His friend Theo, who stood a little way behind him, also looked shocked and upset, as well he might with a dead man on their hands.

James took charge. "Take him over there." Our grooms lifted the dead man and returned him to his cottage, from whence he had run so short a time before. The sooner that grisly sight was out of the way the better. We watched in silence while the two grooms carried him the short distance back to his home, with the gaping door and a white-faced woman standing by it. She watched expressionlessly, as they carried him through the door and out of sight.

"It might be best," James said, "if we continue this indoors. Rose, I'll take you back. You others follow on."

They nodded and began to trudge along the road to the Manor as James remounted and held his hand down, to lift me in front of him. He set his horse to walk back. I nestled against him. My big brother, who had soothed my hurts when I was small. I needed soothing now.

I brought him up to date as best I could on the way back, and asked him to send someone to Mrs. Hoarty to make sure this had not upset her too much. He promised he would send someone and then we arrived home.

I dismounted and went straight upstairs, calling for a maid as I did so. Another gown ruined. I changed quickly and ran back downstairs, to see what developments had transpired.

I found them in the morning room; James, Martha, Tom and Theo, the latter two with glasses of brandy in their hands, presumably given them to calm them after the shock. James was speaking, but he broke off when I came in, and then we heard the front door slam and voices. Richard and Gervase, back from Exeter.

Someone must have told them for within a few minutes they both entered the morning room. Richard came directly to me. "Rose, are you hurt?"

"No, not at all. I saw the start of the brawl, and I came back for help."

He nodded, the fine lines between nose and mouth tight with tension, and took the glass of brandy James offered him with a short word of thanks. "They told me you were in the village when some sort of incident occurred." He took a sip. "I'd like to hear it from the beginning."

"So would I," agreed James. So far, Theo Livingstone had remained silent, but since Tom was showing no inclination to begin, he cleared his throat and glanced at his friend for guidance. Theo was a large man, not overburdened with brain, and I guessed Tom had instigated the affair.

Theo stared at me, as if I was the only person he recognised in the room. He was still taken with the shock. I looked at Tom, trying to reassure him as best I could without words, but he didn't seem to see.

"I was at Peacock's this morning," Theo began in a low voice, "and Tom asked me to help. He told me about the gamekeeper you found the other day, and said we should damned—dashed well teach these smugglers a lesson. I didn't think it was such a good idea, but he was in such a state I thought I should go along and try to stop it getting out of hand."

Richard interrupted him. "Where was his father? Couldn't you have told him?"

"His mother and father were at Fursey's cottage, visiting the poor man's family. He won't like it you know, Tom," he added, looking to where Tom sat, motionless.

Tom shook himself out of his stupor. "That's why I chose to do it when they were out of the way." He took his gaze away from mine, and looked around with a slightly dazed air, as though seeing the room for the first time and surprised to find himself in it. "I only wanted to teach them a lesson, to stop them trespassing on our land again. I knew all about that man, everybody did, and I thought it might serve. He saw us coming and he tried to get away." He lifted his glass to his lips with a shaking hand and took a deep draught. He didn't cough as he normally did after a deep intake of such a powerful spirit. "He ran out of the cottage but we caught him further down the street, and we started to hit him. I saw Rose there, and I told her to go home, but she ran after us."

Richard, sitting next to me, sighed in what sounded like a resigned way, but I kept all my attention on Tom. "She ran off towards the Manor and I thought she was doing as I'd told her and going home. We hit the man, and he fell to the floor, but he must have been hellish strong, because he came up again with that knife in his hand. I don't know what happened then but I was so angry I forgot about any danger and I rushed him. I caught him off balance and knocked him over. And when he didn't come up again we looked a bit closer, and we saw he'd fallen on the knife."

He stopped abruptly and took another drink, emptying his glass. In the silence, we all heard the glass rattle on the table as he failed to control his shaking hand. James sighed. "An unfortunate accident. We should be thankful for that."

"Yes indeed," Martha agreed.

"The Cawntons might not let it rest," said Richard sombrely. "This is the second incident in the village, and they may see it as a campaign against them. They may also see it as the unfortunate loss of a worker, especially this close to a run, and take umbrage. Tom should consider leaving for a time."

"They wouldn't dare hurt Tom!" Martha cried in outrage.

Richard frowned. "They might. It would give his parents peace of mind if he was away from here. Has he any relatives he can visit for a time?"

Tom made a disgusted sound. "I won't leave the high ground to them. They can't run rough-shod over us!"

"They may, in the short term," Richard said regretfully.

Tom was beside himself with indignation "No. They break the law and they put terror in the hearts of ordinary decent people. Do you know our fields empty the day before a run, because they've all been told to rest and prepare for the night's work?"

"No, but it's the sensible thing for them to do," Richard replied mildly. "You can't fight smuggling from here. If you really want to help, get yourself elected to Westminster and lobby there. It's a countrywide problem, even though it is handled locally. It needs to be tackled from the centre, not piecemeal."

"Faugh!" Tom turned away. I was appalled at his lack of control, but Tom was overset by the recent events, and must be at the end of his patience. We sat in silence, until Tom said, in a milder tone, "I beg your pardon, sir. I shouldn't have done any of this. I should go and tell my father."

"Please consider going away for a time," Richard repeated. "They may seek reprisals."

Tom said nothing, but bowed to us, and he and Theo left the room.

Richard sighed heavily. "I'm much afraid the Cawntons won't leave this incident be."

"Is there nothing you can do?" I asked him.

"My dear, what can Strang do?" Martha protested. "He's a man of fashion, not at all concerned with these matters."

Richard shook his head in regret. "We should try to persuade Tom to go away until this blows over. There's a run soon I believe, and they may choose to forget if it's a successful one."

James's eyes narrowed in suspicion. "How can you know that?"

Richard smiled easily. "My dear Hareton, you'd have to be blind not to notice the frantic activity in some areas."

James nodded briefly. "I suppose you're right." He was unimpressed.

"You'd be best advised to leave this alone, Richard," said Gervase gravely. "After all, you have other things to concern you."

Richard looked at me and smiled, an intimate one this time. "So I have," and he said no more on the subject.

Chapter Sixteen

The Earl and Countess of Southwood arrived in Exeter safely. Now Society appeared thick and fast in preparation for the wedding. I found it hard to believe it was all for me, but it seemed so. My worries for Tom not a whit abated, I realised I had other duties, and set about fulfilling them.

Richard took me into Exeter to visit his parents. When I stepped from the carriage outside the house, it brought back all the memories of that afternoon. I felt shy and confused, but I must have been getting better at controlling my feelings, because nobody noticed except Richard, who pressed my hand encouragingly as we went through the front door. This time a superior butler took us all the way up to the drawing room and announced our presence in ringing tones.

There were servants present now, the smell of cooking seeped up from the kitchen below, and there was a feeling of busy habitation, entirely lacking before. I regained my composure, as I climbed the stairs resting my hand on Richard's arm, just like a proper visitor.

The earl and countess formed a formidable partnership. Both unbendingly strict, and determined to have their way in all things, Richard had infuriated them more than once with his wayward behaviour.

At first sight the earl bore little resemblance to his sons, so I could find nothing familiar about him, nothing I could befriend and find sympathy with. He viewed me as a suitable vessel for his heirs, if he thought of me at all. The warmth with which he welcomed me as a prospective bride for his son had a lot more to do with the relief that his heir had finally decided to do his duty than any other consideration. He didn't perceive the affection with which Richard and I held each other, and if he had, he probably wouldn't have cared.

Lady Southwood was a small lady, whose face was the same pointed shape as her sons', and her hair the same golden yellow. The most striking resemblance however was her eyes, which were the same startling clear blue colour.

Unlike her husband, she had perceived Richard's feelings for me, and had declared herself amazed, but in the way someone might be amazed by a performing bear. Either she kept her feelings well hidden, as Richard did, or she had none, and I didn't yet know which.

I greeted Richard's sister, Lady Maria, with genuine pleasure. She was Richard's junior by a full ten years, the last healthy child borne to the earl by his countess after a tragic series of miscarriages and weak babies who didn't survive for long. Maria had been contracted to marry my cousin, the younger son of the fourth Earl of Hareton, but when they saw the state of affairs, Richard and Gervase had strongly advised against it. If it weren't for this, Richard and I would never have met when we did, and matters might have turned out differently for both of us.

Lady Southwood took me to sit next to her by the fire, for it was one of those sunny, chilly days in early spring that can be so deceptively cold despite the bright sunshine. "Are you quite recovered from your dreadful experience of yesterday, my dear?" I stared at her, wondering how she knew. "Strang sent a note," she explained.

"Yes, quite recovered, ma'am. I'm more concerned about my friend Tom Skerrit, who was directly involved in it all."

"The boy seems to have some spirit," Lord Southwood said from where he stood by the window.

Richard strolled across the room to join his father. "Spirit won't get him far with organised gangs like these."

Lord Southwood regarded him with disfavour. "It's the only way to stop these beggars—stand up to 'em."

Richard met his stare dispassionately. "There are different ways of accomplishing the downfall of the gangs that rule the coast, and on the whole I prefer the effective ones. It will take Parliament to properly deal with them."

"Send the army in, that would soon deal with the scoundrels." The earl's face lit up at his solution, and he looked about the room for the expected approval.

He got none from his son. "It would be expensive, in lives and in every other way. Why not cut duty? It would cost the country little, as the loss of revenue would be set off by the increase in volume in legitimately traded goods."

The earl opened his mouth, closed it again, pondered, and then cleared his throat. "There's something to be said for that. But if we cut taxes on liquor, public drunkenness would be even worse than it is now."

Richard said, "Parliament has passed a licensing act, has it not?" His father nodded. "Then if they actually enforce it this time, it should go a long way towards stopping the drink problem. Clean water might help, and in any case, where does all this liquor come from? It will still come from the same source, but it would be legal and therefore easier to control."

Lord Southwood smiled broadly. "Come, we'll make a politician of you yet. That's a well-reasoned, cogent argument. Would you like to be a political hostess, my dear?" he added, turning to me.

I took a sip of tea while I searched for the right reply. I knew Richard had no ambitions in that direction, but I didn't want to antagonise his father unnecessarily. "If Lord Strang should like it, then I would do my best," I said, thinking myself diplomatic.

I warmed to Richard's slow smile of appreciation.

"I'm sure you would make an excellent political wife," Lady Southwood said. "But, Strang, how could you become involved in a brawl in the public street? I can't think you would do such a thing."

His sister gazed at him, her eyes glowing with excitement, but he couldn't give her the description she looked for now, although I thought she might well press him for it once she had him on his own.

His father also expected to him for an explanation, and he was not disappointed. "I'm sorry the story should be doing the rounds of the gossips, and I wish you would depress it for me if you hear it. The truth of it is, that two of the local bullies were beating another man in front of a house where Rose and I were paying a social call. I can't allow such insults to her, so I broke up the fight, that's all. One of them attacked me, so I depressed his pretensions and sent him packing."

"I wasn't aware Miss Golightly was there." Lord Southwood looked at me for all the world as if I was a child who had never seen such a thing. However, I saw where Richard was taking this, so I held my peace.

"I can't permit such insults in her presence," Richard told his father firmly. "It's also true we were visiting an old friend of Rose's, a lady somewhat advanced in years who isn't in the best of health, and the fracas upset her considerably."

"And all you did was break it up?" I wondered why his mother should be sceptical. Richard had been known for his amours, not for his brawling.

"Indeed, Mother," Richard replied. "And restore the unfortunate victim to his family, who lived nearby."

"It sounds perfectly acceptable to me. We'll certainly put paid to that particular rumour." Lord Southwood cleared his throat again, and got out his snuff box, a wonder of the miniaturists' art, flipped the lid and offered some to Richard, who took his usual infinitesimal pinch.

Lord Southwood seemed to enjoy his snuff, drawing it in deeply with an air of satisfaction. "You're not thinking of getting involved with the local riffraff, are you?"

The innocent blue stare fixed on him would have fooled that wily politician, Mr. Fox. "Involved, sir?"

His father, harassed, looked to his wife for assistance, and finding none, returned to his son. "You called it once 'clearing up a small matter'."

"No, I have no such intention." Richard gave his father no clues.

The earl glared at him. "Then you will come to us tomorrow with Gervase?"

"I'll follow in a day or two, sir. I'm helping Lord Hareton with a trifling affair concerning Rose's childhood friend." He made it sound unconnected with the fracas in Darkwater village.

Lady Southwood sighed heavily. "Is this person in trouble?"

"Yes he is," Richard replied bluntly.

The countess raised her hands in the air in a gesture of exasperation. "I knew it. Strang, you're getting married in less than two weeks. Please don't embroil yourself in anything here."

"I have no intention of it, ma'am." Richard left his father's side to cross the room and take his mother's hands. Their hands together looked so similar, except Richard's were larger, but the shape, that long, elegant line was there; something I'd never noticed before.

Richard spoke to his mother directly. "It's rather the other way around. Tom Skerrit was involved in a fracas the other day that resulted in a man's death. It was a clear case of accidental death, but matters would be better resolved if Tom took leave of absence for a while. I hope to convince him of that. I wasn't even there at the time." I hoped they didn't think to ask where I was when it all happened, and connect it with their kind enquiries earlier. They were obviously not familiar with the names of the people involved, or it would have been much easier to put two and two together.

"And you know this Tom Skerrit?" her ladyship asked me.

"He's the son of the squire. We used to play together as children. Richard's trying to help him to scotch any scandal, and if Tom should be absent, then it would all be dealt with more smoothly."

"It seems reasonable," Lord Southwood said doubtfully, and then seemed to lose interest in poor Tom. "But you must come to us soon, Strang. It wouldn't do for you to be married from your betrothed's house."

Richard smiled. "No indeed, sir, and I promise you I will be married from this house." His father was forced to accept his promise. Soon after that the visit came to an end, and Richard took me away.

We spent the rest of the day in visits. All the available fashionable houses in Exeter had now been let, and we toured some of them. We entered fashionable drawing rooms, which contained some of the most important figures in the land, all there for my wedding and, I came to understand, some amusement and a change from the usual fashionable rounds. The story of Richard's run-in with the local villains was repeated more than once, and scotched in the same fashion as before by us both, and by the end of the day I was heartily sick of the story. These people wanted gossip, the same as the local gentry, and I wished them joy of it. They weren't so different after all, but their spheres of influence were larger, their manners more elegant and their clothes grander. Still, I was glad when the day came to an end and I could lean back against the squabs in the carriage with the satisfied sigh of one who has done her duty.

"Such an ordeal," mocked my love.

"It was. I've always found social visits hard work, and I've met more new people today than I ever hoped to. I tried to remember all the names. I hope I've been successful."

"I'm sorry." He took my hand. "I grew up with most of them, you see, and you seemed to fit in so well I almost forgot your sheltered upbringing."

I laughed. "Sheltered? With smugglers on our doorstep and enough gossip to fill any London salon? I would say restricted, but certainly not sheltered."

He smiled. "Restricted then. But I'm convinced you'll slip in to your allotted place as though you'd always been there. I know you were worried about it, but I don't think you need concern yourself any more."

"What do you think they'll say about me?"

His eyes sparkled, and he smiled teasingly. "That you're a pretty-behaved young lady, but they don't know why I should choose you, over their Mary, Elizabeth or Margaret."

"You have, though, and I can't fathom why. I am no different to many of these young ladies, and many of them are superior to me, you know they are." I wouldn't let him interrupt, and I wasn't fishing for compliments. "They're younger, prettier, better educated, and every day I wonder why you chose me. You might regret it one day, but I'm determined to make you as good a wife as you would find anywhere."

"My dear."

"No, Richard, I mean it. I know what I am, and I know what you are, and what you could have for the asking. Any of the eligible young ladies we met today would have had you; at least I'm assured they would by their kindness to you. I'm only beginning to realise how lucky I am."

We were out of the city now, on the country road, so he forestalled any more of my halting speech by taking me in his arms and trying to convince me I was worthy of him.

Chapter Seventeen

Gervase stood in the hall, about to take his leave to stay in his parents' house in Exeter. "Are you sure you won't come?" he asked Richard.

Richard smiled and glanced at me. "In a few days. I want to make sure young Skerrit is out of any danger."

He addressed Martha, who stood behind us. "If it's no trouble? If you're overwhelmed with preparations, I can always go today."

"Not at all," Martha replied, thin lipped. She would never turn anyone from her door, however inconvenient she found it.

I kissed Gervase on the cheek and he smiled, returned the salute, and went out to his waiting chaise.

"The mantua-maker is waiting," Martha reminded me.

After a rueful look at Richard that made him laugh, I followed her upstairs. My trousseau took up more and more of my time—I had never owned so many garments in my life before. The seamstress came every day, and the mantua-maker was here for a final visit to ensure my wedding gown was exactly as it should be.

When I was back to myself, dressed in a simple gown, ordinary again, my attendants left me and I went downstairs to see if I could find Richard.

He was in the small drawing room, talking to Tom, who looked tired, drawn-faced and white. I didn't think he'd had much sleep recently.

Richard seemed calm, reasonable, but he wouldn't relent. "I have apartments in several cities abroad that you are welcome to make use of, but I don't think it will come to that," I heard him say when I entered. Looking round to see who it was, he smiled in greeting, but continued to talk to Tom. "You must have some relatives you can pay a diplomatic visit to."

"I don't see why I should leave the high ground to them," Tom said, his mouth set in a mulish line. "I've done nothing wrong."

Richard glanced with me, his expression serious and concerned. "Tom, you sought this man out, you attacked him in front of witnesses. And if a man is stabbed in this country, the man who stabbed him is automatically convicted of murder, whatever the circumstances. Accidental or not, you are to blame. You're in grave danger." I caught my hand to my chest. I had no idea that was the case.

Tom stared at Richard, amazed. "There was no murder."

"There is strong evidence you're right, not least because he fell on his own knife, but you may find the procedure of proving that difficult," Richard pursued. He tried hard to get Tom to see sense, but I didn't know if it was for Tom's sake or for mine. Any matter that concerned Tom would also reflect on me. I decided I didn't care. If he managed to persuade Tom to discretion, then I'd be much happier to leave my old friend while I left with Richard for my bride-trip. Norrice Terry was a magistrate—he could help in this.

"I won't go," said Tom mulishly, reverting to the language of childhood, and the sulky expression to match it. I'd have laughed had the situation not been so serious.

To my surprise, Richard shrugged. "I've done my best."

"Can't you send word to the Cawntons again?" I crossed the room to his side. Tom glanced up, frowning, but he didn't say anything.

"No, not this time," Richard told me. "If I interfere again they might think I'm taking it personally, that I want to take a hand in it, and then matters might escalate far more than they need. No, discretion is the better answer."

"Do you know these men?" Tom walked across the room to face Richard.

He shook his head. "No, of course not, but if you can remember it, I was involved in a small incident myself when I first arrived. They sent word to me they would leave me alone, but it was nothing like as serious as your misadventure."

Tom accepted his explanation, but didn't look pleased. "I'm sorry, my lord, but I propose to see this thing out. I bid you good day." With that formal salutation, he left the room.

I glanced back at Richard and he grimaced, shaking his head in defeat, so I hurried after Tom. "Let me walk with you." I might persuade him where others could not.

Tom waited while I fetched a cloak and hat, and, his mood restored somewhat, we set out arm in arm for Peacock's.

Tom breathed the air in deeply. "There's nothing like Devonshire air." He showed all the signs of relief that he'd got through a difficult interview.

"Spoken like a true squire," I teased.

"Well, and isn't that what I am? And proud of it. No, these scoundrels won't see me off my own land."

"Richard only suggested a discreet withdrawal for a small time." Once he regained his temper, always volatile but usually overcome by his good sense, he would come around, I was sure.

Walking through one of our orchards, I reached up to drag the branch of a nearby tree, and let it thrash up again to disturb its neighbours, a trick I'd been particularly fond of when we were children.

Tom smiled at the memory I brought back for him, but he wasn't distracted. "If I left, it would seem like a victory for them. My father feels the same way, you know. He regrets what happened, but he doesn't regret who it happened to."

I sighed. "It's not the authorities I'm afraid of. It's the smugglers."

"They won't dare start anything with us." He sounded more

confident than I was feeling. "Don't worry, Rose, I'll be there to dance at your wedding." He didn't say this in a particularly cheerful tone, but I couldn't pursue it, as we had reached the end of the orchard and had to climb the stile into the field beyond.

Once over, I paused to study the field, a gentle slope of green pasture with a wide expanse of clear blue sky above, meeting in a hard line in the distance, fringed at the left side with trees, earth meeting air. Every morning this was as fresh as a newborn baby, memoryless, meeting the world with new moods, new expectations.

I breathed in the sea-scented air. "I shall miss this." I linked my arm with Tom's again.

"What?" This view was so familiar to him he'd never even noticed it, but I, who would lose it soon, was making the most of it while it was still there for me.

I waved my free hand around me. "All this."

Tom gazed around. "Oh, yes. I wouldn't like to live anywhere else but here. I'd feel like a fish out of water in some other place."

"I don't know how I'll feel." Richard had become my home, but I'd come back here from time to time to renew that part of me which had been here before him, and try to keep it, for my own sake.

"I've often thought it's more unfair for women," said Tom, as we strolled across the damp, soft field. "They have to follow their husbands wherever they are, whatever they do."

"Some don't. Some people live completely separate lives after the birth of the heir. They even set up their own households."

"Most do. It's only the high born who can afford to live as two households instead of one."

We walked for a while in silence, listening to the sounds of our county, the seagulls above us, shrieking above the sounds of the birds in the woods we were approaching. I would miss this. "It's been a bit frantic recently. This is much better. I should have come up here before."

"Rose?"

"Yes, Tom?"

He stopped short of the gate into the wood and turned me to face him. "I've wanted to talk to you about that." He studied my face. "Are you quite sure about all this? When I heard your brother had inherited the earldom, I thought you'd stay in Yorkshire, and I might never see you again. Then you decided to come home, and I thought things might settle down. Then I heard you'd decided to marry Lord Strang, a man with a dreadful reputation, and I was worried. I must say he seems a better man than I'd feared, but he's a lord, a member of a world we've never even considered. He's sophisticated and worldly. Are you sure you want all this? Really sure? "

My heart went out to Tom, that he should care so much for me. He was as dear to me as my own brothers. With friends like these, I need never be alone.

"How can I be sure of anything, Tom?" I leant my forehead against his, an old childhood habit of ours. "I'm as sure of Richard as I can be. As for the rest, no, I'm worried and I'm nervous, but I must try. I can't let the world pass me by any more. I must go out to meet it while I have the chance."

Tom withdrew and we opened the gate and went into the wood that marked the start of his father's estate. "I hope you're happy in your new life. For myself, I can't imagine being happy anywhere else."

Gradually, a chill seeped through to my bones, and the lingering dampness crept around me. The arching branches above us cut out the sun. As we walked further up the path, I became aware of the hush in the wood. The birdsong from the field had ceased, and there was none of the usual rustlings of the wildlife amongst the debris beneath our feet. We stopped at the same time, aware that something was different, not quite right.

Tom saw something behind me, and the expression on his face changed to alarm. "Rose, run!"

Without looking back, I took to my heels.

I raced towards the gate, back into the open, back to my home to fetch help, but it was too late. Someone behind me caught my heel, and I fell headlong into the damp earth, kicking to try to free myself from the powerful grasp.

The man pinned my arms to my sides, and fastened them firmly behind my back, then someone else bound my ankles together. I did the only thing left to me. I screamed, as loudly and as long as I could, but a filthy hand clamped over my mouth. When I tried desperately to bite, the hand was removed and a stinking rag tied around my face, choking off my cries. I struggled, but I couldn't prevent being thrown over a burly shoulder, where I could only squirm, like a freshly caught fish in a net.

The man took me back to where Tom lay. Blood trickled from a wound on his head. I was terribly afraid they had killed him, but he was bound in the same way I was, trussed like a cut of meat ready for the spit. He must be alive, or they wouldn't have bothered to tie him.

The fight was getting me nowhere, and sapped my strength to no purpose. When I stopped struggling, the man who carried me smacked my backside. "That's better. You can't get away. We won't hurt you if you behave yourself." He sounded almost cheerful. I could have spat in his face. I still would, given half a chance.

They carried us to the edge of the wood, to a farm track. There, a cart waited, and Tom and I were thrown unceremoniously into it, while the four men who had taken us jumped up behind. We started off.

I lay quietly and studied the men I could see. I didn't recognise any of them. They must come from outside our area, although their accent was distinctively Devonshire. One of them saw me staring and reached for a sack. He lifted my shoulders and pulled the sack over my head. I saw no more. I started to count as a desperate way of marking our progress.

I reached seven thousand five hundred and six when we

stopped. By now the initial shock had worn off, and fear had me in its claws. I'd thought at first they were footpads, but they'd made no effort to search us or steal anything. I still wore my ruby ring, the first thing they would have taken if they'd been common thieves.

That only left one thing. These men were smugglers and this must be some sort of reprisal for Tom's actions. My fear escalated to terror, but I swallowed it down. It was a luxury I couldn't afford to indulge. I couldn't hear a sound from where Tom lay, still as death.

We were lifted off the cart and into a building, up some wooden stairs and into a small space. The difference in the sounds of shuffling feet told me that. I had no idea where we could be but I guessed at an outlying barn of some kind. I remained as quiet as I could, aware my struggles would be useless against four large men. We were laid down and then a door closed.

I lay quietly until sure we were alone, and then I managed to shrug the stinking sack from over my head. I lay for a while, breathing deeply. I felt sick, and I knew that with such a tight gag around my mouth if I actually vomited I could choke and suffocate. I lay still, the taste of filth in my mouth from that rag, until I'd settled my wayward stomach.

I sprawled on floorboards in a room without windows, but light filtered in thinly from somewhere, because I could see Tom's leaden body on the floor in the dim light. By squirming like a snake, I made my way slowly across the floor, inched over to him, and laid my forehead against his in an effort to see if he was still alive. It was a travesty of the friendly gesture of so short a time before.

His forehead was warm, and now I was closer I heard his uneven breathing. I closed my eyes in a short prayer of thanks that he was alive. I rolled over on my side and looked around.

We were in a small room with bare floorboards, and no furniture. A thin stream of light came from several points high up on the wall, dazzling my eyes at the pinpoints where they entered, diffusing into fitful gleams and a dull, all over light below, where we lay. The walls were rough plastered, but the ceiling was a wooden one, and seemed too high in proportion to the walls.

I assumed we lay in a barn or cottage somewhere, not too far away from the wood where we had been taken, perhaps even Darkwater itself, although I doubted that. It would be far safer to take us somewhere more remote. Besides, once Richard knew I was gone he would tear Darkwater apart in an effort to find me and they would know that.

I couldn't think what they meant to do with us, or why they had taken us. I'd assumed they would give Tom a beating for his part in the unfortunate death the other day, but apart from that blow to the head, they didn't seem to have touched him. Did they mean to hurt us? Why would they want to take us otherwise? My head began to ache.

I don't know how long I lay there, stifled by that loathsome gag. My hands tingled, and then went numb under the tight bonds. Then I heard a sound, a groan from Tom.

He opened his eyes and saw me, then instinctively tried to lift his hands to his head, groaning again when he found they were bound behind him. "Rose?"

I made a sound and his eyes widened when he saw I was gagged.

I realised that the fact they had not gagged him meant they were not afraid anyone would overhear us. Perhaps an isolated cottage, then. "God, my head hurts." He tried to flex his arms, but they had tied them just above the elbow. He blinked and turned his head from side to side gingerly, cried out when he felt the spot where they had hit him. "We've been taken?" I nodded.

"Rose, turn around and get really close. I'll see if I can't loosen that filthy thing with my teeth."

I did as I was told. "The knot is only a simple one, I can manage this."

Tom tugged as he tried to loosen my gag and I felt pressure at the back of my head. He worked at it for some time. I lay passive, waiting. I might even have let a tear or two drop, but I was determined not to give way to them. I blinked them back.

Eventually, the tight pressure around my mouth loosened, and I could spit away the rag and move my jaw to get some feeling back. I turned around so I faced Tom. I must have looked a fright, my hair wild around my face, and I must assume, a red line where the gag had been, for he closed his eyes briefly, and his face contorted. "I'm sorry, Rose, I'm sorry." Despair etched his voice.

I coughed, and although my mouth was dry, I found I could talk. "Never mind, Tom. These people are brutes. It's their fault, not yours."

"But if I hadn't had a hand in killing that man…"

"You can't repine on that. We have to think, to see what can be done." He nodded, seeing the sense of that. "Tom, you did well with my gag. Do you think you could do as well with my other bonds?"

I turned my back on him again, and worked my way up so he could see the ropes fastening my arms and hands. "No," I heard him say. "The knots are much better. I'd need a knife to get through these."

I shuffled back down and turned to face him again. "I don't think there's much point shouting or they would have gagged us both."

He agreed. "There might be someone outside on guard, waiting for us to call out. We should stay quiet, and try to think what to do. There might be a chance," he said. "Rose—look inside my coat. There's a small pocket there, where I keep my knife."

Heartened, I nuzzled my way inside his coat, and found the pocket by touch. I used my teeth to pull it open, tearing the seam in the process. There was nothing inside. I went back up to where he waited, anxiously, and I shook my head. "Nothing."

He sighed. "They must have searched me."

"I don't think they searched me." I rolled on the floor and felt the pocket around my waist hard against my leg. I came back to Tom. "I still have my necessaire. There's a small fruit knife in it."

"Where is it?" He tried to work his way down to my waist, wincing from the pain in his head, but then the **door** opened. We froze.

The light from the open door blinded us at **first, and** we both lay squinting against it. Two men came in, **followed by** another who carried two chairs and another with **a table and** candles. The door closed. One of the men placed a **chair** against it and sat down heavily against our only way of escape. The first man sat. Even sitting, his presence was heavier, more commanding than the smugglers we had seen up to now, and I realised we must be getting close to the head of the gang. The man regarded us in silence, and we stared back.

I broke the silence. "Cawnton."

He smiled. Most of his teeth were missing, which didn't improve his appearance. "Miss Rosalind Golightly. Soon to be Lady Strang."

I replied, careful to keep all trace of a tremor out of my voice, deliberately speaking quietly so he couldn't detect my fear. "Now the introductions are over are you going to let us go?"

"I might." His accent was also Devonshire, but not as pure as the men I'd heard earlier. He must have spent some time away from his home county. In the army, perhaps?

"Why have you done this?" Tom demanded. "What do you want with us?"

"Now then." Cawnton rubbed his hands together. "I might want many things, mightn't I? You killed one of my men, and I intend to get his worth, one way or the other. I can't see the law giving me anything, so, as usual, I'll have to take it for myself."

In one unhurried movement, he stood up, moved forward and kicked Tom in the stomach. If Tom hadn't seen his intention and squirmed aside, it would have been in the groin, but it was bad enough. He didn't cry out; he couldn't. All the breath was forced out of him with that one cruel kick. He doubled up and gasped for breath, making small noises.

Cawnton walked back to his chair. "That's just the start. Understand, I have no personal feelings for you one way or the other, but I can't let my men be hurt by other people. I have to keep order." He looked from one to the other of us thoughtfully. "All right then, here it is. Is he ready to listen?"

"No," I said. Tom still gasped painfully. I wet my lips, as I watched him, and although I would have died rather than ask, Cawnton must have seen the gesture, because he came to me and knelt down to where I sat. His eyes were on a level with mine. Grey and thoughtful eyes they were, the eyes of an intelligent man. I flinched and turned my head away, but he held up what he had in his hand. A pewter mug filled with some liquid. He held the back of my head and put the mug to my lips. "It's only small beer. Nothing funny about it."

I had little choice. I drank. Close to him, I smelled him, that rank, damp smell caused by little washing and unhealthy cottages. He must have noticed when I instinctively flinched away, because as I drank he sniffed and commented, "You should see me when I dress for a ball. I smell beautiful then." His two companions laughed, and I feared this closeness. My panic rose at the thought of what they might do, but Cawnton moved away again and sat.

Tom had regained something of his self-control, for he sat up glowering at Cawnton. "My father will find you."

"No he won't," Cawnton answered. "Or at least, he won't find you in time. Don't worry, I may be a bad 'un, but I'm not stupid. Your father will get you back, and you, Miss Golightly, will return to your lordling—if they behave themselves." He waited, smiling for us to give him our full attention. The gloating expression he wore indicated how much he relished the impact he'd made.

I refused to let my face show any of the turmoil I felt. Tom was still recovering from that brutal blow. Cawnton continued.

"There's a run on Friday, a big one. We need all our local hands for it." He nodded at Tom. "Your father will allow us to run our goods through his land this time."

"Never!" Tom gasped.

His brave, pointless words exasperated me. "Oh don't be silly, Tom. Your father will want you back. Cawnton has the right of it. Just listen."

I heard Cawnton's whistle. "Sensible."

I turned back to him. "I don't believe in the romantic notions of villains. What about me?"

"Your little lord caused us some problems a while back, and we've heard he's been asking questions."

"He takes an interest in local affairs," I replied, trying to be cool.

"He does, doesn't he?" Cawnton said. "To be honest, Rose— I can call you Rose? I've always wanted to hobnob with the gentry."

"Call me what you like." I refused to be riled by him.

"All right then—Rose. I didn't really want you taken. Your Lord Strang has somebody in his employ I wouldn't particularly like to cross swords with."

"Thompson." I remembered the note in Richard's pocket that day, and felt relieved that, as Richard had hoped, Cawnton assumed Carier ran Thompson's. Tom stared at me, surprised, but I ignored him.

"He told you, then?" Cawnton said. "Yes, Thompson. He says he's only here for your wedding, but I'm not so sure. He's a thief-taker, and we don't like them here. So, since we've got you, we'll ask your pretty lord to see he does nothing else while he's here. Then we can get on with our run, and you can get on with your wedding, and nobody's put to any more trouble."

At least Richard would be told I was here, wherever here was. Cawnton gestured at one of his men who came over to us. First he felt for Tom's fob, and he pulled that off, then he took my hand and slid off my ring, that gorgeous ruby I had worn for such a little time.

Cawnton whistled. "It would be almost worth killing you for this." He held the stone up to the candle to watch its glitter. "I'm no expert on stones, but I'd say this could buy a run or two. He gave you this?" I nodded. "Well, I'll take it to him to prove you're alive, but I might choose to keep it for myself. It's a bonny stone." He put the fob and the ring away in his pocket. "I've got to show people you can't cross me, otherwise my authority won't be worth an icicle in summer. You understand?" We both nodded this time. "But I'm not an unfeeling man. I'm thinking about releasing you from your ropes, but you've got to understand first it's no use you fighting and shouting. If I don't release you, it could damage you, and I never deliver damaged goods. My bargains are always straight." His two acolytes murmured agreement.

"There's a man outside this door, armed, and if he has to, he'll stop you. He won't come in for any reason at all, not until I get back. You're in a place where noise doesn't matter. Nobody will hear you. You can't get out of here. If I release you, you will wait, or you'll be trussed up like chickens, harder this time and you might end up with useless fingers and toes. Understand?" He glared at us. We both nodded. We couldn't do anything else.

Cawnton held up his hand and waved to the man behind him, his attention still on us. The man came forward, and drew a large knife out of his pocket. He cut our bonds, starting with mine.

Pain shot up my arms as the blood coursed freely through my veins again, and despite my good intentions, my face contorted. I saw Tom, his head down, holding his wrists, and then I heard the furniture being moved and saw they were leaving the room. My little fruit knife seemed like a futile gesture when I saw the man at the door, a flintlock in each hand, and two more stuck in his belt.

A man came in once, and put some things on the floor, and then the door closed and we were left in near darkness.

Chapter Eighteen

They left us a pottery chamber pot, a loaf of bread, a pitcher of small beer and some blankets, remarkably clean ones smelling of lavender. I wondered why they should fritter such luxuries on us, but perhaps Cawnton meant it when he said he was a straight dealer. I was glad of the chamber pot, and Tom turned his back like a gentleman and let me go first. I could have done with some water to wash with as well.

At least I had a comb. I found my little necessaire and emptied it. Together Tom and I examined the little silver fruit knife and agreed I should take charge of it in case they searched him once more. I put it at the top of my stocking, under my garter, where it would be easier to get hold of should they tie us up again. There was also a mirror, a comb, a needle, thread, and my keys.

For something to do, I took all my hairpins out and combed my hair. It was unruly at the best of times, now it was so tangled it would take me a long time to put it to rights.

Tom watched, fascinated. "How can you think of your appearance at a time like this?"

"It's something to do. In any case, I don't want to give them the satisfaction of seeing me at my worst. I want to face them with as much pride as I can muster. And that includes tidy hair." I drew the comb through the only smooth bit I had managed to make so far.

"You have lovely hair," said Tom. "I always thought so."

I looked at him, surprised at the unexpected compliment,

but he began to examine the walls of the room, looking for peepholes or weak spots, running his hands over them.

I got on with my hair and Tom examined the room. He came back and sat down glumly by my side. "If we knew where we were, we might stand a sporting chance. We should try to find that out, first. I say, Rose."

"Yes?" I stopped combing.

"Do you remember when we were children, and you used to sit on my shoulders so we could reach the best apples?"

"Yes." I began to get his drift.

"Do you think you could do it now? You might be able to see out of one of those chinks up there, where the light is coming from?"

I looked up. It was difficult to judge, but it might be possible. "Let's try."

So Tom hunkered down, I sat on his shoulders, after wrapping my skirts around my legs both for modesty, and so Tom could see. Slowly, he stood upright, and he gave a quiet whoop of triumph. "Come on, then." He walked slowly towards the chinks of light. I held tight until we were there, and then, using the wall to support myself, I stretched up as far as I could.

But it was no use. The light was still far above my head, and stretch as I might, I couldn't reach it. It was so frustrating. "I'd need to be an acrobat and stand on your shoulders," I whispered down to Tom.

"You don't feel you could stand?" he asked eagerly.

"No. If I fell, it would make such a noise they'd come in, and we don't want to antagonise them. Not yet, anyway."

He had to see the sense in that. It was one thing being brave but quite another to carry bravery to the point of stupidity. He knelt down and let me off. I stumbled when I stood, and Tom put out his arms to catch me, as he had so often before, but this time it was different.

Instead of releasing me when I regained my balance, he drew me to him and kissed me—not a friendly kiss. It held a passion I'd not been aware of in him before. His tongue probed at my lips and I almost opened, but it felt wrong. It wasn't Richard.

Appalled, I pushed him away. He opened his eyes and stared at me, his eyes filled with horror. "Oh, Rose, I'm sorry, I never meant—oh, God." He turned away, his hand to his head, and I realised he had let something slip, something he'd never meant me to see.

"Oh, Tom, no! Why didn't you tell me before?"

"Before you went away, you mean?" He turned back to me, but I couldn't see his face properly in the gloom, so I moved closer. He made an instinctive gesture, not wanting me to come close, but I took his hand and we sat. He wouldn't look at me. He stared at the floor. "I didn't know myself. It was only when you were away, and I missed you so much I realised I felt more for you than mere friendship, and then you came back betrothed—it was all so quick, maybe you hadn't thought it through, I'd give you time. I don't know," he continued, miserably staring at the planked floor. "And then I saw him, your betrothed, and I knew I couldn't compete with all that, so I decided to keep it to myself."

"Oh, Tom, if this had been two years ago, a year ago even, I would have been so pleased." He looked up at me, hope in his eyes. It broke my heart.

I couldn't let him think there was any hope. I had to explain. I tried to keep my voice steady. I thought if I started to cry he might too. "Although I never loved you in that way, I was always fond of you. We could have had a successful partnership. Love grows between people who marry for other reasons. We've seen it." I kept watching him, willing the misery I saw in his eyes to fade. "But when I met Richard my world changed. Like you, I didn't think I had a hope. You never saw Julia Cartwright, did you?" He shook his head dumbly. "She was so perfect—beautiful, perfectly dressed, rich. I never had a chance, or so I thought. But she turned out to be empty inside and she would have driven Richard mad within a twelvemonth. Still, I tried hard not to think of him until the accident. Then I had no time to think properly, you see, and when he was hauled out of that coach, covered with blood, I thought he might die. All I could think of was to stop the flow and try to save him."

I paused, glancing away, but I forced myself to meet Tom's eyes again. "Then he opened his eyes and looked at me. He said later he fell in love with me the first time he saw me, but I didn't fall for him until that moment." I was quiet then, as I thought of that moment, my despair, my stoical promise to myself to put those thoughts away, and I could imagine how Tom felt—except it probably hadn't been as cataclysmic with him.

"You're in love?" Tom asked, despair etching his voice. "He loves you?"

"Yes. It made me do some stupid things, but here I am, and if we get out of this, next week I'll be Lady Strang, sailing the high seas."

Tom stared at me, puzzled. At least it had made him forget his melancholy. I forced a smile. "He has a yacht, silly."

His face cleared. "Oh, Rose, are you sure he's for you? He's from another world you might not like. You belong here, in Devonshire."

"With the smugglers?" I said scornfully. "No, I belong with him now. Your mother said much the same thing when she first met him, you know, then she spoke with Martha. I let her see a side of him he doesn't usually let people see."

"My mother still has her doubts. Rose, he could hurt you. He's done some things in the past which I don't think you'd quite like."

"I know. I read all about them, and he's told me some of the less disreputable episodes himself. Many of them were exaggerated, but he never excuses himself, or says he had a lot to contend with."

"Like a privileged life, women throwing themselves at him?"

I heard his bitter tone, but I smiled. "No, Tom, like having a brother so close he's almost you, and then seeing him leave for more than ten years, disgraced. Richard was left to bear the whole scandal on his own. That scandal could have broken him, and did make him try to outdo Gervase in outrageous behaviour. But we all grow up one day. He told me he'd done that just before he met me. He was ready for me when I arrived, although he didn't know it."

"Do you know," said Tom thoughtfully, "there's something queer about all that. Why should Mr. Kerre's elopement have caused so much disgrace? Ten years' worth?"

I frowned, and tried to smooth my hair back. It still hung loose, and was beginning to tangle again. "There is something more, but I can't tell you, Tom. It was told me in confidence, and it's not my secret to tell."

He nodded. "Yes, I thought as much. I won't pry. You know what you've told me? About falling in love?"

"Yes." I began to pin my hair back up into place again, as best I could without a mirror.

"Are you sure it isn't infatuation? Are you sure it won't last six months, and then you'll find yourself with a husband you hardly know, who might use you terribly?"

"I know I love him now," I said, despite my mouth full of hairpins, "and I like him, too." I put the last pins in place. "He keeps his promises, he's loyal to his friends, good to his servants, and he will make the best kind of husband. On the other side, he has a terrible temper, mostly under control, he doesn't suffer fools at all and he has a disinclination to let anyone into his life, even his parents. Only two people know him properly—Gervase and myself. He seems unable to let anyone else in." I found it helped to talk about Richard, think about the good things in my life. When I thought ahead there was only a black void. I felt, somewhere deep inside, we weren't meant to get out of this alive.

"It must have been lonely for him," said Tom sardonically.

Having let his guard down so disastrously, we spent a long time trying to get back to normal, as much as we could in this place, but we achieved it by the end of the day. We talked about our childhood, and went over again any plans we might have to get out of this place unhurt.

Tom was every inch a squire's son. His sense of obligation was absolute and his desire for the status quo never to change as entrenched as any other countryman's. The changes in our lives would affect him, too, even if only that he had grander neighbours, but that in itself would bring change to our part of Devonshire. Perhaps his desire to keep everything normal persuaded him to try to keep one thing normal—our relationship. But he couldn't have that. Tom would have to live with it. I hoped it was just a passing fancy, that he'd find someone to care for one day, but I'd always been sure it wouldn't be me. I didn't think I was wrong now. Tom hated change, and I suspected his impulse to keep me had something to do with that. I'd have accepted him gladly, though, had I not met someone else, and I was sure we'd have had a good and productive life together, but I couldn't be sorry now.

We ate the bread and drank the beer, and when the light faded, wrapped ourselves in the blankets and tried to sleep, no nearer a solution than when we had first been brought here. I knew Sir George Skerrit and Richard would do everything they could to find us. I prayed it would be soon.

In the morning, Tom's headache had gone, and he seemed none the worse for the bump. Someone brought us bread, beer and cheese, and dealt with the chamber pot, and when I asked for it, they brought some water in a bowl. I sacrificed one of my petticoats to make a washcloth and towel, and we managed well, considering our miserable situation. I helped Tom rub away some of the thick crust of blood on his head after we'd washed ourselves. Underneath, it wasn't a large wound, and was beginning to heal, which put my mind at ease about that at least.

They left us to ourselves all day. With the chinks in the planking anyone could have been listening and watching, so there was no guarantee we were truly alone. The only way we had any privacy was to get close and whisper, and then they would know we were plotting. So we talked the day away in useless chatter, and the occasional murmur. I was glad I wasn't here alone. I would have given way to despair, but having Tom here meant I had to put up a front of bravery. But I was sorry he was in this mess with me. If he could have got away he might have got help sooner. That went for me, too, but there'd been no chance.

No one came that day, and we were left to manage the night as best we might. It wasn't cold in that little room, so we managed to sleep well enough again, but now the excitement and terror had diluted, anxiety surfaced once again. I thought I would never sleep, going over in my mind what we could do, what they would do to us, if we'd ever be allowed to leave. There was a heavily armed man left outside the door at all times, and for all we knew, another stationed where we couldn't see him.

In a deliberate attempt to soothe my agitation, I mentally went over the night Richard and I had spent together. At least we'd had that. I fell asleep as I had done that night, imaginary arms around me, holding me safe.

It was light when we woke up again, as light as it got in that little chamber. When the man came we asked him for light, but he didn't reply, and we didn't get it. Perhaps they thought we might try to set fire to the little room, an action I would have strenuously resisted, as it would be tantamount to suicide.

We ate and washed in the fresh water they brought us, and then sat down on the floor again. "What day is it?"

"We've slept twice," Tom replied. "It must be Thursday."

"It's my wedding in a week. If I last that long."

Tom reached over and patted my hand. "Of course you'll be there. And I'll be there to dance with you."

I rested my chin on my knees. "We're supposed to go for a rehearsal on Saturday,"

"That might be doubtful now," Tom said with the vestige of a grin. "But you might make the more important appointment."

"Richard will kill them," I told him in a conversational tone.

Tom stared at me in surprise and then laughed. "I know you love him, but really, Rose, what can your popinjay do against a vicious gang of smugglers?"

I didn't want to go into specifics, to tell him about Thompson's, so I held my tongue. And Tom hadn't seen Richard fight off the two bullies in the village that day. He had no way of knowing Richard's fighting prowess.

"I believe Cawnton," Tom continued. "If it's Thursday, the run takes place tomorrow night, and we'll be free on Saturday. He seemed to know what he was about. There is one thing—" He bit off the rest of the sentence, but I couldn't let him leave it at that.

"What? Tell me, Tom, I have a right to know."

He bit his lip. "All right. It only occurred to me this morning. The thing is, Rose, we've seen Cawnton. We can identify him. Nobody has seen him before, except his most trusted men."

I thought this over, digesting the uncomfortable implications. "But if he kills us, there'll be the devil to pay. Richard will let him know he'll be hunted down and executed when he tries to make terms."

Tom could agree with that. "He doesn't seem to be the sort of man who would let an insult pass. Even if he could do little himself, he'd make sure the authorities caught them."

"An insult?" I echoed and only just remembered to lower my voice, so nobody could overhear us. "If I were taken from him after he's let me so far in, it could kill him. It would destroy him as a person. He'd never trust anyone again, never let any tenderness in." I would have cried, had I not been so angry. Not with Tom, but with the thought anyone should hurt Richard to that extent. I remembered what he had told me on that night we spent together; how I would be the last person he lost. I didn't doubt him. My death would mean his death, too.

No one must know the power they had over Richard by holding me. I'd told Tom, but I don't think he believed the half of it. I trusted Tom not to tell anyone, but no one else must know.

I wondered what they would do now, what would be the best course to take. "What would you be doing now, Tom, if you were in your father's shoes?"

Tom had obviously been thinking along the same lines, because he answered me promptly. "I'd alert the authorities, such as they are, get a band of men together and begin to search. It seems the most sensible thing to do. I've been hoping they'll find us, but I've heard nothing, and I've been listening." So had I. "I still have no idea where we are, but they must be sure of us. I think we're in one of those places they use to hide contraband, perhaps in a barn or a cottage."

I thought hard, frowning. I saw the truth of it. "They won't know that. They don't know where we are. I wonder if I'll get my ring back?"

"I doubt it. They won't let a ruby like that go. They'll probably show your family, but keep it. It could pay for a run or two on its own."

"He said it took him some time to find it. He won't want to let them have it."

"I don't think they'll give him much choice."

We had no way of telling the time; they had taken Tom's watch and I hadn't been carrying one, but it must have been an hour or two at least before the door opened and someone stood there, silhouetted in the dazzling light outside. It was someone well dressed, someone who stared at us for some time before he stepped inside and took the chair brought in for him. It was Mr. Norrice Terry.

Chapter Nineteen

Tom and I stared at him, lost for words. A slow smile spread across his heavy features. "You weren't expecting visitors, perhaps?" he asked, his voice thick with what sounded to me like pleasure.

I said nothing. It was obvious he hadn't come to rescue us, so what was the point? Why was he here?

Terry was at ease in this room. I suspected he knew it well. The man behind him held two flintlocks trained on us, not on Mr. Terry.

He fingered the fine lace at his throat. "So how exactly did you think I raised the money to let my wife and daughter live in the style to which they've become so accustomed?"

Tom was seething, but I didn't want him to let his rage boil over. This was obvious provocation, and I wouldn't let Terry have the satisfaction of seeing my emotions. I tried with every ounce of willpower I possessed to stay cool, not to let go. "Do they know?" I asked in tones as measured as I could muster.

"My wife suspects, but as long as the money is forthcoming, she doesn't ask awkward questions. Eustacia doesn't have the least idea. Her mind is on other things."

He looked at me, considering. "She wants your lordling."

"I should be sorry to disappoint her," I replied politely, "but I'm afraid he's spoken for."

"That remains to be seen," said the fat man, sitting back at his ease. "I've promised her she shall have him."

"But the wedding's next Thursday." Tom's impulsive cry gave Terry an opening.

"Not if the bride isn't there. Don't mistake me, you were taken for purely commercial reasons, but if I can do my daughter a favour at the same time by keeping you a few days longer, then I will consider it."

"But he won't marry Eustacia." I tried desperately to think of some way to persuade him to release us.

"He might, if she was there to console him for your terrible abduction," Terry told me. "Who knows? I can only give her the chance. It's the least a man can do for his daughter." He was prepared to go that far then, to let his daughter throw herself at Richard. I supposed Terry thought, along with many other people, that Richard was undiscriminating in his tastes, that any woman would do. But the thought of missing my wedding filled me with despair, and I sank my head forward on to my knees, so Terry wouldn't see the tears.

"How long have you been in league with these people?" Tom must have seen my distress, and I realised he was trying to distract our captor.

"Since the Cawntons came and asked to use my barns. About five years, I suppose. I saw the contraband, realised how much profit could be made, and bought in. I've run the gang in conjunction with the Cawntons ever since. By the way," he added casually, "the view from here could be improved. I've had an ambition for some time now." His next statement came out of the blue. "Miss Golightly, will you do me the honour of removing your upper clothes for me? I would ask for them all, but that will come later."

I felt the colour drain from my face. He continued, speaking in the same tones he used in Martha's drawing room, as he sat back smiling greasily. I met his lascivious stare. "I thought we weren't to be touched."

Terry let his pale stare slip over my body. I felt naked already. "That was Cawnton, my dear. This is me. The first time I saw you I thought you would strip to advantage, and I'd dearly love to see if I was right." His voice hardened. "Do it."

I sat still. The man who had his guns trained on us didn't move, but a smile spread across his face. I would get no help there. Tom, next to me, sprang to his feet, and called Terry all the names he could think of, but the man watched him, and smiled.

"Sit down, Tom," Terry said, then turned back to me with a leer. "If you do this for me, my dear, I'll let you see what's happening outside. I'll wager you don't even know where you are."

The thought came to both Tom and me at the same time. "Penfold," we said in unison.

Terry smiled. "Very good. And in case you wondered, my wife, daughter and most of my household are in Exeter, preparing for your wedding and meeting as many of the great and good as they can. So, there's no one to hear your shouts. No one who cares, that is. But we're getting away from the point. I meant what I said."

He stood up and came over to where Tom sat, and deliberately hit him on the point on his head where he had been knocked out when we'd been taken. Tom fell back, and Terry kicked him hard in the groin. Tom cried out, and his face contorted in pain. Terry drew back his boot for another swing, and I cried out for him to stop. He turned to look at me, still smiling, and I undid the first hook.

He watched while I undid my bodice and loosened the fastenings, releasing the drawstring on my shift, so he could see what he wanted to. I sat with my hands in my lap and met him stare for stare, swallowing the bile that rose in my throat.

He took a long look and then sighed happily. "I knew I was right." The man behind him also stared. I felt like a curiosity of nature, but I sat still, the only expression on my face one of contempt. "When you're in my presence, I want you to appear like that. It gives me something to look at in this featureless place."

He gestured to the man, who crossed the room towards me.

For one moment, I thought he was going to lay hands on me. Listing my rank or the rank of my husband-to-be would garner nothing but derision in this place. I only had my wits and Tom to help me here. I felt sick and afraid, but he walked past me to the wall behind us.

I turned to see what the man was doing, and saw him fiddle with a catch on the floor. A section of the wall opened. Light streamed through, making me lift a hand to my eyes to shade the dazzling stream. Tom, choking from his beating, sat up by my side.

"I'll keep my promise," said our tormentor. "In half an hour I'm to receive some visitors you know well. They'll ask for my help in locating you two. I'm going to let you see them beg."

I couldn't imagine Richard and Sir George begging, but I imagined Terry would try to make them. "Turn back, my dear. I can't see you properly." I obeyed, and he delivered his next speech to my breasts. It made me uncomfortable, to say the least, but I sat still, trying not to give him any provocation either to hit Tom again or to make any move towards me.

"You can watch. But you'll have your hands tied while they're here, and Peter will hold a pistol against each of your heads. If either of you moves or makes any sound, you'll both be shot. I hope that's clear."

He waited until we'd acknowledged him, then he stood up. "I'll see you soon," he murmured, still not looking at my face. He left the room.

As soon as he'd gone I took the drawstring of my shift and pulled it tight, to cover myself again. The man with the pistols didn't stop me, but waited until I'd buttoned my jacket before he went outside and returned with another man who tied our hands behind our backs, this time with broad leather straps. I was glad they hadn't used rope again, because I still had sore, red marks on my wrists from the last time. These straps didn't cut in and hurt as much, but they held us as firmly.

He took Tom and me over to the chink in the wall, wide enough for us to see through, and made us sit. Then he left and the man called Peter came over. Cold iron pressed against my head, and I knew it for the muzzle of a pistol.

We waited in silence, Tom still labouring for breath. We said nothing, not daring to in case Terry's orders were peremptorily carried out.

We stared down into a moderately sized room, a study by the look of it. There was a window on one wall, which showed us we were at least one storey up in the house. This room must be a concealed one, accessible from the room above rather than this one, as our floor was about half way up the wall of the study. Perhaps it was an old priests' hole, or had been deliberately constructed to conceal contraband. There was a large desk in front of the window, and we watched Terry enter in and sit down. He looked up to where we watched and smiled, and then the doorbell sounded.

Within five minutes four people came in, and as they came into our field of vision we saw their unsmiling faces, their short bows to Terry. Sir George Skerrit looked haggard, his usually cheerful face drawn and white. Carier looked his usual stoical self. Richard and Gervase seemed no different. I wished I could see his eyes, see what I could read there. Had he guessed? That Carier was there indicated Thompson's' involvement, but I didn't know, couldn't guess what they planned.

"I'm extremely sorry to hear your trouble," Terry began smoothly, after they had declined any refreshment. "Have you had any word at all?"

Sir George sat heavily and drew out his kerchief. "Nothing, but I can guess what they want." I was so sorry to see him in such a state, and I knew Tom, breathing slowly beside me, was grieved to see his father so affected. His mother and sister must be beside themselves with worry. "We've searched the villages, we've asked everyone, but no one will admit to having seen them."

So far, Richard had said nothing. He toyed pensively with his snuff box, but I saw his quick glances, taking in all the details of the room. "We can only hope they will be restored to you safe and sound," said Terry. His expression would have fooled a paying audience. I had the mad desire to spit on him, but even that wasn't worth my life.

"If they're not," said Richard, speaking for the first time, "others will die."

He put the little box away, and drew something else from his pocket. He held them out, on his open palm for everybody to see. My ring, and Tom's fob.

Richard threw the ring in the air, caught it, and looked up as he did so. So close. I nearly burst. I called out to him in my mind, but he didn't see me, didn't seem to feel my presence.

Terry's heavily jowled face held an expression of mild surprise. "Really, sir, I don't think we need to get so intemperate."

"Yes we do," Richard stated. "We've been making certain enquiries on our rampage through the villages. I never hoped to find them, but I've found out certain other facts, and I've gained some counters. You'll deal with me, Terry."

Terry kept his expression of surprise. "Well, I'll do what I can, as you know I don't hold myself aloof from these people as others do—" He glanced at Sir George enquiringly.

Richard waited for the fat man's full attention. "We know you're more directly involved than that."

"You have proof of this, I presume?" drawled Terry urbanely.

"We don't need proof," Richard said, "since we don't propose to take this to the authorities."

"I'm glad to hear it." Terry leaned back in his chair, his hands steepled, his expression one of polite interest.

What would happen if I screamed? One of us would be shot, but they would hear us, and know. No, it wasn't worth the risk. That man couldn't miss. One of us would die.

"You know us, we know you," Richard said. Terry looked at him enquiringly and Richard sighed. "Very well. You and the Cawntons are in league together and you share the profits of these runs. You know my man here," he indicated Carier with a courtly gesture, and Terry bowed his head low, smiling in mockery. "He has offered to act as go-between, should this business require one."

"I shall appoint my own," Terry said.

So far, Gervase hadn't spoken, but he was looking, looking all the time. While Richard was speaking to Terry, keeping his attention, Gervase examined every part of the room from floor to ceiling. I began to pray.

"You have my property," Richard said flatly. I knew immediately that he, too, had realised what Terry would do if he knew how much I meant to him. "I want it back. In perfect condition."

"It might be a little—sullied." Terry smiled.

Richard's chest rose sharply when he took a short breath, but the expression on his face remained the same. "It would be extremely unfortunate if it were damaged in any way." His urbane tones indicated nothing. He might have been talking about anything, a piece of furniture perhaps, or a dinner service.

"Would it still be acceptable to you?" said Terry.

"It depends," was the measured reply. "What are your terms?"

Terry crossed to the sideboard beneath us and poured himself a glass of wine. The others refused when he motioned at them with the decanter. He went back to his seat and sipped. "Tomorrow night," he said eventually, when they had waited long enough, "is the biggest run of the year so far. It must not be jeopardised, and we need more resting-places than usual. You, Sir George, will provide us with what we need, and you, Lord Strang, will prevail upon Sir James—I mean, of course, Lord Hareton, to do the same. When we have moved the items away, if things go according to plan, this should be Sunday, you will get your property back. Maybe. If you don't comply, you will not see them again."

Richard sighed regretfully. "That's not acceptable."

"You'll find it is," Terry said, a little more strongly.

"No." Richard glanced at Gervase, then Carier, then back at his quarry. "We'll give you your precious run, even the storage space, but the exchange must take place on the night of the run, before the goods are brought ashore."

"Exchange?"

Richard raised a delicate eyebrow in mild surprise "You think I came here with no bargaining counters at all? Cap in hand, ready to capitulate? What guarantees will you give me that you will fulfil your side of the bargain?" He paused. "None at all. Why should I believe you?"

"You have no choice." Terry looked uncertain now.

"We have two counters you might find useful," Richard continued. "They're both called Cawnton. They have information you don't possess. We know you need them, so don't pretend not to care. How do my terms sound now?"

I wanted to clap my hands and shout "bravo!"

Terry finished his drink, frowning. "I misjudged you, my lord."

"But I didn't misjudge you, did I?" Richard said grimly. "The Cawntons brought me the tokens of proof, so I took them as well as their tokens. I can't think what possessed them to come in person, but it was a gift I took gladly." He had turned the exchange. Without a bargaining position, Terry could have killed us, and if Terry thought his secret safe, he would have done so, to keep us from talking.

"Where are they?"

"Where are your hostages?" Richard countered. Gervase still looked about, but I dared not move, dared not let out a sound. Our peephole must be cleverly concealed. His searching gaze had passed over it more than once.

Terry snorted. "The elder Cawnton wanted that ruby."

"He has a good eye." Richard flattened his palm with the ring on it, the ring that had been winking on my finger so recently. "But a little greedy, I think. We'll restore them to you, if you bring my property. We can make this exchange and then we'll go, and you'll have what you want."

"What proof will I have you won't welsh on the bargain?"

Richard shrugged. "None at all, except my word. And the word of the men you've known for many years, Sir George here and Lord Hareton. Our bargain applies to this run only, you understand."

"Of course," Sir George agreed. I thought he could have used a glass of the wine, he looked so worried and upset. My heart went out to him in his distress, forgetting my own concerns in compassion.

"One more thing." Richard looked Terry directly in the eye. "Understand, this is between you and me, Terry, and no one else. If my property is damaged in any way, I shall take advantage of the kind offer your daughter is proposing to me. Lady Hareton has been hard put to it to keep her out of the house this last two days, but apart from one interesting exchange, she has prevailed." I heard Gervase's sharp intake of breath. "Pale, stupid maidens never appealed to me. I prefer the dazzlers. So your daughter will not even have the bliss she tells me she'll achieve in my arms. However, everyone will think I have obliged her. After the stories begin to circulate, no one will touch her again, I promise you, and any social pretensions she might have will be ruined forever." The fashionable exquisite had gone, to be replaced by a man only two people in that room had seen before. And one hidden spectator. "I know she's panting to get me into her bed. I can't turn around without the damned chit drooling over me. When I spread the stories about her lascivious behaviour with me—entirely fabricated, of course—then no one will receive her again."

"If you take advantage of my daughter," said Terry urbanely, "you will marry her."

"No I won't." Richard met his stare. "I will marry Rose Golightly. She is mine, my property, I have bought and paid for her and she brings me advantages Eustacia can't hope to better." His cold demeanour fooled everyone but me, Gervase and Carier. Even Sir George stared at him in horror. "I'm the son of one of the wealthiest and most influential peers in the country. You can never aspire to our power. I'm also a rake, a

libertine, or didn't you know that? It won't affect my reputation
in the least, it will be just another of Strang's cynical conquests
but it will harm poor Eustacia."

After a moment, Terry lowered his gaze. "You sir," he said
to his desk, "are a scoundrel."

Richard laughed, but shortly, without any real amusement.
"Worse than that, as you may have cause to know before too
long. We have concluded our business here. We'll see you at the
cliff tops tomorrow night. What time would be convenient to
you?"

"Nine o'clock."

"We'll be there." Richard glanced at Gervase, who shook his
head slightly. They went out of the room, and left Terry in his
chair, sunk in thought.

I felt bereft. It was one of the worst things I had ever done,
not to cry out, when every fibre of my being was longing to do
just that.

The man Terry had called Peter kept his guns on our head
until we heard the slam of the front door, and the trot of horses'
hooves up the drive. Then, without a word, he released our
hands from the confining straps and left the room. We heard
the outer bolts driven home.

Tom and I moved away, and sat in the centre of the room,
holding each other for comfort. I shook. My recent ordeal and
then seeing Richard so close and not being able to call out to
him undermined any self-control I had left. Tom was still
recovering from the beating he'd received, so we sat, cuddling
each other like children for at least half an hour. We might have
wept a little.

At last Tom spoke. "I'm sorry, Rose. I should have gone
away when Strang told me to."

"Once you'd thought it over, you would have, but they
didn't give you a chance." I straightened up.

With the extra light from the peephole I saw him more
clearly—the marks on his face, the rope burns on his wrists. I
lifted my arms and examined at my own wrists, similarly

marked. "They won't have gone by next Thursday," I said, trying for some levity. It worked to a small extent.

"You'll have to look for some extra lace ruffles," Tom replied. "And I know how much you hate shopping." I grinned. He knew nothing of the kind.

"Don't you think," Tom said reflectively, "that Strang may be walking into a trap tomorrow night? Do you really think Terry will let us go that easily, before he's rid himself of the contraband?"

I remembered a fact that didn't come out in that little conversation downstairs, and it gave me comfort. "I don't think he has any such intention. But Richard knows it." I lowered my voice, and moved closer to him. "There's something I can't tell you now, Tom, not because I don't trust you, but because I don't know who's listening, but we'll be quite safe once we get to that cliff top." I leaned back and Tom nodded, showing me he understood. "Promise me you won't try anything before then. We'll come off all right."

Tom nodded. "Though it goes against the grain to do it. What he did to you, and what he's done to my father, and God knows how my mother and Georgie are—" He broke off, his hand to his forehead. I went to get a drink and let him be.

Chapter Twenty

They left us alone until the following evening, as the daylight began to fade. Tom and I had spent most of the time sleeping, and waiting. I found it helped me enormously to know where we were. I felt more heartened, trying to cheer up an ever more dejected Tom.

Terry failed to appear. I believed he'd taken Richard's threat seriously and would trouble me no more. I didn't want to imagine what Richard would do if Terry raped me.

When the door opened, Tom and I sat next to each other. The chair was brought in and Terry sat down heavily. He stared at me pointedly. "Come on then," he said, roughly. I sat still. "Do it, or I'll hurt him again." He waved a casual hand in Tom's direction.

Sighing, I did as he demanded, despite Tom's pleas for me not to. I had no wish to cause my friend any more hurt, and it seemed a small thing to me, if a distasteful one. It didn't help. I sat next to Tom and watched as Terry got to his feet and walked over to him. First, he struck his head as he had before and then he kicked him in the groin, in an almost detached manner. Tom lay groaning, doubled up with the pain, and I made a move to go and help him.

Terry turned his back on Tom, returned to his chair. "Come here."

I stared at him, debating whether it was worth defying him, but when I saw the expression on his face, I got up and went to stand before him. My stomach turned over, but I was determined he wouldn't see my terror.

There was no mercy anywhere about him. He pulled me down to sit on his lap, and then laid his filthy hands on me. "Very good," he grunted. I stared back, unmoving, feeling those clammy, meaty hands in the places he had no right to be. I called on all my training, everything I'd learned from Richard and Martha to keep my face impassive. He might abuse my body, but I wouldn't let him see how much this hurt me, how devastating this attack was. And my fear of what was to come.

"I went into Exeter last night," he remarked, his hands busy tweaking, pinching, trying to get a reaction, "to see my wife and daughter. And do you know what my little angel told me?"

"I can guess," I replied coldly, trying to keep the tremor out of my voice. Oh no. Eustacia had told him what she knew of Richard and me. I prayed she hadn't told her father of our affection for each other, only the fact that we were lovers.

"You're not the ice maiden I took you for, are you?"

He was so close his smell rose to attack my nostrils, all sweat and bad breath. "My daughter heard some interesting things in that room the night of the Assembly. Though why a man would want to marry a woman he's already taken beats me." He squeezed a nipple hard, and I caught my breath on the pain. "You'll have to get used to that sort of thing. Whores have to put up with a lot worse, you know. Do you know what I'm going to do with you?"

I didn't give him the satisfaction of a reply. He continued to talk without one. He watched me the whole time he spoke. "Skerrit can go back tonight, but I'm not letting you go. Not yet." All the time he talked he pinched and squeezed, seeming to get satisfaction from my pain and humiliation. I put all my effort into keeping my face calm and clear, trying to forget my body belonged to me. "I need a hostage until Sunday at least. I don't place any faith in promises, least of all your little lordling's. But I can do something I've wanted to do for years." He gazed at me, let his attention drift to my lips, my breasts, licked his thick lips with an equally thick tongue. "I'm going to bring you back here, strip you and take you. Then I'm going to give you to anyone who wants you. There's plenty who'll want a piece of a fine lady like you. I doubt if Strang'll want you after what I'll do to you."

Oh God, he would ruin me. Anything Richard and I shared would always have this taint, even if Richard still wanted me after this. Terry continued to taunt me with his hands and his voice, "Two birds with one stone, you might say. It'll give my Eustacia a chance and I can take my fun at the same time. I don't know how it is, but I've always liked to watch."

He reached down, and his gaze lustful on my face, fumbled his way under my skirts. I went rigid with horror and terror. I knew what he meant to do, and I couldn't think of any way to stop him. He was going to rape me now. I closed my eyes, forcing myself to stay calm, not to react in any way.

I couldn't let him hurt Tom any more, and there was no one else here to help me. In desperation my gaze went to the man who stood behind the chair, a different one to the one earlier. He stared at me, his tongue between the few teeth he had left, his pistols trained on Tom. There was no help there.

Tom didn't take this in silence. He sat up again, heedless of any danger to himself. "Leave her alone, Terry. Lord Strang will kill you for this. Think of your daughter."

Terry smirked. "He can't do much damage for all his fine words, and when he finds out what I've done, he'll think twice about wedding this one, and turn somewhere else."

"Didn't your daughter tell you? He loves her. He'll kill you." My heart sank. Tom had put a weapon in his hands.

Terry paused in his disgusting behaviour, and gave Tom his attention. "I don't believe that. Didn't you notice yesterday? When he thought she couldn't hear, he called her his property. That's what she means to him. One breeding machine's as good as another. He might keep this one for fun, but there's a chance for my Eustacia. It's up to her what she does with it. Besides, if he does keep Rose, I'll know I've been there too, every time I look at her. And so will he."

I closed my eyes, and then opened them again. It was worse with them shut. It concentrated my attention on the senses of touch and smell. Terry's rank body odour, together with the feel of his filthy hands on me made bile rise to my throat.

Tom moved to stand up, murder in his eyes, pushing at me to get off his lap. At the same point my body did the deed for me. I was sick, horribly sick, all over Terry and me. It happened so quickly he didn't have time to avoid it, and I took good care to ensure he received as much as I could give him.

Norrice Terry stood up, let me fall to the floor, and cried out, "Whore! Bitch! My new leather breeches, too!" I fell in my own filth, broken, feeling I couldn't sink much lower. He stormed out, leaving me there, and his man followed him, leaving us in the semi darkness we had become accustomed to.

"Rose!" Unhesitatingly Tom lifted me out of the mess and took me in his arms. He let me cry, and he stripped off my soiled clothing for me. I lay in his arms unresisting, sobbing my heart out. This only delayed the inevitable outcome. Terry would make it worse for me now.

By some miracle my shift had escaped the deluge. Tom pulled it up to cover me and fastened the drawstring securely. His stream of invective while he ministered to me would have shamed a sailor, but I let it wash over me. It wasn't directed at me.

When the door opened again, I clutched Tom in alarm, but it was only one of our guards. He dumped a bowl of water down on the floor, and threw a bundle of clothes after it. "He says you're to change," he told us, and left. We heard the bolts shoot home, but this for once brought me relief. It meant Terry wasn't coming back.

I blew my nose and wiped my eyes, then got up and sorted through the clothes. They were probably a maid's by the look of them, but clean. I found an unmarked part of one of my petticoats and Tom tore it up for me to use as a washcloth.

I felt no shame when I slipped my shift over my head, but

Tom turned his head away and gave me some privacy while I washed away all trace of the vomit, and what was worse, Terry's hands. This time they had brought some soap, sweet-smelling ladies' soap. Eustacia's, perhaps. Among the many marks now adorning my flesh, Terry had left a thumb-shaped bruise, on the side of my left breast. I examined it and decided it wouldn't show over my wedding gown. I no longer knew if the ceremony would take place, but I had to behave as if it would. My whole body felt as though it didn't belong to me any more, sore from Terry's fumbles and hurts.

Tom helped me to dress once I was in the clean shift, pulling the stay laces tight for me and fastening some of the tapes at the back. I had to instruct him, as he wasn't at all handy with ladies' clothes. It forced me to think of Richard again, how nimbly he could help me to dress, but I pushed the thought aside, fearing it would weaken me. Once I was decent again in the skirt and caraco jacket I'd been provided with, I sat down on the hard, wooden floor. I took down my hair and combed it until it was silky in an effort to get all traces of the man off me.

Putting myself back in order my mood changed, from black despair to cold, hard anger. If I got away, this would not go unpunished. Fury would have been easier to cope with; this went deeper, searing its way through to an unbreakable resolution.

Tom had not ventured to speak for a while; probably trying to get back his equilibrium. When he did, he sounded colder than I'd ever heard him, even angrier than he'd been before. "When we're out of this, I'll kill him."

I'd already made up my mind to it. "No, I will. No one will look at me and gloat like he'll be able to."

"Do you want Lord Strang to know? I won't tell him if you don't want me to." I stared at Tom, realising how far away he was from understanding. There was no point in arguing. He had never heard me like that, because I could never remember being so shaky, so upset, or so determined.

"Yes. He has to know."

"Won't it—won't he feel—"

"Soiled goods? I hope not. I'll take the chance. There'll be nothing between us, no secrets. We promised." I couldn't live with that locked inside me, it would have been a betrayal.

Tom paused, biting his lip. "You know what Terry said—about you—" He broke off. "Never mind."

"I won't have to, will I?" I snapped, still angry. "It seems the whole world and his wife knows something that is no business of anyone else's. Yes, I'm Richard's mistress, I've been his mistress for the past six months."

"Rose!" If I hadn't been so angry Tom's expression of shocked propriety would have made me laugh. It did help to assuage my mood.

I worked furiously on the knots in my hair. "If you ask me if it's wise, I'll hit you, I swear I will. We were too much in love to wait, at least I was. I'm getting married next Thursday, and I want you there to dance with me." I wasn't sure any more, but to doubt it to anyone else would have been a betrayal.

I flung the hair back over my shoulder so I could look at Tom. He watched me, smiling now. "I'll be there."

"And what," I demanded, my anger fading, "is so amusing?"

"You are," he answered softly, still smiling at me despite our troubles. "Strang's woken something in you. I've never known you like this; you've never been this determined, this sure of yourself. It suits you."

"Thank you, kind sir." I bowed my head graciously, and sat down again to pin my hair up and put on the cap provided.

Time must have been getting on, for as I was finishing my toilet, the door opened again and Peter came back in. He flicked a contemptuous glance at us. "Time to go." He motioned us out of the room with one of his pistols.

It was getting dark, but we still found the light dazzlingly bright when we stepped out of our prison. Another man waited in the little landing outside. He jammed a pistol into my back, urging me to climb a steep set of stairs.

We emerged in what I assumed must be the servants' quarters. The floor was covered with cheap drugget, the whitewashed walls decorated with a few cheap prints. I studied where I was, to find it again if needed. I saw Tom following, the second man behind him.

They took us down to the ground floor and out to the courtyard where several mounted men waited, with horses ready saddled. A heavy, drab travelling cloak was thrown over my shoulders by an unseen hand.

First Tom was put up in front of a villainous-looking man, armed to the teeth. Then Terry reached a hand down and dragged me up to sit in front of him. I would rather have chosen Tom's ride, but I wasn't given the choice.

"It would be madness to try anything foolish," Terry murmured in my ear. "We're taking you to be exchanged. Sadly, I need the Cawnton brothers back. But you will amuse me during the journey, and warm my bed tonight. I shall taunt him with you and take you back."

We set off. Once we were past the gates, the horses settled into a trot and Terry began to fondle me again. I'd tried to make sure my clothes were securely fastened, but he managed to find his way inside. I said nothing, but when he tried to kiss my mouth I turned my head away

He laughed. "I can do without that. Just think—every time your lordling does this—" he tweaked my nipple painfully, "you can think of me." I still said nothing. Any response would probably incite him to do worse. I wanted him to die. "I might let someone else taste your bounties. When I've finished with you. As long as I can watch."

Despite my good intentions, I shuddered. He smiled. "I'm sure you'll come to love it. But you won't have to spend much longer with me. Just long enough to ensure your people don't do anything foolish. You'd already worked that out, hadn't you?" I nodded, but looked away so he wouldn't see my tears. I knew Richard would do something, but I was still afraid. I still had my little fruit knife, and I would plunge it into his heart if I had the chance, but I didn't think, with all his avoirdupois, it would reach that far.

It seemed much longer than usual before we reached the coast, but soon I smelled the tangy sea air, strong and salty, and saw the birds on their nests in the cliffs. We rode to the edge, and Terry dismounted, pulled me down after him and threw the reins to an acolyte. I made out six figures by the cliff edge. They stood still as we approached them. Terry's gripped my waist, holding me close to his loathsome body.

Only the sea breeze ruffled their clothes as they stood completely still, waiting for us. James, Sir George, Carier and Richard, who held the Cawnton Tom and I had met before. Carier held the other. They stood motionless. Richard stared at us expressionlessly, colourlessly while Tom and I were brought to the front. Terry had brought five men with him, and they stood behind him, armed to the teeth. One held a gun at Tom's back.

We stood in silence. Richard avoided my eyes and I knew why. He didn't want to reveal his distress before these people. Anything like that might weaken his resolve, show vulnerability he wouldn't want to display.

"We're here to take our property back," he said, looking straight at Terry.

"Here it is," the fat man replied jauntily. "Safe and sound." He gave me a little shake, but I didn't respond.

"Miss Golightly first," said Richard.

"No," said Terry. "You can have the boy first."

When he nodded the man who held Tom released him, and gave him a little shove. "I'm not going without Rose," Tom protested mulishly.

"Go, Tom," I said.

Richard's head snapped around to me. I don't know what he heard in my voice, but for the first time, his gaze met mine. Hard, icy. I had to stop myself from calling out his name and running forward. Then I saw he was trying to tell me something.

He gave a tiny gesture with his hand, and I understood what he wanted me to do. He knew Terry wouldn't play fair.

Tom moved forward slowly, and crossed the few yards between the two groups. He went and stood by his father. I saw Sir George's hand reach out and touch him, but other than that they stayed still, watching Terry and me.

In response, Richard let his man go, freeing his hands for whatever he had planned. Cawnton strolled across the divide and stood behind Terry. He winked at me as he passed. He looked almost wholesome next to his loathsome backer. I swallowed, waiting.

"Now Rose," said Richard steadily.

Terry sounded conversational, as though they were sitting in Martha's drawing room. "I'm not sure I want to remain entirely without hostages to your good conduct. I might hold on to Rose until next—Sunday, say? Besides, I've not quite finished with her yet."

"What do you say, my love?" Richard looked at me, his tones calm, and unemotional, despite the endearment.

I kept my voice steady, emulating his. "I would like to come home, please."

"You heard the lady," Richard said, quiet and steady. An element of menace entered his voice, something rarely heard in the fashionable drawing rooms of London.

"You can keep your hostage as a token of good faith. I'll keep my charming guest." Terry had one of the Cawntons now, so perhaps he could make do without the other one. He would use me until he was bored with me, and then he would get rid of me.

Richard sighed regretfully. "No, I can't allow that."

He turned around, and when he turned back, he was armed. His sword seemed to have come from nowhere. I guessed it had been speared in the ground behind him. Still without any expression in his voice, he said, "Now."

I dropped to the ground and heard the clash of steel behind me. Rolling over the wet grass, I saw at least eight men who had certainly not been there before, coming steadily up behind Terry and his men. They rushed forward, swords drawn. These weren't dress swords, they were cutlasses and sabres, pointing at the back of every man behind me.

They had been standing on the ledge, that ledge Tom and I had played on when we'd brought the others here that day.

I scrambled to my feet and ran. Richard held out his hand as I reached him and pulled me to his side. "Are you hurt?"

"Yes, but not badly. I'll tell you later."

He searched my face, and I saw the anguish he had been through. He released me, then turned back to Terry. "Our business here is done for the time being. You may go."

At Richard's curt nod, his men dropped the points of their weapons. Terry saw he was outnumbered. I didn't think this would stop a madman like him. I was right.

"This is *my* territory." Terry glared at Richard, angry beyond reason, balked of his prey. "No-one tells me what I can do here."

He drew a gun from his belt and fired as he drew it, but his attitude had warned us of his intentions and Richard leapt to one side while I dropped to the ground. All at once the ordered scene turned into a general melée. The sound of guns firing mixed with the clash of steel as they turned on each other.

I stayed on the ground, picked up the pistol Terry had cast aside and laid about me as best I could with the heavy butt end. I managed to trip a few. I shouted but my voice was lost in the cacophony of male cries. In the confusion I wasn't entirely sure the people I hit were all on the other side, so I made myself stop. I watched the action going on about me, ready to intervene if I could help. Striking out had helped me lose some of the anger I'd bottled up for days.

Tom had acquired a sword from somewhere and was up at the front, fighting to get through to Terry, who had retreated, his men closing about him. Terry had a hand to his arm, and then I saw the gleam of steel at his shoulder. I wasn't sure what had happened until I saw it again; a flash of steel as a thrown knife embedded itself in the back of one of Terry's protective bodyguard. Richard, his sword stuck into the grass in front of him, had a handful of knives. He threw them with beautiful accuracy. Either he wanted to keep Terry alive or his target had moved at the last moment, because the knife buried itself in Terry's right shoulder. The big man bellowed in pain, but he managed, under the cover of the fighting, to run back to where the horses were tethered. He scrambled on the back of one of them. He whipped it up and galloped away, not back inland, but down towards the coastal path that led to the beach.

Terry's men dispersed, leaving us in possession of the high ground. Those of his men who could headed for the beach, around to the side of the cove, scrambling down the steep, perilous path.

One man lay dead, a knife in his back, and another had a cut to his leg, which bled profusely. I didn't feel inclined to help him, but someone must have done. When I took any notice of him again, the wound was tied up and he was sitting at a distance, propped against a tree.

I sat up and brushed myself down with a trembling hand. Richard's arm went about my shoulders as he sat by me. I leaned against him gratefully, but I knew there was something between us, something I had to tell him. Not now, though. Safe at last I felt a strong desire to sleep, but I fought it off, looked up at him, and tried to smile.

He looked bright, alive, excited by the recent action, but in control. He leaned down to kiss me but stopped, and studied me closely. "What happened?" His face clouded with concern. "What did he do to you?"

Tom was sitting on my other side by now. He glanced at me when he heard these words, troubled. "Do you want me to tell him?"

"Thank you, Tom, no. I'll tell him myself, but not here, not now."

"Dear God." Richard guessed some of it. I waited for him to draw away from him. Instead he held me closer. "I'll kill him."

"No," I said calmly, "I will."

He stared at me, startled. "You will tell me."

"Yes I will. But not now."

He frowned, but let it rest. I was too tired and this was too public a place for me to tell him what I needed to.

James came to us, and I showed him a smiling face. I assured him I was perfectly well and none the worse for my ordeal. I had no desire to let everyone know how much I'd been used and humiliated, and I didn't want Terry lynched by vengeful males. I wanted to be there to do it myself. Richard might allow that. James certainly wouldn't.

For the first time since we arrived, I looked out to sea. Smugglers usually preferred a moonless night, but not these people—the moon was full and bright. When the neighbourhood was as much in thrall as Darkwater, concealment gave way to the convenience of visibility.

I saw the bulk of a ship on the horizon, surrounded by the gentle waves of the bay, glinting in the moonlight. The rowboats pulling away from the shore made smaller shadows. On the beach below us, men were active—at least thirty of them at a rough count. They pushed the small boats away, got hurdles ready to drag the goods up the beach and stood guard against anyone foolish enough to oppose them.

"Watch," said Richard. I leaned my head on his shoulder and watched, as if it was an entertainment put on for us, the audience on the cliffs.

I saw the shadow of a small boat, not pulling out from this beach but from another cove, further along the bay. There seemed to be another behind it, but I couldn't be sure.

The little vessel approached the ship, reaching it before the others did. It must have travelled a shorter distance or set off first.

Before it reached the ship, several tiny figures dived over the side of the boat. They headed for the small dot towed behind it, which must be a much smaller vessel, cut it free, and headed back to their cove. The larger boat in front was now unmanned.

The smugglers' rowboats were beginning to draw level with the ship, ready to unload the contraband, but as we watched, the night was rent by a low, ominous boom. On the ship, a great tongue of orange flame shot up to the sky. It caught on one of the sails, sent it up like a torch, spreading along the masts quicker than anything that could be done against it.

"Gervase is an excellent sailor," Richard said. "All I had to do was set the explosive and show him where the slow match went."

Tom dragged his eyes from the scene in front of him to stare at Richard incredulously. Up until now, he had seen Richard as a town dandy, a pretty boy who'd taken my fancy, but not any more. Richard met his astonished stare calmly, great satisfaction in his limpid gaze. "Did you really think I could let them run roughshod over your father and Lord Hareton? And me? They can't profit from what they've done, I simply couldn't allow it." He turned back to the spectacle out at sea. "I've spoken to Cawnton, who seems a reasonable man for a criminal, and reminded him of the downfall of the Hawkhurst gang further up the coast. He'll see sense. From what I've seen, Terry won't." His attention went back to the spectacle in front of us. "We'll deal with him in due course."

I didn't care right now. Fatigue washed over me, and the scene in front seemed unreal, part of a dream. The ship was well alight. Its crew hurled themselves overboard in an attempt to reach the rowboats, heading back to land with all speed.

On the beach, all was chaos. Some men moved about, obviously directing the others, and they dragged the rowboats up the beach, giving no heed to the plight of the crew of the ship, trying to conceal the evidence of their presence now the run had been so obviously aborted.

Richard sighed in satisfaction and stood. "We should leave now. Some of those people may think of revenge, and we could do with a head start."

Everyone looked up, waking as if they had just watched a particularly spellbinding theatrical performance. They started to get to their feet.

Richard turned to the eight men who had been recruited for the evening, presumably from the households hereabouts. I wondered how many dinner parties were a footman short tonight. "Thank you, gentlemen. You'll receive your bonus in the usual way." He shook hands with all of them and they left quietly, after collecting their weapons. One of them pulled the knife out of the back of the dead man, cleaned it on the grass and returned it. Richard took it with a smile of thanks and put it back in his pocket.

He turned to help me up, finding me almost asleep, my chin on my knees. He would have lifted me, but I roused myself and took his outstretched hand. We went to the trees, where several horses were tethered, peacefully grazing in the moonlight. Richard mounted, and said to James behind me, "I don't think Rose is in any condition to ride. I'll take her." It said a lot for his commanding presence that James didn't demur. Instead, my brother gave me a boost while Richard lifted me, and settled me in front of him.

For a moment, I roused, reminded of that nightmare ride with Terry earlier. I sat up straight, and stared at Richard in terror, but I wasn't so far gone I couldn't recognise his face. He met my eyes and flinched, but drew me close. I sank gratefully against him again, and let him wrap me in his travelling cloak. I felt his warmth and took comfort from the gentle words he murmured to me. "Nothing will hurt you now, my love, I'm here, I'll never let you go again," were the tenor of them, exactly what I needed to hear at that moment. Soothed by his words and the gentle movement of the walking horse, I fell sound asleep.

Chapter Twenty-One

I don't know what time we got home, or who put me to bed, but I woke once in the night, stirred and heard a female voice; Martha's, saying, "Go back to sleep, dear. You're safe now." Childlike I obeyed, recognising my own bed. I didn't wake again until the day was well advanced.

The maid came in, saw me and smiled. She bent to light the fire. "Her ladyship says you must rest today, my lady. I'll fetch you some breakfast." I hadn't realised I was hungry until I smelled the hot chocolate on the tray she brought, but I got up, wincing at some of the bruises when I caught them, put on my wrapper, and went to sit by the fire.

I still sat there, my hands wrapped around the warm cup, lost in thought when the door opened and Richard came in. He was fully dressed in his usual style as though he had been to the coffeehouse for an hour, not up all night fighting gangs of free traders.

I was overjoyed, but surprised by his presence in my room. "Martha let you in here?" I asked in amazement.

"Lady Hareton is in bed. She sat up with you all night," he replied, crossing the room to me. "I, on the other hand, slept well. Your brother thinks your maid is here, but I've sent her away."

"Thompson's?" I asked, meaning the maid.

"No, just a good tip." He bent to kiss me good morning, then dropped into the chair opposite mine. "Which reminds me. I've sent to the agency for a maid for you. I hope you don't mind. If you don't like her, you can always send her away, but between ourselves, she's not just the best lady's maid I can find—she has skills in other areas. She'll look after you."

"A bodyguard?" I gazed at him over the chocolate cup. His image shimmered in the steam. He wore blue today, almost the same colour as my wedding dress.

"In a way. Much as Carier serves me. Her name is Adele Nichols. I had to steal her from someone else, but when she heard who it was for, she came willingly."

I sighed. "I'm sure she'll be fine." I didn't really think about it for the time being. I only had one thing on my mind; how to tell him what had been done to me, and what might have been done. Terry would be doing it now if I hadn't broken away, I realised, and despite the warm day and the glowing fire, I shuddered in repulsion.

Richard saw, of course, and leaned towards me, his tone softly tranquil. "You said you'd tell me what was done to you. If you'd rather not, if you can't relive it or you don't want to tell me, we'll leave it alone."

His statement took my breath away. How I loved his concern, his thought for me, and his trust. For all he knew Terry could have raped me already. I could even be carrying his child. But I had to be fair, I had to show Richard, give him the choice. Besides, if I kept it from him, if we were still to be married next week, Richard would find out when he saw my poor abused body on Thursday night. Decisively, I got up from the chair and put down my cup.

My bedroom looked out over the gardens at the back of the house, from two long windows. I opened the shutters out on the right side of one and the left side of the other, thus creating a screen so nobody could see me from outside.

I didn't look at Richard as I dropped the wrapper on the floor and lifted the night-rail over my head.

I stood still, I don't know for how long, and then I dared to glance across to where he sat. It must be obvious what had been done to me. I didn't need to explain once he'd seen the clusters of red pinches and bruises, some of them now darkening to blue, concentrated in the most private parts of my body.

I saw I was right. It needed no explanation. I bent, retrieved my night-rail, and slipped it back on with shaking hands.

White-faced he rose, came across the room, and helped me back into my wrapper. Then he took me into his arms and I rested my head on his shoulder. I let myself cry then, the first time I had allowed myself any self-pity. He stood, holding me in silence until I had myself under control again. He said nothing. There was no need.

We went back to the fire, where he saw me seated before he went into my dressing room, and returned with a damp cloth and a towel. He carefully wiped my face clean of the tears, and gave me the towel afterwards, then took them away again, and came back to resume his seat.

I broke the silence. "It was all Terry. Except the rope burns on my wrists; they were from when we were first taken. He beat Tom until I did what he wanted. He didn't rape me, Richard, although he planned to." If I hadn't been looking I would have missed Richard's slow indrawn breath, a sign that he was fighting to retain control of himself.

I told him everything. I explained Tom's despair, my forced compliance. I spared him nothing, although I dearly wanted to. It was the first time I'd felt any protective instincts towards Richard, the need to spare him, but I knew he had to know now, before any of it had time to fester, or he heard from anywhere else. He listened, still and silent, his elbows on the arms of his chair, his chin resting on his linked hands, pale and grim faced.

When I finished, silence fell once more. I heard the sounds of normal domestic activities over the house, so normal, and I felt at peace for the first time in days. Whatever he decided, nothing was hidden between us. I watched him assimilate what I'd just told him, wondering what his reaction would be, if he would still feel the same about me, whether this would come between us, as Terry had intended it to.

"My poor love," he said after a long time. "I should have thought more clearly. If I hadn't taken the Cawntons, perhaps Terry wouldn't have come near you." He swore softly. "And my damned temper drove him to take you, too. If I hadn't taunted his daughter he might not have taken you, either."

I tried to find reasons for Terry's vicious behaviour. Richard's manner to his daughter didn't excuse abduction. "He seemed eager to get involved in everything. We were held at his house. He wanted to show us how powerful he was, how much under his control we were."

Richard dropped his head into his hands, but when he looked back at my face his eyes were clear, if a little bright, and his face smooth. "I could kill him for this. For what he did, and what he might have done to you."

"Revenge?" I didn't want Richard to sully his soul by doing this. I would not let him do it, because I knew how much his principles meant to him.

"Not entirely. Though that will add spice to the encounter. Terry is a smuggler, and he will be brought to justice. There's no escape for him, we have too many witnesses, too much evidence. If he is tried and convicted, his property will be forfeit to the Crown. His wife, his daughter, all his dependants will be left destitute and the whole district will become notorious."

My brother and Sir George would have to take part in the trial, as witnesses. Nobody won. "So if Terry dies before the trial—"

"Before the authorities come for him..."

I nodded. "I shan't dissuade you. Not this time. I won't bring any discredit to you, and he would make sure ugly rumours were spread. He's seen my body, he knows the natural marks on it and he knows enough to make it believable. That's why I want him dead. Only I want to be there. I want to see it, perhaps even do it myself."

"It's your right, if you wish it. Only, understand if you take a man's life in cold blood it saps some of your humanity, makes you a little harder. Is it worth it?" He watched me intently.

"Yes." I met his direct gaze without a qualm. "I didn't know how vile a person could be until Wednesday. That took away some of my humanity, and forced me to understand a lot more than I ever wanted to. I want this."

"It will have to be soon. Monday perhaps." He still watched me carefully. I could show him no doubts.

I was sure. "Yes, I know, I'll be ready."

I felt the side of my cup to see if my chocolate was still warm enough to drink. It was, so I picked it up and drank, then replaced the empty cup with a sharp click. "Richard?"

"Yes?"

I knew what I wanted to do regarding Terry, but I also knew what he had done to me might put barriers between us, might repulse another man. I didn't think I could bear it. "I don't know how to phrase this. It might be clumsy, excuse me if it doesn't come out right, but..." I paused, trying to find the words, and then gave up, and blurted it out, "Does this make any difference? To us? I mean—can you still want me as you did before?" I stopped, not knowing how else to put it to him. "If you don't want me any more, say so now, and I'll make it easy for you. I'll cry off."

His face darkened. He rose from his chair in one swift movement, crossed to me, and dragged me to my feet. If I had doubted him before, his kiss put all my doubts to rest. Needy, more desperately passionate, he consumed me, burned all Terry's vile touches from my body.

"Blame you for what that bastard did to you?" he murmured, his arms tight about me. "I should sooner blame myself. No, my sweet life, on Thursday next I shall kiss every one of those bruises, do my best to help you to forget there has ever been anyone else there but me." I had to believe him, and the thought of it thrilled me, sent shivers of desire through me. "This changes nothing between us, unless it's altered you."

I shook my head, pulled him down again for another kiss, and then I rested my forehead on his shoulder, dizzy with relief.

"Some men might—oh, I don't know. Only you didn't seem to want to touch me."

"I was too angry, too horrified. Why anyone should want to do that to a woman passes my understanding, much more so because it was you." He kissed the top of my head. "Though I must say I hadn't thought of vomit as a weapon before."

I laughed, despite the memory of that vile room and its owner, and he smiled at me. "Come, that's better. Don't let it defeat you, think ahead. On Monday we kill someone, and on Thursday we marry."

Said like that it seemed unreal, both events so removed from normal existence. I felt lighter, as if a burden had gone from me. I remembered my friend who had shared the ordeal with me. "Do you know how Tom is?"

"His father took him home and said he would put him straight to bed. From what you've said he took quite a beating, but he'll recover."

"He's promised to dance at my wedding," I said quietly, almost to myself. I hadn't told Richard that part—what Tom had said in that little room. I don't even know if I believed it myself now, after so much had happened to us.

He pushed me gently down into my chair again and sat opposite me. "I should never have taken the Cawntons. And that reminds me—" He reached into his pocket and brought out my betrothal ring. He leaned forward to slip it back on my finger, smiled, kissed my hand and leaned back once more.

I looked at the ring and felt all was right again, back in its place, while Richard told me something of his experience. "When the Cawntons came to see us, we didn't want to believe it at first. They showed us your ring, and Tom's fob, and explained it was purely business and no harm would come to you if their demands were met. It was too good to be true— Cawnton came to the house with only his brother for company, trusting in our positions as gentlemen." He gave a sharp laugh. "Idiots. So we took them. When I talked to him he seemed a reasonable man, and I have every hope with Terry out of the way, he'll manage matters much better, with far less violence. He knows what happened to the Hawkhurst gang when they became too violent—" He saw my frown. "No? Well, they found themselves a new leader, and he turned out a brute, ruling by terror, so the authorities found they couldn't ignore him any more. The gang was crushed inside six months."

"Were you—Thompson's involved in any way?"

"Us? No—well, perhaps in a small way." He laughed shortly. "I try not to interfere unless I'm asked. Thompson's may have been in a position to provide the authorities with some information, that's all. But Cawnton knew about it, and he's seen sense. It's the best we can hope for until the business of smuggling is dealt with in Parliament. From your description, Terry seems much more unreasonable. My only excuse is I didn't know how unreasonable he was, how arrogant he had become."

"Did you know he was involved, then?"

"I had enquiries in train when you were taken. He has quite a few Thompson's men in his household, so getting information was easy." He paused. "His wife has delusions of grandeur, of moving in high society. That can be expensive, and may be what drove him to the easy profits he could make from smuggling."

"I don't think so, or not entirely. He thrives on power, on control. It must have been pleasant for him to know he controlled the supply of so many things to people. Whether they knew it or not they were beholden to him."

There was a knock on the door and Lizzie came in. She paused on the threshold as she saw us, and to my surprise, she burst out laughing. "You look like an old married couple, sitting discussing the day's events. Where's the maid?"

Richard grinned. "I sent her away." He got up to offer Lizzie his seat. She declined and sat on the sofa at the foot of the bed, so he resumed his seat. "I needed a private word with Rose."

Lizzie looked at him sharply. "More plans, sir? You're as full of plots as our garden these days."

He laughed. It was good to hear. "It's my nature."

"I only came to see how you were," Lizzie said to me, "but you look much better."

"You saw me last night?" I couldn't remember.

She nodded before she shot Richard another look. "Yes, I've seen the marks," he said. "Rose showed me."

Lizzie's face settled into unaccustomed, stern lines. "Martha and I saw them, but nobody else."

I shrugged. "I'm fine. Only bruises. And no."

I answered her unspoken question and her face relaxed when she understood. I hadn't been raped. "I helped to put you to bed. Strang said you had slept most of the way home, and you were so pale. And where did you get those dreadful clothes?"

"I was sick on my brown riding habit," I told her bluntly.

Richard smiled. "It's about the only good to come out of the whole unsavoury affair. I never liked that riding habit. Brown isn't the best colour for Rose."

"I always told her so," Lizzie agreed.

I let them talk. I found a piece of toast to eat and watched them talk about fashion and colours, wondering not for the first time why he'd chosen me and not my beautiful, frivolous sister. I was content, watching, listening, knowing I was home.

Eventually Lizzie realised I wasn't joining in. "I wish I'd been there last night. To see that ship explode, it must have been thrilling. How was it brought about?"

"Don't ask me," I replied shortly. "A coup I wasn't aware of."

"Gervase," Richard purred, a cat with a bowl of cream. "He's always enjoyed sailing and swimming, and he's skilled at handling seagoing vessels. He reminded me of the Armada—the way the English sent fireships amongst the huge unwieldy ships of the Spanish, to fire and scatter them. It seemed appropriate, here in the county where he was born, to emulate Drake." He grinned. "It worked far better than we'd hoped. Gervase took the fireship as close as he dared and then he and his men took to the smaller rowing boat and rowed back further up the coast, where we'd left horses for them. I haven't seen him yet, he went straight back to Exeter. I plan to go there later today to congratulate him."

"Where did all these men come from?" asked Lizzie, agog.

"I have my sources," he said mysteriously, sharing a knowing look with me. "I can put up a fair muster, if I put my mind to it."

I had a sudden thought. "And those promises you made to Terry—about letting him use the land and barns—?"

Richard frowned. "How do you know about that? Did he taunt you with it?"

"No, we saw it." I hadn't told him about that, restricting my earlier account to the abuses the man had inflicted on us, but now I thought about it, it was a further abuse, to let us watch, so close. "There was a peephole in our prison, and he let us watch the negotiations. He thought he would humiliate you, and he wanted us to see. We couldn't move, our hands were tied and there was a man behind us with a pistol at our heads."

Richard took a deep breath and let it out again. "I did think of allowing him to capture me, to I find out where he was holding you, but my plans weren't complete, and I decided against it."

"We felt helpless," I confessed, "just being able to watch, but he didn't have it all his own way, did he?"

"Not at all. The promises we made were worthless, since I had no intention of allowing the cargo to reach the shore, much less the storerooms he planned to use."

Lizzie laughed. "When I first met you, I thought you were the complete man of fashion. I didn't think you knew any other world."

Richard's long fingers curled round the arm of his chair. "Many people make that mistake. It can be useful. I find it inadvisable to tell people more than they need to know." Looking across at me he caught me holding my hand in front of a yawn.

"We must go now. I need you perfectly restored to health by

Thursday." He stood and came across to me, taking my hands in his. "I'll go and see my brother and my parents in Exeter later today. But I'm not going there again until Wednesday night. I won't leave you now." I was so glad. "When you and Tom were taken we put it about you had both been taken ill. A severe chill, we said, so no one will think it odd if you're not at home to visitors for a few more days." He kissed my hands and dropped them, leaving the room on my smile.

Lizzie stayed to help me back to bed. "I don't know how it is," I confessed, "but I feel tired again."

"Have your sleep out," my sister advised me. "Take your time. As Strang said, you're not at home to visitors for a while."

"Are there many visitors?" I asked.

Lizzie pulled the covers back over me before she answered. "I should say. The world and his wife are beating a path to our door. They all want to see you of course, but they seem to be making do with me." She dimpled prettily, and I smiled sleepily up at her, knowing she loved it all. She bent to kiss my cheek. "So you're not to worry. I'm holding the fort."

Chapter Twenty-Two

I kept to my room until the Sunday, when I attended church. I was relieved to see Tom there, but Richard kept me close, and there were so many people surrounding us afterwards I had no chance of a quiet word with my old friend.

Richard had made his plans, and he told me some of them as we rode towards Penfold Hall on Monday, with only Carier for company. This was in the nature of a quiet ride in the countryside, as far as Martha was concerned, to let me get some fresh air.

Mrs. Terry and her daughter were still in Exeter, living the high life, so Terry would be alone with the servants. I described the room where we'd been kept, where it was and how to get into it, and Richard listened attentively, making sure Carier could hear. "We'll make sure there's no one left there." Carier nodded in agreement. We wanted no witnesses.

We were all armed. A pistol weighed down each of my pockets. Richard had a more substantial sword than his usual dress foil, and a pocketful of those wicked little knives with which he seemed to be so adept. He told me they were Italian, called stilettos, and about the only thing of worth he had brought back from the Grand Tour. "I hadn't the heart for it at the time, but perhaps a repeat visit one day might produce more. Should you like that?"

I smiled at him. "I should like it much. I've often yearned to see more than my own native shores,"

"Then you shall," he said warmly. I knew he was trying to

lighten my apprehension. It didn't work.

I hadn't felt at all nervous as we rode together towards Penfold. However, when the roofline of the house loomed before us out of the horizon the bile rose in my throat. I knew if Richard suspected I was in the least worried, he might well send me home, so I fought to stay calm. I must see this through, for my own peace of mind, so the smile stayed on my face and I held my head up to the wind when we rode into the courtyard.

Carier took the horses to the back of the house, so they wouldn't be seen by any casual caller. Then he would go up to the secret room and make sure no one was secreted there.

Someone let us in immediately, before we had time to sound the knocker. They must have seen us coming. A superior-looking footman in livery took us straight up to the study.

The house was quiet with most of the occupants absent, and our footsteps on the wooden stairs reverberated around the house. Terry waited for us. He didn't stand when we entered, but leaned back in his chair, smiling broadly.

"Stay outside," he said to the footman, and the man went out of the room to stand guard on the door.

Terry put his hand to his chin, and regarded us thoughtfully. "A pleasure to see you both. Won't you sit down?"

Richard seated me and then himself, on two of the hard chairs available. It was a larger room than it had seemed from my prison on high, and well kept, smelling of lavender and polish. It would have been a pleasant room, if not for its occupant.

Seeing him again brought back my ordeal like a blow to the stomach, and I was glad I hadn't eaten much that day, because I didn't want to spoil the beautiful riding habit I'd borrowed from my sister. Terry's body spilled out of his clothes, as though it tried to escape him; the gloating smile was as loathsome as I remembered. He poured some wine for us, though neither of us made a move to touch it.

"You owe Miss Golightly an apology," said Richard, at his most glacial.

Terry's smile was greasily gloating. "She told you, did she? I'm sorry she did; I would have liked to tell you myself. Cosy armful, ain't she?"

Richard said nothing for the time being, just let him talk. Perhaps he wanted to see the man's ugliness for himself. "Don't suppose there's any chance we could share her? No? Pity. Some men prefer to share, you know. I've often taken advantage of it myself."

"I take it you're not prepared to offer the apology I require?"

"No, on the whole I don't think so. You've cost me a lot of money, my lord, and I might take it in kind." He stood. He was armed; he must have been holding the gun all the time under the desk. Neither of us turned a hair. Richard had warned me to expect something of the kind.

The sound of a horse outside did make us start, however, not least Terry, who glanced behind him out of the window. "How cosy. Young Skerrit. Perhaps I'll have all three of you seen to at the same time." He raised his voice to the man outside. "Let him in."

He kept his gun trained on us, and soon Tom was ushered in. He stared at us in surprise, but we merely smiled in greeting. We could have been in a fashionable drawing room, both of us careful not to reveal anything.

"Have you taken his weapons?" Terry demanded of the servant. In reply the servant took a brace of pistols out of his pocket, and let them drop back again.

"How pleasant to see you." sneered Terry, once his man had gone back to his post. He was sure of his control over us. "So soon after your last visit, too. Though I shall remember you best doubled up on my floor, watching me as I played with my new toy."

"You bastard!" Tom shot forward impulsively.

What stopped him wasn't Terry, but Richard. Without raising his voice, his commanding, "Sit down, Tom," had the required effect. Tom put a hand on the desk to stop his forward rush and stood, breathing heavily to regain his temper. Then he meekly fetched a chair and sat next to me, watching Terry.

"What stupidity made you come here?" Terry asked Richard then.

"Several reasons." Richard crossed his legs, supremely at ease with this man, in control. "Mostly to kill you. But I've always found it helps to know what sort of person it is I'm to kill. I can't think of many more people more deserving of it than you."

"What a coincidence, since that's precisely what I thought I might do with you. Shall we drink to it?" Terry poured Tom a glass of wine and placed it in front of him.

Terry returned to his side of the desk, still holding his pistol, picked up his glass, and held it to his lips. He held it in the air, and let the daylight gleam in its depths. "Shall we say, a quick and easy end?" he said, motioning for us to drink. Richard made no move, but Tom, with the habits of good behaviour drummed into him picked up the glass, and I leaned forward to mine.

Richard's calm voice prevented us. "After you."

Terry didn't drink, but put his glass down.

Richard quirked an eyebrow. "Laudanum? Or something a little more professional?"

The fat man smiled. "Someone with the same impulses as myself. I would have enjoyed getting to know you better, sir, had your imminent end not prevented it."

"Tell me—how do you propose to carry this out?" Richard used tones worthy of the drawing room, but the chill remained, in cut glass precision.

Terry smiled broadly. "You'll be taken with your horses, and thrown over the cliff. A tragic riding accident. I'd like the opportunity of finishing what I started with Miss Golightly here. In fact I might still do so."

Tom picked up his glass and threw it to the floor. Richard turned to him in polite enquiry. "Why did you come here, Tom?

You should really have left it to us, you know."

"I couldn't leave matters as they were," Tom said. "I had to do something, and it seemed no one else would do anything."

"How wrong you were. So, another member of our exclusive society I think, my sweet." Richard smiled, the query in his eyes only for me. With him, I had no problem. I smiled back serenely.

Terry motioned at Tom negligently with his pistol. "This boy told me you love this lady. He must have mistaken the physical act with the mental one, don't you think? I'm surprised you're still planning to go ahead with the ceremony. You've had what you wanted, after all. Is she that good?" He looked at Richard with genuine curiosity in his protuberant eyes.

Richard didn't rise to his bait. I was sure now that Terry was provoking him, trying to get him to attack so he could shoot; trusting in the mangling the cliff would give his body to hide the evidence. "How's your shoulder?" he asked.

"Sore," replied Terry immediately.

Richard smiled, the only thing to disturb his glacial calm so far. "Good."

"I trust my servants relieved you of those wicked little knives?" Terry asked, a glint in his eye. "I've a good mind to practise with them myself. Do they cut faces well?" His attention turned to me, his meaning clear.

"Sharp as razors," Richard put his hand to his pocket, and let the knives click together, so Terry could hear.

"Good God, they were supposed to take all your weapons away. He called out to the man outside the door. "Hey you!"

Two armed footmen entered, and behind them was Carier. "Anyone?" Richard didn't look around.

"Cawnton," said Carier. "I sent him home. He saw reason."

"Good."

Terry wasn't pleased at the intrusion, but the sight of the two armed men seemed to put his mind at ease. "See no one comes in," Richard said to his man.

"Yes, my lord," said Carier, for all the world as if Richard had asked him to pass him his coat. He left.

Terry turned on his men. "You were supposed to see all the weapons were confiscated. Strang still seems to have weapons in his pocket, and I hope that scabbard's empty."

In reply, Richard lifted his coat and let Terry see the hilt of his sword under it. His eyes never left Terry's face. "Give the boy his guns back." One of the footmen obeyed. Now Tom's face was a picture of bewilderment.

Unhurriedly, Richard crossed the room towards Terry, and went behind the desk. In a last gesture, Terry raised his gun and fired at him.

The gun clicked uselessly. Before he could turn it round and use the butt, Richard took the barrel in his hand and wrenched it out of Terry's grasp. At the same time he dipped his hand into his pocket and drew out his own flintlock. He put the barrel against Terry's temple and in a voice of steel, said, "Unlike yours, this one is loaded. Sit down."

Such was the force of his voice we all sat, except the servants who stood silently behind.

"You may go," Richard said to them, and without a word the two men bowed and left.

Terry sighed heavily. "How much did they cost you? It must have been a pretty penny, because I pay them extremely well."

"I know," said Richard. "I set their salaries."

Terry's head jerked round, but the gun stayed firmly against his temple. He stared Richard straight in the eye, and Richard gazed back at him, pure and innocent. "You've heard of Thompson's?" he drawled.

Terry shrugged "We get most of our servants from there, I believe. What of it?"

"I'm one of the principals of the company." Richard spoke slowly and clearly, waiting for his prey to catch up with him. "It's a useful sideline, and it's becoming more profitable every year. A portmanteau, you might say, several uses all rolled into one. It's the best domestic agency in the country, a spy network and a private army."

Terry was silent. He stared up at Richard, and realised how he'd contrived all this, how he'd been defeated. "Aren't private armies illegal?"

"Not as illegal as smuggling," Richard answered.

I glanced at my friend. "Do close your mouth, Tom." He obeyed.

Richard moved the pistol against Terry's temple. "On Thursday night, didn't you recognise any of the men I conjured up? Or don't you recognise them out of livery?"

"I don't believe you," said Terry. "They'd never dare disobey me."

Richard smiled. "Only if I ask them. Some of them owe me their good name and others are only drawn to me by the promise of filthy lucre. None of them have ever peached, and never will."

"Peached?" Terry repeated.

"Not all my experiences have been as salubrious as you might suppose." Richard looked as though he was in a drawing room chatting, not standing against a window holding a gun to the head of the vilest man I'd ever known. "I called a muster. I was, I admit, surprised to receive replies from under this roof, but they were the most enthusiastic members of the venture. I spoke with some of them. I thought they exaggerated somewhat, but they swear they did not." He looked down at Terry, contempt etched into his elegant features. "I don't propose to repeat them but it seems you enjoy making people suffer, including your own family. Miss Golightly prevented me from giving your daughter a serious set-down at Exeter Assembly Rooms. Now I know more about you I can only thank her for it. It isn't Eustacia's fault she has turned out thoughtless and selfish. It must have been her only defence against you."

"What do you know?" Terry snarled. "Women need to be kept in their place, something you'll learn only too soon if you still intend to marry this piece."

"What's all this about?" Tom managed, his voice obeying

him at last.

"You weren't meant to be here, Tom," I reminded him. "Did you think we'd come here without any preparation, without even a plan?"

"Do you think I would bring Rose here if there was any danger at all?" Richard added softly. "Since everyone here is sworn to secrecy—including you, Tom—" Tom nodded dumbly, "—I needn't scruple to tell you I love her more than life itself, and I would never voluntarily put her at any risk. I only brought her because she needed to see for herself, to put her mind at rest."

"You couldn't have stopped me," I said, smiling at him.

"Short of locking you up, no. But if you hadn't come, you would never have been completely sure in your mind."

Tom looked from Richard to me and sighed. "She was always headstrong as a girl. I could never manage her."

"She doesn't need managing," Richard looked at me with the expression he reserved for me alone. "She knows her own mind as well as I know mine. She will do as she thinks fit, and she'll make me proud of her." Tom sighed again, heavily than the last time.

My love looked across at me and smiled, meeting my eyes. "Do you want to stay, sweetheart?"

"Absolutely," I replied.

When his attention went back to Terry his face hardened again. "The only men in this house are Thompson's. My men. All the others have leave of absence, supposedly on Terry's orders."

Terry broke in, his harsh voice intruding on the quiet one. "Tell me what you want, and then go."

"Yes, of course." Richard's gun never wavered. "First of all, the apology. You offered Miss Golightly a deep insult. Several, in fact."

"Very well." Terry was back in control of himself again. He stared across his desk at me and he grinned, the spirit still there, the memory still in his mind. "It was worth it, though."

Without warning, Richard swung the butt of the pistol and struck him in a backhanded swipe that knocked him sideways. Terry would have fallen out of his chair but for its arms, which kept him in place. Richard coolly reached down, hooked it into Terry's collar, and hauled him back into place.

The fat man's temple bled freely, but he didn't try to staunch the wound in any way. He seemed to be stunned, shaking his head to try to restore his reason. Richard waited. I didn't move, although the force of the blow and its cold, deliberate delivery made Tom wince.

"The apology," Richard reminded him, when Terry had recovered a little.

The man reached for his wine, and then snatched his hand back.

"Are there any unpoisoned decanters?" Richard asked him.

"All the others." Terry held his hands to his head in an effort to steady himself. Richard glanced at Tom. "If you wouldn't mind?" Tom silently went and poured a drink for Terry, brandy by the look of it, which the man took and drank straight down without a pause. He put the glass on the table with shaking fingers.

Richard leaned forward and moved the glass out of his reach. "I should hate to see you try to spoil my looks."

Richard held the pistol still unwaveringly trained on Terry's temple. "I see you've recovered your usual good temper. Please—let's waste no more energy on this."

Terry stared at me, blood seeping from the nasty wound on his head. I sat still and straight. "I seem to have offered you some insult," he said in a formal tone. "I regret the incident, and I offer you my heartfelt apologies."

I nodded. "Look down, away from her," Richard ordered. Terry obeyed, staring at the polished desk top in front of him. "Now then," Richard continued, to Tom and I. "Should it be suicide—or an accident?"

Chapter Twenty-Three

Tom's head jerked up, white and shocked. "My God, Strang, what are you saying?"

Richard's celestial blue eyes opened wider in surprise. "Did you think I would take his word? Did you think it was going to be a polite apology, shake hands and go home? What do you take me for?"

"A murderer." This choked out from Terry, rigid under the muzzle of the gun.

"A considered cull," Richard corrected him. "I've consulted with my principals, and we're all agreed. I haven't asked Tom what he thinks, though. Perhaps we should ask him now and leave your fate in his hands."

I opened my mouth to protest, but something in Richard's eyes kept me silent. "Well, Tom?"

Tom stared, appalled, from Richard to me and to Terry and back again. Then he swore, and stood up to help himself from the decanter he'd recently used to give Terry his drink. "You mean it?"

Richard nodded, an eyebrow raised in query. "If it's suicide, the Crown has the right to confiscate his goods. His wife and daughter would be left destitute and although they usually choose to return a portion, because of Terry's involvement in the smuggling, it's more likely they'll choose to take the estate. But if he died cleaning his gun, it's an accident and his family will be provided for. Personally, I would opt for accident. I don't think this should affect anyone else more than it has to. I'm not saying Eustacia Terry will at once become as sweet as Lizzie Golightly, but it may make her more content." He paused. "Of course, I'm a good deal more compassionate than some of the other principals in the enterprise. And you, Tom, saw his excesses first hand. I've only seen the results."

Tom blinked at me, surprised. "You showed him?"

"Yes of course," I answered. "He would have seen it soon enough, and I've no intention of spoiling my wedding night by shocking him with it then."

"I don't think I know you at all, Rose," Tom said.

"I hardly know myself." I put my hand out to him. "I only have one constant, these days. Come, Tom, choose."

"Your word must count for a great deal," Richard added. "Think about that room, what occurred in it, and—"

"All right." His hand shook, where it lay in mine. "I can't bear the thought of him doing it to anyone else, and I don't think this was the first time he's abused someone in that way. But—I can't say it—" He broke off, biting his lip.

"Take your time," said Richard. It had taken me no time at all to make my mind up, but then, Tom had some time to think and recover from the ordeal, and perhaps a decision made out of reason might have more weight than mine. I glanced at Richard and saw there was no escape for Terry. There was nothing left for him now.

"There're others," Terry said. "When I had her on my lap, there was a man covering us all the time. They saw what I did, they'll speak up."

"Who would believe them? Ruffians, thieves like them. In any case, there were two, the one you called Peter and one named—Griffiths, I was told. They are being dealt with as we speak." Richard gave a smile that had nothing of amusement about it. "To put your mind at rest, their widows will be taken care of." I didn't know if he told the truth or not, but it had the desired effect. Terry visibly winced and Tom gasped as though he had received a blow to the face. Richard accepted his stare. "There are two things at stake here, Tom. Firstly, Rose will marry a Kerre on Thursday. There are some things a family such as ours is entitled to, and I will make sure the criteria are fulfilled. Understand this is nothing to do with position, scandal, and society gossip. It goes far, far deeper than that. It's to do with respect and decency." Tom nodded slowly. "And then there is what is to most people the lesser consideration of the insult done to Rose and, by implication, myself."

"You could drop her," Terry suggested. "I'll take her off your hands if you think your family can't stand soiled goods."

Richard looked down at Terry in mild surprise, as though he was a servant interrupting his betters. Expressionlessly, Richard put the muzzle hard against the wound and cocked it. The only movement in the room was his thumb on the hammer as he pulled it back, and the only sound the click when it locked into place. Terry drew a breath, sharply, knowing he'd come to the last. "All right. You've won. I'm afraid. I apologise without any reservations, I'm in the wrong. I swear not to tell anyone what has happened in this room today, and I'll make any reparation I can." His breath rasped heavily in the otherwise silent room.

Richard still held off. I began to think he would really let Terry go. "The latter consideration is to me the deciding factor. I'm sorry, Tom, I've waited long enough."

He pulled the trigger.

Where there was order before, now chaos reigned. Blood and brains spattered the carefully polished surface of the room and where there had been a living being, now lay a bloody, spongy mess. Richard pushed the back of the chair hard with his knee and Terry slumped down on to the table in front of us.

I leapt to my feet, afraid the blood had spoiled Lizzie's habit and I would be forced to burn it, but I couldn't see any marks. Richard had shot Terry from the side, and all the mess had gone away from us.

After the first recoil Richard leaned over the body. He put the gun in the dead man's hand, where it might have fallen if Terry had shot himself. "I think we must leave the powers that be to decide on the suicide or accident verdict." He glanced up at Tom, who stood still, his hand clamped over his mouth. "For God's sake don't be sick, Skerrit." Then he looked at me. "Rose?"

I stared at the thing on the desk, shocked I felt so little. I'd seen dead men before, from accident or old age, but never the result of an action like this. It didn't seem to matter. The shock had come before, when I'd realised how much Terry had fooled us all, and for how long. This seemed to be an anticlimax, not the horror it should have been.

Richard would have taken my hand and turned me away, but I leaned forward, forestalling him, and picked up the two untouched wine glasses and the two tumblers used for brandy, all now spotted with blood. "These must be washed." I left the glass Tom had thrown to the floor. One glass would not be remarked on.

Richard nodded, and took my arm. "We have to go now."

Tom looked up from where he stood staring at the body, and numbly followed us out of the room. The footman outside hadn't moved. "Give us ten minutes and then raise the alarm," Richard ordered.

"Yes, my lord."

Richard took the glasses from me and put them on a table by the door "Make sure these are washed and put away." The second footman picked them up and indicated we should follow him with a little bow. "The back stairs are clear, my lord, and they lead straight to the courtyard at the back of the house."

We followed the man down the cold stone steps to the back door where Carier waited.

There was a small lobby before the door. As Tom and the footman passed through it, Richard caught my arm and pulled me back.

His face was white, his clear blue eyes completely paralysed. He dragged me to him and held me tight, his head buried in my shoulder. He threw his head back and took several deep breaths, then looked at me, not smiling, with such need in his eyes I wanted to take him to my bed and hold him until he'd forgotten what he'd done, so there was only us again. "I told you, my love. An act like this takes a little of your soul, but I could see no other way." I admired him deeply, even more now I knew what it had cost him to take this step. My husband-to-be respected life more than anyone would ever know. Except me.

He forced a smile, and took my hand. We went out into the yard together.

Richard cupped his hands and helped me into the saddle. Then he mounted his own horse. Tom, still dumb with shock, waited for us. We wasted no time putting Penfold Hall behind us. I welcomed the release, and galloped up to the ridge beyond, letting my horse have her head. I didn't think of anything except the wind at my ears trying to free my hat where I had jammed it hard on my head as we left.

Richard let me go. He must have seen my need to release some of the tension I felt, to try to deal with my feelings, but I was always aware of him riding closely behind me.

Once over the ridge, the house out of sight, we deliberately slowed down. If anyone had seen us going hell for leather it would have seemed suspicious, when the tragedy at Penfold Hall was discovered, and after a while we stopped completely. Richard helped me down and I didn't let him release me when I stood on the ground. "I took Rose out for a gentle ride today," Richard said to Tom, his arm still around my waist. "She is, after all, still convalescent. We met you and you rode with us for a while. We know nothing about any other occurrences, of course."

"Of course," Tom repeated. "What made you do it?" he cried, his voice cracking.

Richard touched his hand in a steadying gesture. "It was needful. Apart from all other considerations, Rose wouldn't have slept soundly for a long time to come if she knew he was doing what he did to her to anyone else, someone without protectors. The man would have caused the death of many other people, and perhaps started a war to gain territory. He was greedy and he wouldn't have stopped. I've seen his kind before. We both have."

He glanced across at Carier who concurred with a dour nod. "Not too many times, my lord, but I can recall one or two."

"Left to themselves they get worse," Richard told a silent Tom. "In this instance, the moment he laid a finger on Rose, he was dead. I was planning to ruin him, was plotting with Cawnton to take over his part of the smuggling enterprise, and although it would have taken much more effort and money, it might have been worth it."

"You love her that much?" Tom asked, wonder in his eyes.

"Oh, much more than that," Richard assured him. His hand tightened briefly around my waist. "Other women are presented with jewellery and money as proof of devotion. If I started to present mine with dead bodies, society might begin to wonder."

Richard waited while I gave Tom a hug.

Then he took me back to my horse and helped me to mount, and we continued on our way.

Chapter Twenty-Four

I was weary when we got home, and I spent most of the rest of the day in the small parlour kept for family use, reading the papers with my feet up. Richard joined me for much of the time, and we sat in companionable silence, recovering from the ordeals of recent days. Once I asked him, "Have you done this often?"

"No," he answered. "Sometimes the authorities deal with it, sometimes the family themselves, if it avoids a scandal. I've killed before, but not usually in cold blood."

"Could it have been avoided?" I was concerned for Richard's welfare more than anything else.

"No. I could have got someone else to do it, but this one was mine."

I didn't ask any more.

I was in my room getting dressed for dinner when Lizzie hurtled in with the news. "You'll never guess."

"What?" I knew from the look on her face, excitement suppressed by concern, what the news was.

"It's Norrice Terry. He's been found dead in his study."

"Good God." I kept my eyes on the mirror, marvelling at the calm expression on my face while my stomach churned.

Lizzie noticed nothing amiss. She continued to talk, telling me all about it, and all I could see was that comfortable study, and the thing on the desk. "They found him in his study at about twelve o'clock with his gun next to him on the desk. He'd killed himself, they said. At least he won't come to trial. Or perhaps one of his lowlife friends murdered him. What do you think?"

"I'm not going to think about it. It's a shock, but not that much of a shock." I rummaged around on the dressing table in the pretence of searching for something there. "I'm not even going to speculate." I met her eyes in the mirror. "But I'm glad he's dead," I added, with no particular emphasis, deliberately taking the heat out of my voice.

"He was a wicked man," Lizzie agreed, serious for once. "When I saw what he'd done to you—" She broke off. I sighed when I remembered the conversation I'd had with Martha about my bruises. More perceptive than Lizzie, she'd seen where the marks were clustered and it took some time before I could convince her that he had done nothing else. "Rose, you're getting married on Thursday and Strang has seen the marks., so it's as well he killed himself or whatever happened, because I can't see your husband-to-be leaving that one alone." She turned to me in shock. "Rose. Do you think...?"

"Don't be ridiculous," I snapped, picking up my nail buffer. "What time has he had? He was with me all day today, and we met Tom when we were out riding."

"Do you think Tom might have done something?" Lizzie asked, balked of her original prey.

"Even less of a chance than Richard, I'd say. And in any case, he wouldn't do anything in cold blood like that. Did you say he was found at twelve o'clock?"

"Yes."

"How long had he been there?"

"I don't know," she confessed.

I smiled in satisfaction. "Well then, if the servants heard the noise and came immediately, Tom couldn't have done it, because we met him at least half an hour earlier than that."

"Oh." She was more relieved than disappointed, and I hadn't actually lied to her. I knew now I could live with what we had done, and I felt easier Terry wasn't going to torment me or anyone else any more.

If I could live with this, I could live with Richard as proprietor of Thompson's and all that went with it. He needed it as a basis for his own power. If I had insisted, he would have given it up, but he must see that we were both safer with the company behind us rather than with no protection at all. He had let me in to every aspect of his life now, nothing hidden from me. I had to honour that and take him as he was, not as I might wish he would be. He wasn't a country squire, he was the heir to one of the principal peerages in the country, sophisticated, powerful, and he would never be any different. I would have to learn how to be the best wife I could be to him, in public and in private. Private was easier.

This was the end of my life as a spinster sister in rural Devonshire. I wasn't sure what lay ahead, but I knew one thing. Richard was the centre of it. He always would be.

About the Author

Winner of two EPPIEs, Lynne Connolly is the best-selling author of sensuous romance, including the Triple Countess series, the Secrets trilogy and the Richard and Rose series. Lynne fell in love with the Georgian era at primary school, and never fell out of it, visiting historical sites, towns, battlefields and houses in her home country of England.

Lynne writes sensuous historical romance, and gives the reader a real flavour of what it was like to live and love in the eighteenth century. But she likes the twenty-first century fine, and she also writes paranormal romance set in bustling, modern cities. She lives in England with her family and her Muse, a cat called Jack. She writes surrounded by the doll's houses she enjoys making and filling.

She has a website at www.lynneconnolly.com and a blog at www.lynneconnolly.blogspot.com. She'd love to hear from you—write to her at lynne_connolly@yahoo.co.uk

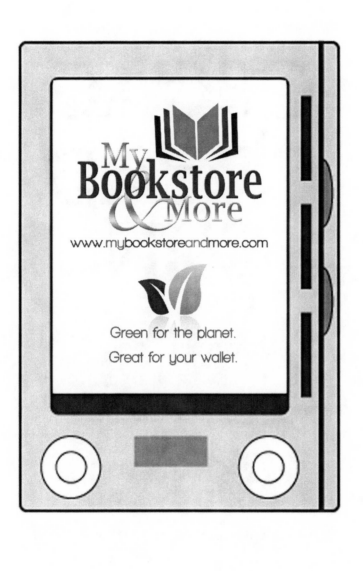

GREAT CHEAP FUN

Discover eBooks!

THE FASTEST WAY TO GET THE HOTTEST NAMES

Get your favorite authors on your favorite reader, long before they're out in print! Ebooks from Samhain go wherever you go, and work with whatever you carry—Palm, PDF, Mobi, and more.

Samhain
publishing
Ltd

WWW.SAMHAINPUBLISHING.COM